THE LIGHTNESS OF WATER

Water Witch ~ Book One

TONI CABELL

CHAPTER 1

"Solace, are you nearly ready? Everyone's waiting!" Arik tapped on the door to her bedroom. Solace tugged on the bright blue tunic she'd made for her Naming Day, smoothing it over her worn gray leggings, and buckled on her mother's leather belt, soft with age. This was her seventeenth Naming Day and the third without her mother. Solace dreamt of her again last night. They were sitting on the porch swing out front, gently swaying as they sipped sassafras tea. Solace reached out her hand to grasp her mother's, and that's when she woke up, the ache in her chest still fresh.

"Who's everyone?" she teased Arik, trying to shake her off mood.

"Everyone who loves you."

Solace heard the yearning in his voice and sighed. Any other girl would have encouraged Arik, with his warm brown eyes and easy-going ways. An added bonus, he wouldn't have to spend twenty years fighting the king's wars to earn a soldier's reward of forty acres. His father had done that for him, serving under Solace's father. Both men had earned their forty acres the same year and selected side-by-side plots, farming the dry land together.

"Tell my adoring fans I'll be along in a minute." Solace straightened her bedroom, barely larger than a closet, before stepping into the cramped main room of the stone cottage she shared with her father. The kitchen took up almost half the area, with a scarred wooden table occupying the middle of the room.

"Happy Naming Day!" said Arik as he kissed her cheek, his beard rough against her skin. Taking her hand, he led her to the table where their fathers sipped their morning coffee.

Solace slipped her arms around her father's neck. "Good morning sleepy head," said Soren, patting her hand affectionately. It was true; Solace *had* slept in that morning, the one morning of the harvest season she wasn't up before dawn preparing breakfast. Her father smelled of fresh hay—he must have been out to the barn early, handling her morning chores so she could sleep an extra hour—and the pungent tobacco he smoked in his pipe.

"Take a seat, milady," said Arik, as he pulled out a chair for her and placed a homespun napkin in her lap. "Your breakfast awaits you!" He bowed low as he poured her a mug of coffee, and she shook her head at him, smiling. Arik had started the Naming Day breakfast tradition after her mother died, when Solace's grief wrapped around her like a dark veil. Arik and their two dads had struggled to find a way to reach her.

"Any plans for your special day?" asked Gordo, Arik's father, as he dug into his scrambled eggs, ham, and biscuits. Gordo looked like a leaner, shorter version of her dad, with the same weathered tan skin, dark eyes that missed nothing, and gray hair and beard.

"This is special." Solace waved her hands at the table where several packages wrapped in brown paper and twine sat waiting for her to open. "I've got the sheep to look after this morning and then a divining at the Thieler's." Solace, like her mother before her, could divine for water in the severest of droughts. Even traveling merchants from neighboring Toresz knew of the Yeloshan hill girl with the rare gift for water divining.

"I wish one of us could take you to the Thieler's and wait for you." Soren drew his eyebrows together. "I don't like you coming back at night alone."

"You've got the harvest to worry about—the weather's started to turn. And I won't be alone. One of the Thieler boys will take me back in their cart." Solace had no qualms about traveling through the hills—her hills, where she'd been divining for years—in the dark.

"The oldest boy can't be more than twelve. Not much help if you run into trouble," pointed out her father.

"Stop worrying so much!"

Soren grunted, "May as well ask me to stop breathing!"

"Reminds me of that time you'd been knocked unconscious and were barely breathing," said Gordo. Solace suspected he was trying to distract her father. "We'd lost more than half our men and were outnumbered ten to one at least."

Soren nodded, his gaze wandering to a distant battlefield. Gordo described how they had tracked and ambushed the larger army. Solace and Arik had grown up listening to their fathers tell of their military campaigns. Solace had heard their stories so many times she could recite their battle plans from memory.

She shrugged at Arik, who interrupted the storytelling. "Let's have Solace open her gifts before we head to the fields." Arik handed her an awkwardly wrapped gift, and Gordo sat up straighter, watching as she pulled off the twine and paper. She pulled out a braided cord, about three feet in length, with a leather cradle woven into the middle. One end of the cord had a loop just large enough for a finger to slip through, while the other end of the cord was knotted. She found a second cord, identical to the first, curled inside the wrapping paper.

"New slings! Gordo, thank you! My old slings are fraying badly." Like other children raised in the hill country, Solace had received a sling as her first toy. These days, she used her sling as a weapon; she never left the stone cottage without a sling wrapped around her waist or tucked into her pouch.

Gordo nodded. "These braided cords will hold up better than your old rope slings. I added a bit of length, too, so you can hurl stones farther than before."

Solace reached for the smaller of the two packages, tore off the wrapping, and pulled out a polished, brown leather pouch with an adjustable shoulder strap. She turned to Soren. "This is just like the one you saw me admiring in the market last spring. But you didn't buy it that day, so how did you..." A small line creased her brow. "So *this* is what you've been working on whenever you went to 'check on something' in the barn. I should have known! I love it!"

She went over to her father and kissed his grizzled cheek. Soren patted her on the head like a young girl. "You deserve it, and much more besides. No one could ask for a better daughter."

"And here's my gift," said Arik. Solace took the large package from him, their fingers brushing lightly. Ripping it open, she gasped as she pulled out a thick woolen cloak, woven from brown and beige and taupe yarn to create a dappled effect. It would be the perfect camouflage when she was protecting her sheep from wolves and jackals, and yet striking enough to wear proudly to the market. A cloak this well made must have cost Arik three-months' earnings, maybe more.

He was doing everything he could—short of actually saying the words—to demonstrate his feelings. And Solace knew her feelings wouldn't change. She'd never be content as a farmer's wife, scraping out a living from the dry soil of the Yeloshan hill country, and occasionally divining the best location for a neighbor's well. She swallowed down a lump in her throat, wishing things were different, that she was different.

"Arik, this is beautiful. And far too special for a hill girl like me!" She squeezed his hand. "Thank you."

"You're no ordinary hill girl." Arik's voice was husky.

"Here, here!" said Soren, as he raised his coffee mug in a toast to his daughter.

Solace stood up and started clearing the table, but Soren said, "Leave it be. We can clean up after ourselves. Go run off to your sheep and that book you're itching to read." She grinned at her father, who knew her so well, and carried her gifts into her room.

Solace transferred the new slings and one of her mother's old books to the brown leather pouch. She added her comb and pearl-handled dagger, and slipped on Arik's cloak, running her hands down the soft, nubby fabric. She slung the pouch cross-wise across her left shoulder. Before leaving, she returned to the kitchen to slice off a thick slab of cheese and a piece of ham, wrapped them in a cloth napkin, and stowed them in her pouch. She picked up a water skin, which she'd fill up using the pump outside.

Arik and Gordo had already cleaned up their dishes and left. Her father pulled on his work boots and turned toward Solace. "You're going to need to tell him, you know."

Solace's hand rested on the doorknob. Soren had spoken of Arik's feelings for her once before. And then, only to tell her to think with both her heart and her head, because they needed to be united, not divided. "I don't want to hurt him."

"He's already hurting. Right now he's stuck fast, hoping you'll come to him. Be kind and tell Arik the truth. Release him to find someone else."

"Release him?" Solace frowned. "But I've never promised him, never said—"

"And you've never said no, either. So release him."

Solace nodded slowly, her stomach churning at the thought she'd somehow misled Arik. "Won't he hate me? And what about Gordo? He's your best friend—won't he hate me too?"

Soren walked over to Solace and put one roughened hand on her shoulder. "Gordo can see plain as day you're not in love with his son, and he'll not hold that against you. As for Arik, he'll be disappointed, but probably also relieved to know where he stands with you."

"Thanks Dad," Solace whispered. She grabbed her staff, yanked open the door, and bolted toward the sheep pen. If she stayed any longer, she'd burst into tears.

Solace gently prodded her sheep out of the pen, calling out to the last few stragglers, "Alright, Maisie and Pawl, let's go!" Barley, her brown and black border collie, ensured the sheep followed her up the hill behind their cottage, nipping at the heels of any unwise enough to wander away.

Solace led them along a flat, rocky path, stooping occasionally to pick up a stone and rub it between her fingers. Only the best stones, round and smooth, wound up in the drawstring bag she'd tucked inside her leather pouch. She climbed into the adjacent hills where the grazing was better. After checking that all sheep were accounted for and Barley was keeping a sharp lookout, Solace sat beneath a flinty crag that curved out above her head, offering some protection from the wind. She leaned back, wrapped herself more snugly in her new cloak, and opened her book with a happy sigh. She paused in her reading periodically to check on the sheep and share her lunch and water with Barley, who dutifully bounded after a particularly stubborn sheep and chased him back into their grazing spot.

Solace had just reached the part of the story where the prince was trying to decide whether he could ever love the poor maiden, when Solace heard a low rumble from Barley's throat. She carefully put down the book, reached into her pouch for her sling and stones, and slowly stood up. She pulled out two stones because she knew there was never enough time for a third shot.

Barley's rumble turned into a full-throated growl, and Solace saw why: a large black-backed jackal stood on the crag above them, eyeing Pawl, the stubborn, straying sheep who at that moment wandered next to Solace. As the jackal crouched down, ready to pounce, all the hairs on Solace's neck stood up.

Solace went rigid with fear, watching as white foam dribbled out of the jackal's jaws, packing a death sentence in every bite. She dropped one of the stones inside the cradle of her sling and slipped her middle finger through the looped end of the braided cord. Gripping the knot at the other end of the cord between her thumb and forefinger, she rotated the sling in an arc above her head.

Before the jackal's hind legs could push off the crag, Solace released the knotted end of the cord. Her first stone hit the ground next to his front paws. Hissing at her poor aim, due more to the newness of her sling than to her skill as a slinger, she took a deep breath and tried to steady her thundering heart. She repeated the steps, praying she had enough time for one clean shot: seat the stone inside the cradle, grip the knotted end of the cord, and rotate the sling.

The jackal drew back his lips in a frothy snarl and leapt into the air, aiming for her and Pawl as Barley barked and ran in anxious circles. Solace followed the jackal's snout, aiming just behind his jaw line. She released the knotted end of the cord, this time adjusting for the fact Gordo had added to its length. The stone projectile whizzed out of its cradle, found its target, and sank into the jackal's eye. The jackal gave a strangled half-yip and fell to the ground.

Solace leaned over and put both hands on her thighs, waiting for her knees to stop shaking. Pawl and the other sheep scattered, and Barley, barking and nipping, began rounding them up again. She picked up her staff and offered a silent prayer of thanks as she approached the lifeless jackal.

She heard the crunching of stones and pebbles and looked around to find Arik scrabbling down the hill. He ran to her breathlessly and grabbed her by the shoulders. "Solace, are you hurt?" Glancing down at the jackal, he added, "He's rabid! Are you sure he didn't bite you?"

Solace shook her head but didn't trust her voice just yet.

"I saw you take aim as the jackal leapt down. What a shot —I don't think I've seen any better!" He looked from Solace back down at the jackal. "Let's get the sheep and Barley out of the area and away from the carcass."

Arik went over to where she'd been sitting and scooped up her things, and then he helped Barley round up Pawl, Maisie, and the other sheep. Once they were moving along, away from the carcass, he handed over her leather pouch and book.

"Thanks," she said, dropping her sling and book into the pouch. She added as an afterthought, "Why are you here, instead of out in the field with our dads?"

"Because the Thieler boy showed up in his pony cart looking for you, so I offered to fetch you and bring the sheep back."

Solace marked the position of the sun against the tall oak that stood at the bottom of the hill, near the cottage. "He's a bit early."

Arik laughed. "He seems eager to watch you at work."

"Ah yes, let's all gather round and watch the strange girl who can divine for water. Is she a witch? Or just a freak?"

Arik took her hand and said, "No one thinks you're a witch or a freak or strange in any way. You're gifted and special."

Solace blinked and bit her bottom lip, knowing she had to say something to Arik. She squeezed his hand as her stomach twisted into knots. Her words tumbled out quickly, before she could recall them. "You're kind and loyal and my best friend. I wish that I could make you happy, because I do love you. And yet I know that you love me more, and that's not fair to you. So I'm releasing you." Solace let go of Arik's hand and took a few steps away from him.

Arik grabbed her left arm and swung her around to face him. Dropping her staff on the ground, she used her free hand to swipe at her eyes, which threatened to spill over. He pushed a lock of dark hair away from her face and asked, "Is this what you really want?"

Solace swallowed down a lump in her throat and nodded. "I want you to be happily married to a woman who wants nothing more than to be your wife."

"And you want something more?"

Solace nodded again. "I'm sorry."

Arik drew her against his chest in a bear hug. "Me too. I've been hoping you'd want to be with me, and yet deep down knowing that you needed something I can't give you."

She wrapped her arms around him and hugged him back, her eyes burning with unshed tears. Arik kissed the top of her head and pulled away. He said shakily, "You'll always carry a piece of my heart."

Solace's voice sounded watery to her ears. "And you'll carry a piece of mine. Let's wrap those two pieces in brown paper and twine, and place them carefully in the past."

Arik compressed his lips and nodded. "In the past." He picked up her staff and carried it for her.

They walked silently downhill toward the cottage, herding the sheep along. Arik nodded at a boy sitting drowsily under the oak tree, his pony tethered nearby. "I'll take care of the sheep and Barley. You go on now with the Thieler boy. And be careful coming back tonight."

A single tear escaped down her cheek as she mumbled her thanks.

She hailed the Thieler boy and climbed stiffly into the cart. The boy jumped up, untethered the pony, and sat down next to her. Glancing over at Solace, who stared straight ahead, he asked, "Don't you need something more? A divining kit or something?"

Solace shook her head. "I have all I need. Please, let's go."

❧

A small crowd had gathered to watch Solace search for the best location for the Thieler's new well. The boy dropped her off near the old well, at the base of a rocky hill. *Poor Mr. Thieler,* thought Solace, *his forty acres are drier and rockier than Dad's.* Still, she knew she could help him find a water source, because underground springs crisscrossed the Yeloshan hills. But without a water diviner to guide the digging, the springs were nearly impossible to find beneath sixty feet or more of stony ground.

Solace knew there'd be no fresh water beneath the old well, and so she walked south a hundred paces, over rough, bumpy terrain, all her senses alert. She looked for the slightest change in the color of the rocky soil but saw the same brownish-beige hue wherever she looked. And she listened. Sometimes she could hear the sigh of an underground spring gurgling below the surface.

Bending down, Solace grabbed a handful of pebbly dirt and sniffed. She let it sift through her fingers, sprinkling the earth below. She rubbed her fingers together and brought them back up to her nostrils. *Nothing.* Not the barest scent or texture of moisture nearby. As she suspected, but she always tested the ground to be sure. She had a decision to make: walk another hundred paces south and test the soil again, or head east or west, and search closer in. She decided to walk farther south.

The onlookers followed her soberly, curious about her gift,

which was well known by now, and also a bit wary of her, even somewhat scared. She was certain some of them did think she was a witch, regardless of Arik's protestations otherwise. *Let them think what they will. Their silver helped Dad and me—and Arik and Gordo, for that matter—when the crop failed last year, and it'll help us again, to be sure.*

She covered the terrain more slowly this time, looking for any variation in the soil and listening, straining her ears. Still nothing. She tested the soil anyway, something her mother taught her to do, since sometimes the other senses could be fooled.

Solace squinted into the sun. Another hour of light left. She sniffed the air and cupped her ears. A few onlookers shuffled their feet, breaking her concentration. She glared at them and they backed away, bowing their heads in a kind of apology. She had a mental map in her head of all the wells she and her mother had divined across these hills, and an image of how the water sources connected below them came to her. She closed her eyes, licked her finger, and held it up in the air. No one moved. A baby started to cry and the mother hushed it, walking away from the gathering.

West, her gift told her, *head west now.* Solace nodded to herself and turning west, walked a hundred paces downhill. *There,* her gift shouted in her head, *right there, where the soil looks as if a shadow has brushed past it.* Solace knelt down, pressing her ear to the ground. She heard the whisper of water beneath her. Raising her head from the ground, she scooped up the soil and rubbed it between her fingers. She brought a handful to her nose, inhaling the loamy scent of water buried far below. Finally she tasted the soil—it was the only way to gauge how deep the farmer had to dig the well. Sixty feet, but worth it. For there the Thielers would find a water source that would last them into the next generation, maybe longer. She stood up, smiling.

She motioned to Mr. and Mrs. Thieler, who walked over to

her expectantly. Pointing at the ground, Solace shouted so the entire crowd could hear, which was something else her mother had taught her, explaining that a bit of showmanship now ensured new divining requests later. "Dig right here, sixty-five feet down. There's a good underground spring, for you and your family, bubbling right below us!" She always added five feet to her estimate, because the men would strike water sooner and be thankful for it.

Solace pulled a handkerchief from her leather pouch and wiped her mouth and the side of her face. Tucking a loose strand of hair behind her ear, she waited. The small crowd broke into applause, and then a few of the boys started whooping. Mr. Thieler threw back his head and laughed, and Mrs. Thieler invited everyone to share some bread and soup back at their cottage.

Solace's stomach growled as they walked back uphill to the cottage, and the older woman patted her arm kindly. "Your mother found our first well for us, and it ran true for eighteen years. It's nice to know you've inherited her gift, lass."

After dinner and some lively fiddling from Mr. Thieler, Solace stifled a yawn and rose. It was getting on toward midnight, and she'd have to be up at first light to start her chores. Mrs. Thieler came over and pressed three silver coins into her hand. They both knew the Thielers were paying Solace in good faith, based on her reputation and gift. They also knew if the men dug and the ground came up dry, the coins would be returned. This had never happened to either Solace or her mother, and so payment was made on the day of the divination.

The Thieler's eldest son brought the pony cart out, and Solace climbed in, stifling another yawn and thinking fondly of her bed. The boy guided the pony across the ridge and downhill toward Solace's home. He kept looking up at the sliver of moon in the sky. Enough to see by, but barely. Solace got the feeling he was afraid to travel too far away from his mother's embrace and the warm bed he shared with his younger brothers.

"You can leave me at the next hill, it's on our property. I can walk the rest of the way."

He wavered and then shook his head. "Father says to take you to your door."

Solace smiled. He was putting on a brave front. "It's fine, Timor. It's our land, and I know it like the back of my own hand. I can walk it."

Timor shrugged and when they reached the hill, he pulled up the pony. "You sure it's alright?"

"Of course." Solace climbed out of the cart, raised the hood of her cloak, and adjusted her leather pouch. She waved and Timor turned the cart around.

Afterward, she couldn't be sure if it was pure exhaustion— divining took a lot out of her—or the emotional drain of finally telling Arik her feelings, but all she could say for certain was that her sense of hearing failed her utterly. She never heard him coming. She'd walked maybe thirty paces, guided by the thinnest sliver of moon, and then all went black.

Solace struggled inside the blackness, pushing against whatever held her. The blackness felt scratchy, almost like she'd walked into a burlap sack. She kicked and screamed, but someone wrestled her to the ground. Clapping a strong hand over her mouth and nose and cutting off her air, a man's voice growled through the darkness, "If you want to live through the night, keep your mouth shut—" and then the sharp pinch of a dagger pressed against her throat.

CHAPTER 2

The pressure from the dagger eased at Solace's throat, and she felt a piece of rope being dragged across her shoulders. She screamed as loud as she could, kicking and punching wildly. Solace made contact with something, a shin or knee perhaps.

"Oof!" grunted the man. "Don't make this any harder on yourself!"

Solace twisted out of his grasp and started running blindly, the sack still on her head and dangling below her knees. Her kidnapper caught up with her in a few long strides and tossed her to the ground. Solace felt him straddle her, and she screamed harder, terrified of what he had in mind. The man clamped his hand over her mouth and leaned down to hiss in her ear. "Stop now, or your family is next."

My family? He must mean Dad, and Arik and Gordo. He's been spying on us! But why? We're nothing but poor hill people. Solace squeezed her eyes shut and sniffled. She had to keep her father and the others safe. She'd cooperate for now—until she could figure out a way to escape.

"Can I remove my hand now, without you caterwauling to the moon?"

Solace nodded and bit back a snarly reply. Her captor made quick work of trussing her up like one of her Naming Day packages, and then he tossed into the air. She swallowed down a scream as she landed, presumably on a horse, because she heard him snort and paw the ground. Someone—probably the same knife-wielding man, because he seemed to be acting alone —jumped into the saddle and adjusted her so she lay across the front of the saddle, with her head bouncing below the horse's withers. She sensed a flick of the reins and the horse took off at a gallop. They were followed by a second set of hooves hitting the rocky soil somewhere behind them.

Solace tried listening to the horses' hooves striking the ground to figure out their direction but she soon gave up. They rode for what seemed like days, but was probably a few hours, Solace rocking and bumping along until she wanted to retch. She squirmed about in her sack until the man yelled, "Be still! You're upsetting my horse."

She yelled back, "And you're upsetting me! My head's splitting, and I'm going to be sick all over this burlap in another minute!"

The man reined in his horse and they slowed down to a trot, then a walk, and finally they stopped, Solace's stomach in her throat and her head throbbing.

"I'll remove the ropes and sack so you can have some fresh air. No funny business or you'll regret it."

"Am I supposed to thank you?"

"I don't expect gratitude, but I demand obedience, or the sack will go back on your head for the duration of the ride. And I can assure you, it's a very long ride."

Solace listened closely to his pronunciation of certain words; his enunciation was too refined to be from the hills of Yelosha, which was the only accent Solace could identify. He might be from one of the cities along the western coast, beyond the Hawxhurss Mountains that split Yelosha in half—the western half lush and green and prosperous—and the eastern half arid and brown and poor. Or maybe he wasn't Yeloshan at all.

Solace felt herself being lifted from the back of the horse, more gently than she'd been tossed onto it, and then one hand gripped her waist while the other hand unwound the ropes. The man let go of her momentarily, and in her disorientation, she tumbled to the ground, still swaddled in burlap. Her head struck something sharp, a rock or tree root. As she drifted into unconsciousness, she thought she heard him exclaim, "Are you alright? I didn't mean to—"

Solace woke up thirsty, her head pounding, lying under a blanket inside a two-person tent. She rolled onto her side and cried out from the pain. Bringing her hand up to her bandaged head, she probed around and discovered an egg-sized lump on her forehead.

The tent flap was drawn back and a large shadow loomed in the opening. All Solace could make out was the silhouette of a tall man, framed by the sunlight outside the tent. *How long have I been lying here?* A frisson of fear crept up Solace's spine, and she paused, trying to figure out whether she hurt anywhere other than her head. She took a deep breath and exhaled. *No, I think it's just my head—for now.*

"Would you like some water?" he asked, with none of his previous gruffness.

"Aye," Solace whispered. If she spoke any louder, her head might explode.

The man entered the tent, stooping over because of his height, and knelt down beside her with a water skin in his hands. He wore the black leather duster and large-brimmed hat of a trader or merchant, but he'd pulled the brim of his hat low, so she couldn't see much of his face other than his dark, well-

THE LIGHTNESS OF WATER

trimmed beard. He moved like a younger man, more like Arik than her father.

Solace noticed the palm of his right hand sported the calluses of one who wielded a sword regularly. She'd asked her father once about the bumpy calluses across his palm, and he had pulled out his sword to show her where the hilt fit snugly over them. Even though her father had replaced his sword with a plow, the calluses were a permanent reminder of his old life. *Could this man be a mercenary? He was no ordinary soldier.* She shuddered to think about his plans for her.

Slipping an arm under her neck, he carefully propped her up so she could have a few sips. Coughing, she said, "Enough." She almost said thanks, but decided it was ridiculous to thank the kidnapper who'd caused her injury, simply because he gave her a drink of water.

"Get some rest. We ride at sunset." Since she'd been knocked out sometime after midnight, and the sun was well up, she realized his kidnapping timetable must be seriously off schedule. *Good, maybe Dad or Gordo are tracking us now.* Her father and his best friend had been considered the finest scouts —and trackers—in the king's army. More enemies surrendered while en route to battle than engaged in actual fighting, when they spotted Soren, Gordo, and an entire battalion galloping toward them.

"I don't think I can."

"You will ride," he snarled—his unpleasant side was back with a vengeance—and stormed out of the tent. Despite her best efforts to stay awake, Solace slept soundly until a shake of her shoulder roused her.

"Dad?" she asked groggily.

"Here, you need to eat," a rough voice answered. Then he added, "It'll help you feel better."

Solace gingerly sat up and the tent started spinning. She closed her eyes and gritted her teeth, willing herself not to be sick all over the tent. A minty aroma wafted under her nose, and she inhaled. Her nausea lifted somewhat, and she opened her eyes.

The man handed her a battered tin bowl filled with mint-scented porridge, and a small round-handled spoon. Solace's stomach gurgled, and she reached for the bowl. After eating, she wiped her mouth on a clean rag nearby and took a long swallow of water. She did feel better but didn't want to admit it to her captor.

"We'll be leaving in five minutes. Take care of any personal business and be ready to go," he nodded and turned to leave.

"Wait."

He turned around and looked at her, one dark eyebrow raised. He must have adjusted his hat, since the brim no longer obscured his face. Her kidnapper looked to be in his early twenties, and under other circumstances she might consider him good-looking. Chiseled cheekbones, brown-black eyes, and the same tawny complexion as hers. Hill people often joked their complexions matched the color of the hills, various shades of tawny beige, tan, or brown. Perhaps he was from the hill country of Toresz, on the other side of the Yeloshan border, which might explain his accent.

Yeloshans and Toreszans shared a common ethnic heritage and culture. The nations were allies, their two kings joining forces against stronger foes and otherwise leaving each other alone. While traders and merchants moved freely across the border, there was little migration back and forth. Deprivation and failed harvests occurred on both sides of the border, although Solace heard rumors that King Neuss of Toresz was an especially harsh ruler.

"What's your name? Where are we going? And why me?" she asked.

"You can call me Rhees. And you'll find out soon enough, Solace Blu." He spun on his heels and left.

So he knows my name. But that still doesn't answer "why me?"
Solace had no more time to puzzle it out. She stood up stiffly,
stepped out of the tent, and took care of her personal
business behind a large boulder. She briefly considered trying
to make a break for it, but she had no idea where she was. The
sun had set, and she still had the remnants of a headache, so
she trudged back and watched as he expertly took down the
tent.

"My leather pouch, I had it on me earlier. Where is it?"

Rhees walked toward the horses. She must have ridden the
bay stallion, a huge animal, sixteen hands tall at least, because
the smaller mare carried the tent and packs. Rhees pulled her
pouch from one of the saddlebags and tossed it to her. She
opened the flap and found her book and a comb inside. Her
slings, three silver coins, and dagger, which she wished she had
at the moment to use on Rhees, if that was even his real name,
were gone.

"Where's the rest of my stuff?" she asked, shaking her
pouch at him.

"You mean your weapons—quite an assortment for a young
hill girl—

and your coinage? I confiscated your weapons and
borrowed your coins."

Solace snorted. "Right, you 'borrowed' my coins."

Rhees drew himself up to his full height. Towering over her,
he folded his arms. "I intend to repay you when we...ah, when
we reach our final destination."

Solace rolled her eyes. "Sure. Whatever you say." *A
kidnapper and a thief. And probably a mercenary too.* She pointed to
the packhorse, still trying to make out where her weapons were
hidden. "What's her name?"

"Caya." The mare gave Solace a placid glance.

Rhees pulled his brim down low and indicated she should
climb into the saddle, but the bay stallion was much taller than

the farm animals she'd grown up with. She patted the horse and asked, "What's his name?"

"Jenx. Now stop stalling. Up you go." He picked her up at the waist like a child and plunked her into the saddle. Stepping onto his stirrup, he swung one long leg over the saddle and settled behind her. Solace sat up straighter, trying not to make physical contact with him, an impossible goal for two people sitting astride a horse, even an oversized horse like Jenx.

Two leather-clad arms reached around either side of her and flicked the reins. The horse took off, thrusting Solace back into Rhees's chest. She instantly pulled herself up by grasping the saddle horn, and Rhees actually chuckled. Her temper flared, and she sidled forward a couple of inches in the saddle. Rhees started to laugh.

Solace hated the man even more than she had the day before.

~

They rode all night, pausing when the horses needed a break, and rode again until sunrise. They climbed into the hills, where Rhees found a small hollow, invisible from the valley below, to set up camp. *He's taking no chances being spotted during the day,* Solace thought grimly.

Solace slid out of the saddle and glanced around, trying to determine their location. Unfortunately, the hill country of Yelosha, which stretched from the Hawxhurss mountain range in the west all the way to the eastern border with Toresz, looked pretty much the same: brown hills with patches of wild grasses, and carefully irrigated fields, the farmers relying on wells, watering holes, and the short rainy season to sustain them and their animals in the arid Yeloshan countryside.

Nothing looked even remotely familiar, and Solace couldn't see the Hawxhurss Mountains anywhere, so she guessed their destination must be Toresz. Fresh anxiety fed the knot in her stomach. They hadn't passed any farms during the past few hours, nothing but brown, rocky hills everywhere she looked. *Even if I manage to escape, where would I go?*

A cold wind whistled through the hills, whipping their clothes and faces, and blowing Rhees's hat off his head. His dark, wavy hair flew in all directions as he ran after the tumbling hat and scooped it up. Returning briefly to her side, he dropped a saddlebag by her feet and turned to walk away.

"You will cook for us while I brush down and feed the horses," he said over his shoulder. "The supplies are in my saddlebag."

Solace clenched her fists, anger blooming in her chest. She called out to his departing back, "You may be a kidnapper, a mercenary, and a criminal, but you *could* say please."

Rhees paused and turned around to face her. "And you *could* thank me for healing your headache this morning, but I heard nothing." Solace noticed he didn't deny any of the names she'd called him.

"Do you really expect me to thank the man who took me from my home, dropped me on my head, and holds me captive against my will?" Solace put her hands on her hips.

"I did not drop you on your head."

"You let go of me when I was wrapped in a burlap sack and dizzy. Same thing."

"You will cook for us now," Rhees said and busied himself with the horses.

"Hateful man." Solace muttered under her breath. She unbuckled the first flap and looked inside: packets of coffee, tea, and herbs, as well as dried meat and vegetables. Underneath the other flap she found a cooking pot, serving ware, utensils, and a few extra packets of preserved vegetables. She flipped the bag over and looked around for a false lining. Her slings and dagger had to be hidden somewhere.

"Your weapons are not in the saddlebag, so stop stalling and make dinner."

"You didn't throw them away, did you?" Solace glared up at him. He was a tall man, taller than her father and Arik by half a head, at least.

"That is not your concern."

"Aye, it is my concern! Everything you've done is my concern!" Solace threw the saddlebag at him. "You can cook for yourself."

He took four large strides and loomed in front of her, thrusting the saddlebag at her chest. "You will cook for us, one way or another. I suggest you choose the easier way," he said in a raspy voice, barely above a whisper, his eyes flashing darkly.

Solace glowered at him. He glowered back.

"I have nothing to start the fire with," she said in an even voice. She'd not give him the satisfaction of seeing her cower, even though his raspy-voiced threat did scare her. Besides, she was famished and couldn't go on much longer without food. She would eat to maintain her strength and find a way to escape.

Rhees pulled a flint from one of the pockets of his duster and handed it to her. "The wild grasses will burn fast. You'll need to gather some sticks and branches, as well."

He returned to Jenx and spoke soothingly as he finished brushing him. Jenx flicked his ears forward and nuzzled Rhees's neck. Solace shook her head. The horse had extremely poor taste, but then again, the animal had about as much choice as she did at the moment.

Solace managed to get the fire going while Rhees set up the tent. She concocted a stew from some dried tomatoes, onions, a bit of salted pork, and a packet of herbs, carefully adding water from one of the water skins. He walked over and sat down across from her, the small, smoking fire forming a hazy barrier between them. Solace handed him a bowl of the stew and one of the peculiar round-handled spoons. They ate in silence. He handed his bowl back to her for a refill. When they finished eating, she cleaned the bowls, utensils, and cooking pot with sand and stowed them in the saddlebag.

Rhees put out the fire with several handfuls of sand and said, "Best to turn in now, as we'll be up before sunset."

Solace didn't answer but walked toward the tent, exhaustion coursing through every limb. She knew she should change the bandage on her head, but that would have to wait. She couldn't do one more thing. When she pulled back the tent flap to enter and saw Rhees was following behind, she spun around, her hand flat against his broad chest.

"Whoa! I might cook for two, but I sleep alone."

Rhees lowered his dark eyebrows and glared. "I have one tent and we will share."

"You can sleep outside."

"I will freeze outside," he said sharply, taking a step toward her. "We will share this tent. Now step aside."

"I sleep alone," she repeated, her voice shaking.

Rhees paused as the meaning behind her words slowly sank in. He looked down at his scuffed boots and shook his head. "No harm will come to you. I give you my word." Removing his hat, he looked directly at her, as if to demonstrate his sincerity.

Solace rolled her eyes, her fear making her bold. "Really? The word of a kidnapper?"

Something like shame flitted across his face, but his voice was steely. "I kidnap out of necessity, not malice. Step aside, now!" This last part was said with particular vehemence, and he lifted her by the waist, swung her roughly behind him, and stalked into the tent.

Solace took several steps away from the tent and dropped down to the ground, shivering in the wind. She pulled the cloak Arik had given her more tightly around herself and thought of her Naming Day—could it have been just two days ago?—and all the love that surrounded her in that cramped little cottage. Curling up on her side, the tears spilled over. She'd been holding them back since that horrid man had dropped the sack over her head and stole her away, but she let them come now, wracking, painful sobs that made her head hurt again and gave her hiccups.

After she cried herself out and grew quiet, save for an occasional hiccup, she heard the tent flap open. Rhees walked out, sighed heavily, and handed her a handkerchief. She mopped her face and blew her nose.

Rhees knelt down beside her and said softly, with none of his usual arrogance, "I give you my word."

She nodded, too worn out to fight back. He reached out his hand toward her. She allowed herself to be pulled up from the ground and led into the tent.

CHAPTER 3

olace noted there were two bedrolls on the floor of the tent. Rhees pointed to the bedroll farthest from the tent flap. Naturally, he'd be sleeping in front of the tent entrance, so she couldn't possible slip outside without waking him.

She dropped onto her bedroll, slipped under the blanket fully clothed, and rolled on her side with her back to Rhees. Holding herself rigid, she waited to see whether he came near her. He fumbled with the tent flap—it had ties to close it—and then she heard him removing his duster, folding it, and putting it on the ground. When she heard him pulling off his pants, one leg at a time, she squeezed her eyes shut, her heart pounding in her chest, and clutched a fistful of blanket in each shaking hand.

But he pulled back his own blanket and slid underneath. After a while, Solace heard the steady breathing of a man asleep. She rolled over onto her other side and stared at him for a while, trying to figure him out. She finally gave up and closed her eyes until the smell of coffee woke her up.

Rhees pushed aside the tent flap and handed her a mug.

"I'll change that bandage when you've finished your coffee," he said and went back outside.

He addressed her in a normal tone of voice. No arrogance or gruffness or raspy-voiced threats for a change. She took a swallow of hot coffee and warmed her hands on the mug. Her fingers and toes had gone stiff with cold during the night, and she wondered, not for the first time, where they were going and what would happen to her when they arrived.

When she finished her coffee, she unwound the bandage from her head and tossed it aside. The knot in the center of her forehead was still tender, but the swelling was down. She searched her pouch for her comb, unbraided her hair, and tried untangling the worst of the knots before re-braiding it again. *What I wouldn't give for a warm bath.*

Standing up, she removed her travel-stained cloak and smoothed down her rumpled blue tunic. Pulling the cloak back over her head and grabbing her pouch, she carried her tin mug outside and set it down next to Rhees's saddlebag. A coppery sky stretched overhead as the sun sank into the hills.

Rhees motioned for her to join him at the smoky fire where he'd brewed the coffee. When she sat down next to him, he reached over to probe her wound. "Ouch!" she said and started to pull away, but he put his hands on her face and held her head steady.

"Better," he said, examining her forehead. He reached into a small bag at his side and pulled out a jar of ointment. He smeared some over her bruised forehead and then unwound a clean piece of gauze, which he expertly wrapped around her head, tying it neatly in the back.

"You seem to have some skills as a healer," she said, curious about the ointment and the minty-porridge he'd fixed for her the previous day.

"My mother was a healer," he looked down into his mug.

"Ah," she nodded. "Healing skills are useful for mercenaries."

Rhees slammed his tin mug on the ground, hot coffee sloshing over the rim and splashing his hand. He hastily grabbed a rag to wipe off the coffee and asked in an angry huff, "Why do you persist in calling me a mercenary?"

Solace plowed ahead, undeterred by his temper, and ticked off the reasons on her fingers, "One, you're dressed as a merchant or trader, but since you're a kidnapper, you are likely neither. Two, the calluses on your right palm are from using your sword. Only soldiers or mercenaries have calluses like that. Three, your accent is not from around here. Most men in the Yeloshan coastal province purchase their way out of military service to our king. It's only the poor Yeloshan hill men, like my father, who serve in the army. Which means you're from Toresz, where the king's soldiers are required to wear his uniform. Given these facts, you must be both a kidnapper and a mercenary. And so healing skills would come in handy in your *profession*." Solace emphasized the last word and calmly waited for another outburst from Rhees.

But Rhees's mouth was open, and a look of surprise and something else, maybe fear, crossed his features. He denied nothing and spoke in a low raspy tone, the one he used to make threats. "You are highly observant. Perhaps it comes from growing up in these hills, among wolves and jackals and water shortages. However, if you share your observations with anyone else, both our lives will be forfeited."

"Who could I possibly share my observations with out here?" Solace waved her hand around them. They were the only people for many, many miles.

"Enough said. We ride." He tossed the rest of his coffee, put out the fire, and took down the tent. Pointing to the saddlebag and bedrolls, he told Solace to secure them on Caya. When they were ready to leave, Solace glanced back at the campsite. Rhees had eliminated every trace of their presence. Clearly he knew how to avoid being found, and she realized, with a sharp ache in her chest, her father might never track her down.

~

For six more days they followed the same pattern, riding at night, allowing Jenx and Caya to graze when needed, and stopping when the sun rose. As they rode, Solace discovered the mental map of subterranean water sources she always relied on began to fade, until one day she felt no connection to the water at all.

Squinting, she noticed no color variations in the soil, and when they stopped to rest the horses, she heard not even the faintest murmurings of running water anywhere. The land they were riding through was more barren than any she'd seen, and it left her feeling breathless, almost panicky, to be so disconnected from the water deep within the earth that fed every well and spring in the Yeloshan hills.

As they traveled, the horses drew moisture from the wild grasses, and when they were really thirsty, they pawed at dried creek beds, uncovering isolated pockets of muddy water trapped beneath the clay and sand. That worked fine for the horses, but not for Solace or Rhees. By the seventh day, they'd run out of food, and their water skins were nearly dry. As they drew closer to Toresz, Rhees's temper grew shorter. When the sun set on the last evening, Solace roused herself from a fitful sleep and finding the tent empty, went outside to discover Rhees brushing down Jenx again, which he'd done before turning in.

"Are we leaving?"

Rhees growled, "We wait here."

"Why?"

Rhees threw his brush on the ground and stalked over to her. "Why must you ask so many questions? If I had any idea you'd drive me this crazy I'd never have—"

Solace narrowed her eyes and shouted, "Never have what? Kidnapped me from my home? Forced me to cook for you and clean for you and ride with you all these nights past? And forced me to go hungry and thirsty too?" Solace shoved Rhees out of the way and he lost his balance. Realizing it might be her only chance to escape from him, she started to run. She didn't care if she died in these hills, she couldn't stand one more day in his presence. Jenx neighed, and she whispered as she ran past, "It's not you; it's him I hate."

Solace heard Rhees cursing and then taking up the chase behind her. She ran downhill, her footing slipping several times, and her breath coming in short gasps. She ran until she thought her heart would explode, all the while hearing his long strides gaining on her.

She looked behind just as he caught up with her. Wrapping one muscled arm around her waist, he tackled her to the ground and they both tumbled downhill another twenty paces, finally coming to rest against a large boulder. He snarled in her ear, "You little fool! Do you have a death wish? We're in Toresz now, and a girl traveling without protection in these hills will be killed as easily as a rabbit, but only after she's been assaulted by King Neuss's men."

Tears coursed down Solace's face and a few fell on his hand. Rhees looked at the tears and rolled away from her. Sitting up, he ran a hand through his unruly hair; he'd lost his hat somewhere above them. More quietly he asked, "Are you injured?"

Solace wiped her tears on the sleeve of her ruined cloak and shook her head. "I don't think so." Rhees stood, pulling her up with him, and kept a firm grasp on her arm as they climbed back up to their campsite.

As they neared the top of the ridge where they'd camped, Rhees stopped and pulled her closer, putting a finger to his lips. They heard a rustling that wasn't the wind coursing through the hills or creatures stirring in the grasses. Rhees cupped one hand, all the while keeping his other arm wrapped around her waist, and whistled. Solace knew her birdcalls, but she didn't recognize this one. They heard another whistle echo in reply. Solace could sense some of the tension draining from Rhees, and he practically ran the rest of the way, with Solace stumbling along beside him.

"Chelyss! Well met!" Rhees dropped his arm from around Solace's waist and grinned at the man he called Chelyss, who looked about Soren's age, with gray hair peeking out beneath his peaked cap and a fringe of gray whiskers framing his lean face.

"Well met, Rhees! You're late, as usual, and Fenwith's been worrying, as usual!" Chelyss ran over to Rhees, clapped him on the shoulder, and handed him his hat. "Found it on the ground over there and figured you'd run off in a hurry."

Turning to Solace, Chelyss swept his cap off his head and bowed. "Solace Blu! Well met, young lass, well met!"

Solace was taken aback by the warm welcome and the man's use of her name. Her mother had taught her to be polite in all circumstances, although even her mother hadn't anticipated Solace being kidnapped and then greeted by the friend of her captor.

"Well met, Mr. Chelyss. And thank you for the warm welcome. It is good to meet a Toreszan with manners!" She flicked her eyes at Rhees, who drew his eyebrows together in a scowl.

Chelyss glanced at Rhees and guffawed. "The lass has your measure, Rhees, and pretty quick too!"

"Aye, well, it's past time we left these hills. We haven't eaten since yesterday morning," Rhees grumbled.

Chelyss sobered quickly. "Fenwith figured you'd run out of food by now, so I brought some bread and cheese." He pulled a knapsack off his back, rummaged around, and withdrew a slab of cheese, cut up in chunks and wrapped in a cloth napkin, and a loaf of crusty bread.

Chelyss offered the cheese and bread first to Solace, who took a small portion of each despite her hunger, and then she passed the food to Rhees, who took half and pushed the rest back at her. "You haven't been eating well, even before we ran out of food. Take more." He made it sound more like a command, so she ignored him and pushed the food back at him.

"Thank you," she said to Chelyss and bit into a piece of cheese.

Chelyss nodded and then offered them a full water skin. After they slaked their thirst, he withdrew two apples from his knapsack and offered them to the horses, grazing on the wild grasses nearby. Caya nibbled at hers, while Jenx wolfed his down in two bites, and then he took Chelyss's cap between his teeth and tossed it to the ground playfully.

Chelyss and Rhees made quick work of taking down the tent and breaking camp. Solace's head was spinning with questions but she held her tongue, figuring if she were really quiet, they might forget she was present and speak more freely. Rhees pointed to Jenx. "You will ride," he said curtly.

He made a move as if to hoist her into the saddle but Solace put up her hand, palm out, and said, "I've got this." Solace used to exercise her father's draft horses when they weren't needed for farm work, and she'd taught herself various types of mounts. There was one mount she'd perfected, which she thought would work well with Jenx, who was about three hands taller than her father's largest horse. She would have preferred to try the mount on Jenx in private first, but she'd worked it out in her head, in much the same way she worked out where to aim the stone of her sling or exactly how deep to dig a well. And she didn't want Rhees tossing her into the saddle anymore.

Solace ran toward Jenx and pushed off the ground with both her feet. As she leapt in the air, she grabbed his saddle horn in her left hand and gripped the back of the saddle with her right. She swung her right leg over Jenx's broad back, lifting her right arm out of the way of her leg, and landed gracefully in the saddle. Solace rubbed Jenx's mane and whispered her thanks.

Chelyss whistled, and Rhees's scowl deepened. "Nice trick," he muttered and reached for the reins. Chelyss and Rhees walked in front, leading Jenx and Solace and Caya down the hill and into the valley below. Solace strained her ears, catching snippets of conversation.

"...papers are ready, as you requested," said Chelyss.

"Good," Rhees replied. "And the scrolls?"

Chelyss mumbled something and then added, "...will pass muster with the king's men."

"Do they suspect anything?"

"I had a couple nosing around yesterday, asking after you, but I said you were still in the hills."

"Well done." Rhees squeezed the older man's shoulder affectionately.

Chelyss pointed a thumb back at Solace and asked, "Is it true, what we've heard?"

Rhees said, "Saw it with my own eyes." He hesitated and then leaned over to whisper in Chelyss's ear, "...confirmed...a perfect record..."

Solace couldn't hear anything until Chelyss exclaimed, "Could be the saving of us..." and then he lowered his voice and continued speaking. She almost gave up attempting to eavesdrop, but her ears perked up when she heard Chelyss conclude, "...a brilliant plan. Keeps her under your protection and safe."

Rhees snorted. "Although she's quite a handful. A regular harridan at times." Solace didn't know what a harridan was, but she could tell it was an insult. *What a hateful man!* She gripped the saddle horn tightly and leaned forward to catch his next remarks.

Chelyss said something about making allowances, and Rhees replied, "But you're not the one who'll be marrying her!"

CHAPTER 4

"**M**arrying? You and me? I'd rather die first!" Solace shouted down at the back of Rhees's head. She felt like a pawn in some crazy game where the rules kept changing. Nothing made sense, and she was tired and hungry—she should have eaten more—and wanted to go home. Every time she thought of her father, and how frantic with worry he must be, her stomach turned into tight, painful knots.

"Hush now, lass, these hills have ears." Chelyss left Rhees and dropped back to walk alongside her. "'Tis not what it seems. We'll talk more later, when we're safely within four walls."

Chelyss rejoined Rhees and they didn't speak again, but continued their descent through the hills, until Rhees said, "I see Fenwith has left a candle burning." Solace spotted a pinprick of light in the distance, somewhere in the valley below them.

Rhees and Chelyss picked up the pace, both clearly anxious to be inside. Solace didn't think they feared crossing paths with four-legged creatures such as wolves or jackals, but it was the two-legged variety that had them worried. She peered around uneasily, the darkness surrounding them like a shroud.

Solace heard Chelyss curse under his breath when a torch appeared on the path in front of them, held high by a uniformed man, probably a border guard. Several more guards bearing torches, the flickering flames casting orange halos across their faces, blocked their path.

"Names and papers," stated the lead guard.

Rhees slowed his pace, coming to a stop while still in the shadows, outside the circle of light cast by the torches. Chelyss stepped forward and spoke formally, "Well met, Guardsmen."

The lead guard waved his torch in front of Chelyss's face. "Name?"

"You know my name well enough, Petr. You see me three times a week at least purchasing water in Shulamorn."

"So? The king's protocols must be followed to the letter. Names and papers, now!" Petr looked like he wanted to pound the torch into the palm of his hand for emphasis.

Chelyss sighed dramatically and flicked his left hand ever so slightly behind his back. Rhees moved forward and clapped his hand on Chelyss's shoulder, and Solace saw something passed between their hands so quickly none of the guards took notice.

"Come now, uncle, let's cooperate with these good men. After all, they're just doing their jobs." Rhees laughed a bit too loudly, but Solace noticed the lead guard relaxed slightly.

"Rhees Demore and my fiancé, Lace Blusari." Rhees made an elaborate show of thoroughly searching the various pockets of his leather duster for his papers, and Solace's pulse quickened as each pocket came up empty. Although she hated Rhees, with good reason, she had to admit he'd been true to his word. He hadn't laid a hand on her while they slept side-by-side in the same tent for the past week. But the hungry way the guards were looking at her turned her stomach. She tried making herself invisible by withdrawing more deeply into the folds of her cloak.

"Ah, here they are." Rhees produced the papers with a flourish and handed them to Petr, who took Rhees's papers and then looked at Chelyss expectantly.

Chelyss reached into the breast pocket of his jacket to retrieve his papers. "Chelyss Demore," he mumbled as Petr removed the papers from his hand.

Petr motioned to one of the guards, who joined him a short distance away, while the other two stood stolidly in front of them, waiting for further orders. Jenx pawed the ground, snorting, but Solace patted his neck and he settled down.

The second guard returned to Chelyss, handed his papers back to him, and growled, "All in order. You may go. But don't try our patience again."

"I'll wait for my nephew and his fiancé, if you don't mind. They're my guests."

"As you wish."

Petr walked over to Solace and Jenx, holding his torch high so he could examine her face and clothes. She knew she looked a mess—more than a week on the road, no way to bathe or comb out her hair properly, her clothes travel-stained—even the beautiful cloak Arik had given her was ruined.

"Your fiancé looks as if she's been dragged kicking and screaming all the way to the altar." Petr addressed Solace. "Where did you say you hail from?"

Before Solace could answer—she had no idea what those papers said, and she trusted the guards even less than she trusted Rhees—Rhees stepped between Petr and Jenx, who was shifting nervously on his hooves. "She didn't say, but the papers state clearly that my fiancé is from Yelosha, the Warovryss Province." Solace knew the Warovryss Province, about a hundred miles or more to the north, shared a border with Toresz. Traveling from there through the hills would help explain her bedraggled appearance and her Yeloshan accent.

Speaking to Solace again, Petr asked, "And are you formally betrothed to this man?"

Solace hesitated a fraction of a second, wondering what would happen if she denied it. But she covered her hesitation with a yawn and said, "Aye sir."

Petr led Rhees back to where the second guard was standing and spoke to Rhees in low, urgent tones, gesticulating with his torch in one hand and the papers in the other. Solace feared he might set the papers on fire, either by accident or possibly on purpose, and she suspected those papers were the only thing keeping her safe at the moment. Rhees raised his hands, palms up, and Petr and the other guard glanced directly at Solace, as if she were a pig at market and they were calculating her value.

Rhees coughed and gestured to Petr, who impatiently waved his torch. Rhees fished around inside his duster, and pulling out several coins, dropped them in Petr's palm. Petr turned them over to examine them. "Why are you traveling with Yeloshan silver?"

"That's my fiancé's dowry you're holding," said Rhees.

Solace gritted her teeth, furious at Rhees for using her coins to pay off Petr. For a second, Petr looked like he was going to object, but Solace heard Rhees say, "Search us if you will, but that's all we have."

Petr hesitated but the second guard leaned over, glanced at the coins, and said, "Petr, let's go. It's well past dinner time and the boys are famished."

Petr pushed the papers back at Rhees and said, "You may pass." Waves of relief washed over Solace. To think she felt safer with Rhees and Chelyss than with Petr and the guards made her almost laugh out loud.

Rhees thanked him, returned to Jenx's side, and picked up

the reins. They followed Chelyss along the main road until the ground leveled off. They left the road, walked several hundred paces across rocky ground, and pulled up in front of a large stone cottage with a single candle burning in the front window. As Solace slid off Jenx, her legs collapsed underneath her, and she landed in a heap on the ground.

The door to the cottage burst open, and a sixtyish woman with a complexion several shades darker than either man ran out. The woman wore a thick sweater over her cotton work dress, her silver hair pulled back into a tidy bun. She bent down to help Solace stand, tut-tutting all the while. "This poor lass. Rhees, what did you do to her? She's skin and bones and shaking all over!" The woman put her arm around Solace and helped her into the cottage. Their homey front parlor could have swallowed Solace's cottage twice over. The older woman whisked Solace, whose legs were shaking badly, through a doorway on the far side of the parlor. They entered a sizable kitchen, lit up with several candles, where a brass bathtub stood on curved legs in the corner, waiting to be filled with water.

"Don't blame me if she didn't want to eat! She's stubborn as a mule, that one," Rhees grumbled as he followed behind them.

"Here, lass, sit down." The woman pulled out a kitchen chair for Solace and scolded Rhees. "Manners, young man, watch your manners. She's far from home and frightened half to death."

Turning back to Solace she said, "Don't mind him, he's been like that, well, since the troubles began."

"Fenwith, let's not be going into all that history," Chelyss interrupted.

Fenwith said, "Help me, old man, with the tub. We need to heat the pots of water whilst I fetch the lass a cup of tea. Her teeth are chattering, and her lips are blue with cold." Fenwith picked up Solace's ice-cold hands and tut-tutted again. Solace shivered inside her cloak.

Solace saw Rhees glance her way and an odd look flitted across his face, as if she were inconveniencing him somehow. "What's wrong with you?" he frowned. "You were fit and feisty the entire ride here."

Fenwith rolled her eyes. "Out of the kitchen, Rhees. I'll let you know when you can have the tub. I've laid out a cold supper for you in the parlor."

"Wait a minute, you expect me to bathe second, after *her*?"

Fenwith put her hands on her hips and stared Rhees down. He left the kitchen grumbling to himself.

A large fireplace occupied one wall in the kitchen, where Chelyss heated pot after pot of water, while Fenwith plied Solace with chamomile tea. When Chelyss declared the water hot enough for bathing, Fenwith shooed him as well from the kitchen, closed the door, and helped Solace undress and step into the tub.

Fenwith handed Solace a small piece of soap and then proceeded to unbraid Solace's hair and shampoo it for her. Solace wasn't sure whether it was Fenwith's kindness or the touch of her fingers on her hair, but tears welled in her eyes and traveled down her cheeks. When Fenwith spotted the tears she said, "I know you're missing your home, and you're wondering whether you're safe, but I promise you, no harm will come to you in this household, nor while you're under Rhees's protection."

When Solace didn't answer, Fenwith knit her brows and asked, "Did he mistreat you, lass?"

Solace splashed water on her face to wash away the tears and took a deep breath. "Not physically, no."

Fenwith sighed and finished rinsing Solace's hair. "But he was difficult to travel with, ornery even?"

"Ornery, arrogant, demanding...you get the idea."

Fenwith picked up an oversized towel from the oak table in the center of the room, and held it up so Solace could step right into it. Solace sat down in a chair near the fire, all bundled up and feeling almost human, as Fenwith towel-dried her hair.

"I'm not making excuses, mind you, but Rhees has a strong sense of duty, which drives everything he does." Fenwith handed her an ivory satin nightgown with a matching dressing gown, and a pair of ivory satin slippers.

Solace had read about satin but never touched it before. The silky smoothness of the fabric felt too rich for a hill girl from Yelosha, too rich for Fenwith and Chelyss, for that matter. Solace ran her fingers across the delicate piping along the neckline of the nightgown before slipping it over her head. She belted the dressing gown around her waist and slid her feet into the dainty slippers, which wouldn't last five minutes on a Yeloshan farm.

It was Rhees's turn for a bath, and as Solace was leaving the kitchen, she put her hand on the older woman's arm. "If his sense of duty drove him to kidnap me, then he must be a mercenary or worse."

Fenwith looked horrified. "Oh no, lass, Rhees isn't a mercenary. Nothing could be further from the truth."

Rhees chose that moment to walk into the kitchen with a couple of towels and a change of clothes. He dropped his towels in the doorway and stooped to pick them up, although he couldn't take his eyes off Solace, dressed in ivory satin, her black hair released from its tight braid and tumbling about her shoulders.

Solace tightened the belt on her dressing gown and waited for Rhees to move out of the doorway, but he seemed to want to linger. He looked at Fenwith and said in a husky voice, "I hadn't realized you'd saved any of her things."

Solace heard the catch in his voice and wondered whom he

was remembering. Rhees continued staring at her, his eyes taking on a glassy sheen.

Fenwith nodded. "I saved some of Ellanora's things, those that reminded me most of her. And just as well, since this lass's clothes are ruined. She's almost the same size as your mother too. I'll just need to take in a few of the dresses."

So Rhees lost his mother, just like me. But it seemed to have made him a harder, unyielding sort of a man.

Solace was determined to learn something about Rhees that might explain why he'd taken her. "What exactly is your profession?" She braced herself to hear anything from poacher to slave trader.

"It's nothing you've guessed; I can promise you that." Rhees said, and nodding at her ivory satin ensemble, he added, "You look...healthier."

Solace folded her arms across her chest, feeling more self-conscious than she had in the cramped two-person tent they'd shared all week. "Well, are you going to answer me?"

"I am employed by King Neuss."

Solace snorted. "Just as I thought. You're one of his henchmen, what my father would call a 'fixer.'"

Fenwith interrupted, "You've got Rhees all wrong, he's not —" But Rhees held up his hand.

"In a manner of speaking, that's true enough. I do fix things, like books and scrolls and such," he answered with a half-smile.

"You fix books? And scrolls?" Solace's brow furrowed.

"I work in the Great Library of Toresz. I'm a librarian."

CHAPTER 5

Solace stared at Rhees, her frown deepening. *A librarian? A kidnapping librarian with the calluses of a master swordsman?* Before she could form a response that was polite enough for Fenwith's ears, Rhees held the door open for both of them and said, "Ladies? If you please, I'd like to bathe now."

"Of course, we'll be on our way," Fenwith replied and then said to Solace, "You go along, dear, and sit by the fireplace in the front parlor. Your hair is still damp, and I don't want you to catch another chill. I'll bring out your supper in a few minutes." Solace nodded her thanks and left the kitchen without another word to Rhees.

Chelyss pulled up a chair next to the fireplace for Solace, who was relieved to sit on a cushioned seat rather than a hard leather saddle. As she fluffed out her damp hair in the hopes it would dry faster, she looked around the cottage. While it was larger and better furnished than her own simple home, nonetheless, Solace noticed the fraying seat cushions and threadbare rugs. A cracked mirror hung near the front door. The Demore family had fallen on leaner times, no different from any other family of the hills, whether Yeloshan or Toreszan.

Fenwith brought her a plate of sausages, a sliced apple, cheese, and fresh bread. She sat next to Chelyss on a sofa covered with throws strategically placed to hide the tattered fabric underneath, and inquired about their trip through the hills. Solace ate slowly, savoring every bite, while Chelyss explained about running into the king's guards and the bribe Rhees had to pay.

When he was finished, Fenwith shook her head. "Petr's mother would rattle in her grave if she knew how he was throwing his weight around. It's pure greed that's driving him and the others."

"It's a good thing I met up with Rhees when I did. Without the papers for the lass, and Rhees claiming they were betrothed, we'd be having a different conversation right now."

"I didn't like the way those men stared at me." Solace placed her empty plate on a spindly end table. "Do they treat all women that way around here?"

Chelyss got up to toss another log onto the fire and sat back down next to Fenwith. Scratching his gray beard, he asked, "How much do you know about what's been happening here in Toresz since King Neuss murdered his way into power ten years ago?"

"We're too busy trying to survive on our Yeloshan farms to seek out news about Toresz," said Solace. "However, we've heard from traders passing through on market day that King Neuss is a harsh, greedy ruler who makes his people pay dearly for everything they eat and drink and wear."

"Aye that's true, but there's more. Neuss encourages lawlessness because it allows him to tighten his grip. He lets his guards take young women who are not under the protection of a man, whether a husband, father, brother, or fiancé, and they're not seen again. And even when a woman is traveling with other men, the guards expect to be paid a bribe, as you saw tonight."

"What happens to the women they take away?"

Chelyss drew his bushy silver eyebrows together. "The guards assault those poor lasses, sometimes kill them, and other times they sell them to traffickers. The lucky ones wind up working in the mines or the fields. The unlucky ones—"

"I think my uncle has explained enough for you to grasp why we must claim to be betrothed, and why we must sound believable. Unlike tonight, when your slight hesitation could have been fatal," said Rhees, who re-entered the front parlor wearing a loose-fitting chambray shirt open at the throat, his damp hair neatly combed and curling over his collar. He'd traded his dusty denims for lightweight grey pants. Rhees pulled up another chair in front of the fire and angled himself so he could look directly at Solace. A bath and a meal, and being among his family, must have released the pent-up tension she sensed whenever he was around. He seemed almost relaxed and looked at her not unkindly.

Solace took a deep breath and asked the question no one had answered for her yet. "Why did you take me?" She prepared herself for another angry outburst but it didn't come.

Instead, Rhees ran his hand through his dark hair and grunted, "I told you it was out of necessity, not malice, and that's the truth." Rhees paused, glanced at Fenwith, and softened his tone. "Even though I live and work among books, and I started reading before I learned to hold a sword, words fail me in this. I'll have to *show* you why I brought you to Toresz. It's the only way you'll understand and perhaps see that I mean you no harm."

"Wait just a minute." Solace put up her hand, skepticism etched on her face. "I know you to be a skillful tracker and kidnapper, a hard man who forced me at knifepoint to travel across the Yeloshan hills. You claim that you're a librarian, a man of learning and books." Solace shook her head. "I may be a simple girl from the hills, but I was raised to think for myself, and defend myself and my sheep, since I was a small child. You're hiding more than you're telling."

Rhees stood up abruptly and snapped at Fenwith, "See, I told you. She's impossible!" Turning back to Solace, he growled, "You're right, I am a hard man. And if you want to live long enough to see your next Naming Day, you'll keep your opinions to yourself and do what I say. I'm to bed." He stalked out of the parlor and headed down the narrow corridor to the right of the front door, which Solace assumed led to the bedrooms.

She pointed at his retreating back and said loudly enough for Rhees to hear, "And *that's* what I've been dealing with since he snatched me from my father's farm." Rhees squared his shoulders, opened one of the bedroom doors, and slammed it behind him.

Fenwith and Chelyss exchanged a look, the kind of look that couples who are married a long time will exchange, which is full of meaning only the two of them can interpret.

Fenwith said, "There's a lot we're not saying because it's too dangerous to even whisper aloud, but he's a better man than you give him credit for."

"Aye, a much better man," added Chelyss. "Though I will acknowledge he's become a hard man over time. The only way for him to survive."

Solace folded her hands in her lap, realizing she wouldn't learn anything more from Chelyss or Fenwith that night. Compressing her lips, she said, "Very well. I have no choice but to go along with whatever that man has in mind, *if I want to live*, that is. And since you don't intend to tell me anything more, then there's nothing more to be said. Could you please show me where I'll be sleeping?"

Fenwith's hazel eyes looked sad, as if she wanted to say something but couldn't or wouldn't. She rose from the sofa.

"Of course, lass, let me show you the way. I've given you Ellanora's bedroom." She lit an extra candle, placed it in a holder, and led Solace to the bedroom at the far end of the corridor. Fenwith handed her the candle and bade her goodnight as she closed door. Solace was alone for the first time since Rhees had taken her.

It was too dim to see much of the bedroom, but the rug on the wooden floor was plush and soft under Solace's satin slippers. She placed the candle on the nightstand, removed her dressing gown, and tossed in on a nearby chair. Pulling back the heavy down comforter on the bed, she blew out the candle, burrowed underneath the soft cotton sheets, and curled up on her side.

∼

Solace woke up to a gentle rat-tat-tat. She opened one eye, trying to figure out where the sound was coming from. *Had a kangaroo rat gotten into the tent again?* She'd laughed out loud a few nights ago when Rhees jumped up from his bedroll, shrieking at the wandering rat that had the nerve to peek its head underneath their tent flap. The rat scurried away and Rhees had stomped out of the tent in a huff.

Solace yawned and pushed away the thin blanket of her bedroll, but found her hand grasping a soft comforter instead. Then she remembered where she was and sat up in bed—in the largest bed she'd ever seen—large enough for an entire family to sleep together.

Someone knocked at her door more firmly this time. Solace pushed her mass of black hair away from her face and called out, "Who is it?"

Fenwith said through the door, "'Tis Fenwith, here with your breakfast, or lunch, as it were. May I come in?"

"Of course."

Fenwith opened the door and entered with a tray. "I thought you might like breakfast in bed, seeing as how you've had to rough it for a while, and Rhees says you'll be leaving early tomorrow morning."

Solace nodded, wondering where Rhees would be taking her next. "Thank you." Fenwith placed the bed tray squarely across Solace's legs. Solace inhaled the aroma of freshly brewed coffee and took a sip from the porcelain cup. She lifted the linen napkin from the tray and found a steaming bowl of oatmeal and a quarter-cup of raisins.

"After you've eaten, we'll pull together a wardrobe for you. I'll take up my needle and thread, and we'll have you fitted in no time." Fenwith brushed a strand of hair out of Solace's eyes and said softly, "I'm sorry, lass. Sorry that I didn't stop Rhees. Not that he would have listened, but I could have tried harder to talk him out of this crazy scheme of his."

Solace looked at the older woman, her eyes reddened as if she'd been crying, and squeezed her hand. "I appreciate your kindness. And I've no doubt that man would have ignored your advice anyway."

Fenwith patted Solace's arm. "Take your time. It'll be your last free morning for quite awhile."

Solace took her advice, enjoying breakfast in bed, a first for her, and savored her solitude until a flood of homesickness washed over her. She missed her father and Arik and Barley and her sheep. She missed her old life. She forced herself not to think about it too much, because she'd start crying again, and she'd learned quickly during the past week how much that infuriated Rhees. Solace swallowed the ache in the back of her throat and removed the tray to the nightstand.

She stood up, curling her toes into the blue and gold floral-patterned rug. She walked around the entire bedroom and examined the rich mahogany furnishings that seemed too large for the room, and out of place in that cottage. Returning to the bed, Solace noticed a round seal stamped into the center of the headboard. She climbed back onto the bed to examine the seal. A golden lion's head sat above two crossed swords inside a lapis blue circle. Gilded olive leaves edged the rim of the seal. It seemed an odd sort of decoration, and she wondered whether all owners of enormous beds carved inlaid gold crests into their headboards.

Belting the dressing gown around her waist, she left the bedroom, carrying the tray with her. She padded into the kitchen, where Fenwith was scrubbing down the table. There was no sign of Rhees anywhere, which suited Solace just fine.

Fenwith looked up when Solace entered and smiled. "Good timing. I'd much rather be fixing up your wardrobe than cleaning the kitchen. Let's go!"

Fenwith took Solace back to the bedroom and began opening dresser drawers, pulling out undergarments, tunics, leggings, and dresses. She stacked the clothes in neat piles on the bed, more clothes than Solace had seen in a month of market days: cotton and linen undergarments, more satin nightdresses like the one she was wearing, silk stockings, soft wool leggings, lightweight tunics and tops, skirts, and dresses for summer, and warmer clothes for winter, in flannels and plaids and soft worsted wools, and evening dresses for formal occasions with matching overcoats, shoes and gloves.

"You told Rhees you saved a *few* of Ellanora's things," said Solace, surveying the clothes spread across the bed.

"A small white lie, and he'll be none the wiser," said Fenwith with a wink. "We'll sort through and select an assortment for your trip to Urhl. Your clothes must be appropriate, well made and yet understated, for Lace Blusari, the fiancé of the Chief Librarian." Solace knew that Urhl was the capital of Toresz, and she'd heard it was a huge city, much larger than any city in Yelosha, including the capital.

"So he really is a *librarian?*"

"Aye, Chief Librarian."

Solace snorted. "I'll believe it when I see it."

"Well, Lace—Rhees says we have to start using the name on your papers—you'll be seeing it soon enough."

Over the next few hours, Solace modeled the various dresses and tunics for Fenwith's critical eye. She let Fenwith decide which clothes to alter and pack for the trip and which to leave behind. Rhees had instructed Fenwith to fit Solace's entire wardrobe into two saddlebags, which was no small feat of engineering.

When they were finished, Solace had a full wardrobe for every season, making her wonder just how long Fenwith expected Rhees and Solace to be in the city. Solace learned there was no point in trying to ply Fenwith with questions; she was fiercely loyal to her nephew, even when she didn't agree with his methods.

Fenwith told Solace to select something to wear for the rest of the day from the "reject" pile, and Solace picked a grey jersey dress and black tights. For the next morning, Fenwith had already laid out a smart navy-striped tunic with coordinating leggings, and a tanned leather traveling cloak lined with flannel. Solace found several sturdy leather belts in the bottom of the dresser, and a good thing too, since she'd lost her mother's belt during the journey through the hills.

"I'd best be getting some dinner together. Those men will be looking for their food soon enough," said Fenwith on the way out of the bedroom.

"I'll help you."

Fenwith turned back to Solace, her eyes growing moist. "You're offering to help me in the kitchen? A girl that's been stolen from her family, offering to help an old woman like me, who knows it's wrong to keep you here, but is agreeing to it anyway?"

Solace smiled wistfully. "You're doing it because you trust

your nephew. And while I don't trust him, I need him to survive whatever's coming. So yes, I'll help you with dinner. Besides, I've been working since I could walk. I'm not used to idleness."

Fenwith went back to Solace and threw her arms around her, drawing her into an embrace. "Perhaps some good will come out of all this. Rhees thinks so anyway." Then Fenwith wiped her eyes on her apron and left for the kitchen, with Solace following behind, puzzling over Fenwith's words.

They entered the kitchen to find Rhees and Chelyss sitting at the table, examining several maps spread across the entire surface.

"It's about time you turned up, old woman," said Chelyss affectionately.

"Afraid you won't have your supper, old man?" teased Fenwith. Solace sincerely hoped she'd never wind up calling her husband "old man" and would absolutely forbid her husband from calling her an "old woman." She lifted her shoulders slightly at the old man-old woman exchange, and then she glanced at Rhees, who also shrugged. She found it strange, being in sync with Rhees on anything.

"Lace, come here; I want to show you our route to Urhl." Rhees didn't apologize for calling her *impossible* the previous evening and storming off like a spoiled child. Nor did he say *please* when he addressed her. And no one seemed to expect him to behave any differently.

"Lace?" Rhees repeated, impatience creeping into his voice.

"Why can't we use my real name, at least when we're alone?" She walked closer to the table but remained standing. She refused to be ordered around by Rhees.

"Because the smallest slip of the tongue could mean imprisonment or hanging, that's why. I was going to drill you later tonight on your new identity, but we may as well do it now. Here." Rhees handed her a handwritten note. She

50

frowned at a few of the letters, which seemed to have extra curlicues on them.

"You can read, can't you?" he asked, trying but failing to keep the sarcasm out of his voice.

"Aye, I can read. Unlike you, I learned to use a weapon, my sling, *before* I learned to read, but I'm as good a reader as anyone I know." Solace scowled at him.

"Then let's hear you read that aloud."

"Fine." She didn't want to let him upset her again in front of Fenwith and Chelyss. She recited the basic facts of her new life from the note in her hand:

Name: Lace Blusari
Age: 17
Birthplace: Warovryss Province, Yelosha
Father: Jakob Blusari (b. East Yelosha Province)
Mother: Nila Milss (b. Warovryss Province)
Betrothed: Rhees Demore (b. Shulamorn Province, Toresz)
Occupation: Catalog Assistant

"Very good!" Rhees sounded surprised she could read so well.

"What's a catalog assistant?" Solace asked, curious despite herself. Her mother had told her about a trip she'd taken as a young woman to one of the coastal cities, where she'd visited a building packed floor-to-ceiling with books on every subject imaginable. Solace made her mother promise to take her to a library one day, but they'd never traveled farther than the hills of their home.

"You'll work in the Great Library of Toresz, helping to catalog the books and scrolls."

"But I don't know anything about cataloging."

"So long as you can read, which you've just demonstrated, you can catalog. I want you to memorize those facts by this evening, and then return that note to me."

Solace handed him the note immediately. Now it was his turn to scowl. "You've memorized it already?"

Solace nodded and then repeated the contents back to him. He nodded curtly and said, "Now that's done, come look at the maps."

Solace leaned over the maps to have a look. Rhees had pieced together several maps so he could show her the entire journey from one end of the table to the other. He plotted their route, which zigzagged across the hill country of Toresz, dipped into a series of valleys where farmers were even now planting their winter wheat, and ascended into the higher elevations where the king's mines were located.

"Why are we zigzagging our way to Urhl, when we could follow these trails through the Orpash Plain here and arrive days sooner?" Solaced traced an alternate route on the maps with her finger.

Rhees arched one dark eyebrow. "You are one of the few women I know who can read a map, let alone knows how to navigate using one."

"My father and most of our neighbors served in the Yeloshan army, and they'd often draw maps in the dirt when they described some of their battles. Besides, I nearly always have a map in my head, a mental image, of the water sources running beneath Yelosha, which helps me when I'm divining for a new well."

Everyone fell silent and looked at Solace expectantly. She felt nervous all of a sudden, uncertain why they were staring at her.

"And do you have a mental map right now, of water sources beneath us here?" Rhees asked quietly.

Solace shook her head. "I seem to have lost my mental map

about a day ago, probably because I was too hungry and exhausted to concentrate. But when I'm outside again, walking or riding in the fresh air, I'll probably start connecting new water sources together in my head. At least that's how it's always worked before." Frowning, she added, "Why are you so interested all of a sudden?"

Rhees said, "Pure curiosity, having never understood how water diviners work."

"Oh, I see," said Solace, although she really didn't. "Well, while the mental map helps, in the end it takes all five senses to divine for water." She paused to remember her question. "So are you going to explain more about our route? Why are we taking the long way?"

"As to that, the answer is simple," said Rhees. "We're going to visit some of my friends along the way, and we're going to do our best to avoid getting killed while en route."

CHAPTER 6

"Just how many enemies do you have?" *And how many friends can a hard man like you really have?*

"Enough. But the chief danger will be from highwaymen, which is why we'll avoid the main roads. Under Neuss's reign, Toresz has been overrun with roving gangs who attack people in broad daylight. Some will merely steal us blind, others will steal and kill."

"Why do the people put up with it?"

Rhees shook his head, his fingers resting lightly on the maps, "Because they're so downtrodden they haven't the will to revolt. They're half-starved and frightened. And in desperate need of hope." He looked at Solace, as if willing her to care about Toresz, about his people.

"You sound as if you actually care about them."

Rhees slammed his fist on the table, scattering the maps. "Of course I care about them, what do you take me for?" His brown-black eyes flashed at her.

Solace folded her arms and shrugged. "A man of many secrets. And too many secrets can get us both killed."

Rhees stood up from the table so abruptly his chair fell

over. His gaze locked on hers, and he clenched his jaw. Solace knew she was pushing him, but she decided now was the time to push, while Fenwith and Chelyss were around as a buffer.

Chelyss cleared his throat. "The lass makes a good point. Maybe it's time to tell her—"

"No!" Rhees picked up the chair he'd knocked over and set it down with a loud thump on the wooden floor. "She's too young and unseasoned to understand. And I don't trust her."

Solace glared at Rhees defiantly. "The feeling is mutual, because I certainly don't trust you."

Rhees exhaled and dropped his glance first. He stared at his boots, running a hand through his hair, and then he asked his aunt and uncle to give them some privacy. The older man gave Rhees a quizzical look as he pushed away from the table. Chelyss and Fenwith wordlessly left the kitchen, Fenwith patting Solace's shoulder on the way out and closing the door behind them.

Rhees pulled out the same kitchen chair he'd just knocked over and said, "Would you please take a seat?" Surprised, Solace rewarded his sudden display of good manners by complying. He sat down opposite her.

"I know that what I've done—taking you from your home and forcing you to travel with me to Toresz—is unforgivable. You have every right to never trust me. In fact, I'm sure you must hate me."

Rhees paused, and when Solace didn't respond, he continued, "But I promise if you cooperate with me, when this is all over I will take you home."

Solace sat up straighter. "You will? How long will everything take—I mean, until I can go home?" This was the best news Solace had since Rhees had tossed her onto Jenx's back in the dark.

"At least six months, maybe a year."

"A whole year? That's such a long time!" Solace thought of

her father and how anxious he must be, searching for her, and not finding her—and how after a while—weeks? months?—how sad and lonely he would become. Her lower lip quivered and she bit down on it hard so hard she drew blood.

Rhees reached into his pocket, withdrew a fresh handkerchief, and handed it to her. She dabbed her lower lip and swiped at her eyes.

"We'll be busy and the time will pass quickly."

~

They were outside before dawn the next morning, just as the first few pink streaks slashed the sky above the hills. Caya, Jenx, and another horse, a sleek black stallion, stood impatiently in front of the cottage, straining to be on the road. Rhees and Chelyss were checking saddles, ensuring bags were stowed, and speaking in low, rumbling voices, patting the horses.

Solace pointed at the third horse and asked Fenwith, "Is Chelyss coming with us?"

"No. Rhees wants you to ride Jenx. He says you and the horse have bonded. He's taking Zirott."

Rhees overheard them. "We can make better time if we're riding separately, and since you're already familiar with Jenx, I thought it made sense for you to have him."

"But isn't Jenx your horse?"

"So is Zirott. I generally travel with both horses, plus Caya, when I need to cover a great deal of ground in a short amount of time."

Solace nodded, thinking he still sounded more like a mercenary than a librarian. She knew from her father that traveling with multiple horses was a common tactic among the king's knights and soldiers like her father, who'd ridden in the cavalry. Caya's saddlebags bulged with supplies, and two water skins were strapped to her back. Jenx and Zirott each carried an extra water skin, topped up for the trip ahead.

Turning back to Fenwith, she hugged the older woman. "Thank you for everything. I hope I can see you again one day." Surprising herself, Solace realized this was true. She'd grown fond of Fenwith and wanted to see the older woman again.

Fenwith gave her a fierce hug in return and repeated an old blessing common among the hill people of Yelosha and Toresz. "May you traverse these hills in safety, may you find rest when you are weary, and may your labors be honored and your water be plenty."

Solace walked over to Jenx and rubbed the side of his neck. He blew air through his nostrils and gave a soft whicker. She mounted him the same way she had earlier, by vaulting onto his back and then picking up his reins, drawing a gasp from Fenwith. Chelyss came over to make final adjustments to the stirrups, which he or Rhees had already shortened. Patting Jenx's flank, he said, "Peace go with you, lass."

Rhees pulled up alongside her on Zirott. "We have a long ride before we stop for the night. Stay close." He flicked his reins, and Zirott trotted ahead.

Rhees had told her the first three days of their trip would be the most dangerous. They'd be passing through disputed territories under the control of various gangs. He'd insisted she study various alternate routes on the maps after dinner, memorizing how to reach each destination on their roundabout journey to Urhl. However, when Solace had asked him to return her slings and dagger, he'd arched an eyebrow and snorted. Meanwhile, he traveled with a long sword, a short sword, and several knives. So much for trust.

They rode hard each day, taking few breaks, and were careful to avoid attention when they stopped each night, which meant cold suppers and no campfires. Solace could sense Rhees's unease the deeper they traveled through the lawless lands. As they rode, she periodically picked up slight variations in the color of the soil, a sign that water might be below the surface. Even so, she noticed no watering holes nearby, and no wells. A general sense of deprivation hung about the brown Toreszan hills, and Solace hoped no families were attempting to eke out a living among them.

Toward sunset on their third day, Solace was beginning to think Rhees had exaggerated the dangers of traveling through the isolated hill country. They hadn't seen anyone or anything, other than a lone mountain lion and several desert hares, until a horse and rider crossed their path and pulled up short.

Rhees slowed down enough to decide he didn't like what he saw and whistled loudly. Caya broke into a gallop behind them, heading deeper into the rock-strewn hills and away from the group. Jenx and Zirott galloped straight ahead, veering around the lone rider at the last minute. Solace pulled in front, gripping the reins so hard her fingers cramped as Jenx continued to gallop. She knew something was wrong but couldn't ask Rhees any questions. The din of hooves pounding the dry ground drowned out every other sound. All she could do was hold on and hope they were riding away from danger.

She thought they might be safe, until two more horses appeared out of nowhere, galloping along either side of her, drawing so close they cut off her exit. The riders had wrapped large scarves around their heads to obscure their faces and pulled the brims of their hats down low, which Solace took as a bad sign. Boxed in by the horses on either side, Jenx neighed and rose up on his hind legs, trying to break away. Solace flung herself forward and grabbed his mane to keep from flying off his back. Her pulse thundered in her temples, and she wondered whether she would escape this time, whether Rhees had any money left to pay off these men.

Behind her, she heard the clang of swords, but she couldn't swivel her head far enough to see who was fighting.

Was it Rhees and the first rider? Were several riders attacking? Cornered, the larger of the two men reached over and yanked on Jenx's reins. Solace tried holding on, struggling to retain the reins, but the second rider reached a beefy arm around her waist. He roughly pulled her toward him and kicked his horse in the flank. The horse took off in a burst of speed, with Solace's legs dangling in the air and her back pressed into the rider's side. Based on the smell emanating from the rider's clothes and body, Solace reckoned he hadn't bathed in months.

"C'mon, lads! I got the grand prize!" The man slowed down and turned his horse around. Solace screamed and struggled to free herself, but he tightened his grasp, crushing her against himself. She punched at his leather-clad arm and tried wriggling free, cursing Rhees for not returning her weapons— she could have helped even their odds. The rider laughed at her feeble efforts to escape and growled in her ear, "Ye won't be so fit an' feisty when I'm through with ye, sweetheart!"

Solace screamed louder and then felt something whiz past her head. Her captor's arm went slack, and she fell to the ground. Solace scrambled to roll away, terrified of being stomped by the horse's thundering hooves. The horse jogged another twenty feet, and the man toppled off, a knife stuck fast in his throat.

Solace spun around and saw the two other riders sprawled on the ground, their horses wandering nearby. Jenx trotted over to Zirott, and the two of them ambled toward her, side by side, with Rhees leaning forward on Zirott as if he were searching for something. Solace waited until he was closer before asking, "What are you looking for?"

Rhees ignored her question and asked gruffly, "Are you injured?"

She shook her head. "That was a lucky throw on your part. Another inch and I'd be dead."

"Luck had nothing to do with it," he muttered. "I'm thirsty, I think I might like to stop."

"Here? But we're out in the open, totally exposed!" Before Solace could press the matter, Rhees pitched forward onto Zirott's neck. She ran over to him and saw a trail of blood running down his left arm and dripping onto the ground. Solace was reluctant to move him enough to examine him, because she knew she'd never get him back onto the horse to transport him. *Wait a minute. What am I doing? If I left now on Jenx, he'd never be able to track me.*

Solace stared at Rhees, trying to decide if she owed him anything at all. True, he had just saved her life, but she'd never have been in danger in the first place if he'd left her in Yelosha. Jenx nosed Solace's shoulder and snorted.

"Fine," she said to Jenx. "I'll get him to a safe place for the night, and then we'll see."

Glancing around, she tried to find any landmarks to orient herself. According to the various routes Rhees had made Solace memorize, there were a series of cave systems dotting these hills. The mines of Toresz were famous for their rich veins of gold and silver, providing King Neuss with his primary source of income. She mounted Jenx, picked up Zirott's reins, and led the horses higher into the rock-strewn hills.

They had just entered a small clearing punctuated by several boulders when Solace heard something rustling nearby. She froze, her heart lurching in her chest. The rustling became louder, and Solace realized another horse was heading toward them. She had no weapon, nothing she could use to defend herself. Rhees's swords were tucked underneath him, and she'd never dislodge them in time.

Jenx and Zirott neighed, and Solace cried, "Caya!" as the mare trotted into the clearing. Sliding wearily from Jenx's back, Solace coaxed Zirott around several boulders, finally stopping at the entrance to a cave. She helped Rhees off his horse—he was feverish and had no idea where he was—and got him into the cave, where he dropped to his knees and rolled onto his side.

Solace grabbed the healer's kit from Caya and returned to the cave. She unbuttoned Rhees's leather duster and struggled to pull it away from his left side, where he'd been wounded. She removed both his swords, set them aside, and finally wrestled him out of the duster. When Solace laid him back down, she saw that her hands were covered with blood. She didn't have time to start a fire and boil water. She had to find his wound and stop the bleeding, or he'd not last the night.

She ripped his shirt off and sucked in her breath. He'd been stabbed through the shoulder, and the deep gash was bleeding steadily. She grabbed the water skin and poured water onto his wound. Rhees thrashed around and cried out, but remained unconscious. "Rest now," she said quietly. It was easier for her to work on a man who wasn't moving around.

After cleaning the wound thoroughly, Solace covered it with a tincture of white sage, followed by strips of clean cloth. She bound the entire wound with several larger strips, and rummaging through Rhees's bags, she found a clean shirt, which she put on him. She covered him with a blanket and went outside to see to the horses, waiting patiently for her to remove their saddles and bags and brush them down. One by one, she led them over to the wild grasses that wound around the hillside so they could graze. She'd observed that Rhees's horses didn't need to be tied up; he'd trained them to never wander far. Exhausted by this point, Solace had a few pieces of dried meat, a few gulps of water, and promptly fell asleep next to Rhees.

She woke with a start the following morning. After checking on Rhees, who was still asleep, she went outside to see to the horses. Three pairs of solemn brown eyes stared back at her. Solace was grateful the horses were accustomed to taking care of themselves in the hills, finding muddy water beneath the dried creek beds and filling their stomachs with grass and berries. She walked up to each of them and patted their necks, saving Jenx for last. "What do you think I should do?" Solace whispered, half hoping Jenx could advise her.

If she left now, she could probably make it to the Yeloshan border in three or four days, so long as she avoided any more gangs or guards. Once she crossed the border, she'd still have another eight or nine days of riding through the hills before reaching home. It was dangerous but doable, particularly since she'd grown up in the hills and had learned how to track and hunt and survive from her father. She'd need to find her slings though.

A loud squawking interrupted her calculations. Looking up, she saw carrion birds circling in the distance. With a shiver, she realized they were feeding on the three men lying below. Something shifted inside her, and Solace realized she couldn't leave Rhees lying in the cave, unconscious and defenseless, no matter how desperately she wanted to go home.

Sighing, she returned to the cave and changed Rhees's dressing. At least the wound was no longer oozing. He moaned a few times, but his eyes remained closed. She forced some water between his lips and let him sleep. Then she dragged every single saddlebag and pouch into the mouth of the cave, where the sun's rays cast some natural light, and methodically went through each one. She found the papers claiming she was Rhees's fiancé and snorted out loud.

Examining his coin purse, Solace discovered he'd kept back one of her silver Yeloshan coins, presumably for payment of another bribe. The other coins were of little value and made of brass or copper. He hadn't lied when he told her he needed her coins. She pursed her lips, wondering how a librarian of such meager means would pay her back, as he claimed he would. She could forego the money. It was his promise to take her home that she'd hold him to.

She pulled out all of his clothes, unfolding and refolding each piece, searching for her weapons. She finally found them stowed among his undergarments. Perhaps he thought she'd be too ladylike to sort through them, but she'd spent the last three years caring for her father and had laundered more than her share of men's undergarments during that time.

The last saddlebag contained several illuminated scrolls that looked very old. Partially unrolling the first scroll, Solace studied the hand-drawn illustrations and unfamiliar language but could make no sense of the story. She rolled the scroll back up and placed it with the others, wondering whether these were the scrolls that Chelyss had mentioned to Rhees.

Solace decided to risk a small fire before nightfall, so she could brew medicinal herbs for Rhees and concoct a stew from their food supplies. Carrying an overfull cup of medicinal tea into the cave, she wondered how she was going to get an unconscious Rhees to drink any of it.

"What are you making?" Rhees asked, his voice sounding thin and reedy.

Startled, Solace spilled a few drops of hot tea onto her hand. "Stew, but first you need to drink this." She put the tea down on the ground and helped him into more of a seated position, propping a saddlebag behind his back.

"Easy now, you don't want to start bleeding again." She knelt beside him and handed him the tea. Rhees's eyes flicked over her face and then focused on the ground nearby. Spotting her slings and dagger lying next to her bedding, his mouth opened but no sound came out. He took the tea from her and sipped it, grimacing at the bitter taste.

She started to rise but his much larger hand closed around hers. "Why?"

"Are you asking me why I saved your life? Or why I haven't escaped yet?"

"Both."

Solace pulled her hand away and rose. She couldn't explain it to herself, let alone to Rhees. Shrugging, she said, "I figure I'll have a better chance of getting home if you're around to help me. That is, if you keep your word and turn out to be the 'better man' that Fenwith says you are."

Nodding curtly and sounding almost Rhees-like, she grumbled, "Now get some rest."

CHAPTER 7

Solace insisted that Rhees rest for another full day before attempting to leave the safety of the cave. He was a cranky, uncooperative patient and she found herself wondering whether she should have left him to the birds. On the morning of their departure she readied the horses, saddling them and stowing their bags, and she ensured they'd left no evidence behind of their campsite, except for the bloodstain on the floor of the cave.

When she tried to help Rhees mount Zirott, he waved her away with a scowl. "I'm not an invalid, thank you very much." He mounted his horse stiffly and stifled a gasp of pain as he swung into the saddle.

"Uh huh," she said. "You're in no shape for travel or for a sword fight. I'll ride in front." She'd scoured the ground the day before and filled the drawstring bag attached to her belt with stones for slinging. One of her slings was looped over her saddle horn, the other was tied around her waist, and her dagger was hidden inside the lining of her cloak. Solace had caught Rhees silently watching her arm herself that morning.

"The devil you will!" He guided Zirott alongside her. "We'll ride side by side."

Solace figured that was a concession of sorts and said nothing. They rode in silence, more slowly than they had during their first three days, passing through a dusty plain with barren brown hills rising on either side. Near dusk they came upon the saddest-looking cluster of shacks Solace had ever seen. She looked at Rhees with a question on her lips.

His face was pinched with pain from the constant riding motion. She hoped he hadn't re-opened the gash in his shoulder, which would take even longer to heal. Rhees nodded at the mining settlement, sitting at the base of a dry, rocky range of hills. "These are friends, as you'll come to see."

When they were still several hundred yards away, a giant of a man emerged from one of the shacks and shouted, waving in their direction. Rhees and Solace picked up their pace, and the large man ran out to greet them.

"Well met, my friend!" said the man as they pulled up their horses. Peering closer at Rhees, he added, "You look unwell."

"I met up with a sword a couple days back," Rhees said. He paused and added more quietly, "I'm afraid you're going to have to give me a hand, Wilhm."

Solace dismounted quickly and went to Rhees's left side. "I knew you were too ambitious today. And now you've probably re-opened your wound." Turning to Wilhm she said, "He's got a deep gash in his left shoulder."

Rhees grunted as his friend helped him dismount. "Wilhm Imyns, please make the acquaintance of Lace Blusari."

Wilhm broke into a wide grin. "Well met, Lace Blusari."

Rhees added with a hint of irony, "My lovely and unassailable fiancé."

"Then you're well suited," said Wilhm. Rhees's eyebrows rose in surprise.

"Well met, Mr. Imyns," replied Solace, curious about the history behind Rhees's friendship with this impoverished miner.

"Please, call me Wilhm."

As they led the horses toward the settlement, Rhees asked, "How's Maysel and your boys?"

Wilhm looked down at the ground and kicked a stone. "We lost young Wils to the fever. He wasn't strong enough to fight it. Maysel's taken it hard." A tear rolled down the big man's cheek, and he didn't attempt to wipe it away. Solace's heart twisted inside her, moved by the man's raw grief. If the dilapidated conditions were any indication of what they'd see inside the Imyns's shack, she presumed that poor Wils didn't have enough food to eat, and he'd succumbed to the fever that swept through the hills at the end of the summer.

"I'm sorry to hear it," Rhees said. "He was a fine boy."

Wilhm sniffed and squinted behind them, staring in the direction they'd come. "They're pushing us harder than ever. I reckon they'd not miss a couple of men and their families. There're plenty of farmers desperate enough to throw in the towel and try the mines."

A thin woman stepped out of the nearest shack and walked toward them, wiping her hands on her faded apron. "Rhees, we'd begun to worry." The woman's wan smile didn't reach her eyes. Even though Solace guessed she was about Rhees's age, she was prematurely stooped over and looked closer to forty.

Rhees introduced Solace to Maysel, and she invited them into her home. This was no modest but snug stone cottage like the one Soren had built for his family, but a tilting shack of paper-thin wooden slats, so poorly constructed the wind whistled through the gaps. They stepped into a single room, with a fire pit at one side that vented out of the roof. A small pot of something, probably gruel, hung from a hook over the open flame. Twin boys, about two years old, sat on a blanket on the floor. They had their mother's eyes, large, brown, and mirthless.

Solace was no stranger to poverty or food shortages, especially at the end of winter when the pantry ran bare. She'd gone to bed many nights without supper. But the Imyns were barely subsisting, and this year's harvest had been a good one. She worried about the children. How would they survive the fever next time around?

Rhees handed Maysel a package wrapped in brown paper containing a wheel of cheese and several links of sausage. She thanked him and carried the package to her worktable as if it were the rarest of treasures.

Solace said to Rhees, "We need to check your shoulder and apply a new dressing."

Rhees removed his long duster to reveal a blood-soaked shirt underneath. Solace frowned. "Why didn't you stop sooner? We didn't have to push so hard." She didn't wait for a reply but helped Rhees peel off his shirt. "We'll need to clean this wound with hot salt water."

Looking at Maysel, she asked, "Do you have a pot of water that you can begin heating for us?"

Maysel's bottom lip quivered and she glanced at her husband. Before Wilhm could explain, Rhees spoke up. "Lace, they don't have any spare water. They pay the mining overlord, who in turn pays Neuss, for every drop of water they use. The king owns all the water in Toresz."

"What? But water belongs to the people who live and work in these hills." Solace had never heard of anything so outlandish as a ruler owning the water supply and then forcing his own people to pay for it. As a water diviner, she felt especially outraged by the idea of hoarding water. "Water should be free to all!"

"Well said," replied Wilhm, "but unfortunately that's not

true here in Toresz under Neuss's reign. We're forced to pay dearly for our water."

Rhees reached into his coin purse, pulled out a brass coin, and handed it to Wilhm, but Wilhm put up his hands. "I can't accept that, my friend."

"But I won't take your drinking water to clean my shoulder."

"You misunderstand me. What I mean is that I can't bring a brass coin in the middle of the workweek to the overlord without raising suspicions. He'll assume I've come by that coin illegally, since I've already purchased my water rations."

Solace stretched out her palm. "Give me the coin. I'll go out and purchase the water."

Rhees squinted at Solace, his brown-black eyes assessing her. Turning to Wilhm, he said, "Would you please go with Lace to ensure she's not harassed by anyone and help her carry the water? I'd do it myself if I could."

"Of course," said Wilhm. Grabbing a water urn, he led Solace outside and through the crowded settlement, past shacks sagging from overexposure to wind and sun and man-made misery.

"Thank you for coming along with me." Solace could sense the man's unease, and for the first time she felt anger swelling inside her at the Toreszan king.

"Rhees is a good friend, and I'm happy to offer what little help I can."

She decided to satisfy her curiosity about Rhees and Wilhm. "How long have you known Rhees?"

Wilhm smiled. "Since we were boys. Chelyss and my dad worked together for years during King Meade's reign, and the families have always been close. Although Chelyss retired about the time Rhees was born, he'd trained generations of the king's knights, while my dad trained the king's horses."

Solace recalled her father and Gordo discussing the brutal

rebellion led by Neuss and his fellow deserters from King Meade's army. She'd been seven at the time and remembered her father shaking his head in disgust. Neuss and his men had staged a coup in the castle, murdering King Meade, his children, and all his knights and servants. His wife—the queen —had been dead a long time by then. At least the queen hadn't lived long enough to see her children murdered before her eyes. Solace shuddered involuntarily.

"What happened here when Neuss overthrew King Meade?" she asked.

"Rhees lost his mother and I lost my dad on the same day." Wilhm looked down at his worn boots. "The only reason Chelyss survived was he'd long since moved to Shulamorn, a far-flung border town that no one cared about."

"But I thought Rhees's mother also lived in Shulamorn, with Chelyss and Fenwith. How was she killed?"

"King Meade had sent for Ellanora because the princess was taken ill. The king wanted the best healer in the country to look after his daughter. We heard later that Ellanora and Meade were slain together, along with the princess and prince." Solace felt a pang of sympathy for Rhees. She'd found it difficult enough to lose her mother to illness. She couldn't imagine how Rhees must have felt when he'd lost his mother to Neuss's assassins.

They approached the well where two armed guards stood watch. The surlier of the two ignored Wilhm and sauntered over to Solace. He stuck his face inches from hers, his rank breath blasting her. "Water rations have already been given out. Move on."

Solace stood her ground. "I am a visitor here and need to replenish my fiancé's water skins for our journey."

"This ain't a charity, lady. Move on."

"Who said anything about charity? I'm willing to pay for our water."

Wilhm intervened at that point. "Please, sir, the lady needs to purchase enough to be able to travel on to Urhl. Her fiancé works for King Neuss."

The guard pushed out his bottom lip and considered. "How much?"

Solace opened her palm and showed the guard the brass coin. "How much water can I buy?"

The guard snatched the coin from her palm and nodded at Wilhm, "Go on, fill up yer urn. And be quick about it, before I change my mind."

As soon as they were out of earshot, Solace burst out, "How can you stand it? I had to bite my tongue to keep from answering back."

Wilhm shrugged. "What choice do I have? I need to feed my family. If I so much as speak back, I'll be sacked and whipped and tossed out of the settlement along with Maysel and my little ones."

"I know you can't act alone, but if there were others willing to help, maybe there could be a way."

"First thing we'd need is our own water supply. If we had water, maybe we could grow a few vegetables in our yards, keep a chicken or two, have something to eat besides gruel and something to drink besides our own sweat."

A thought tickled at the back of Solace's mind. "Have you and Rhees ever talked about this?"

"All the time."

"And?"

"And Rhees says he's working on a plan." Wilhm glanced at Solace. "Has he said anything to you?"

"Not exactly. But I have no doubt he's planning something." *Like kidnapping a diviner so she can help him find the water hidden in these hills.* Solace drew her brows together and tried to recall what Rhees had said to her, something about their work being risky and even dangerous.

From what she'd observed, sneaking around Toresz trying to secretly locate water sources was more than just dangerous. It was suicidal.

~

Rhees and Solace left the next morning, promising to visit again in early spring. Solace was relieved to ride away from the forlorn settlement, but she soon discovered that Rhees's zigzagging route to Urhl included stops at several more impoverished settlements along the way. At each stop, she met men and women who were as desperately poor as Wilhm and Maysel, and just as grateful for whatever gifts of cheese or sausage Rhees managed to bring them. They also seemed to look upon Rhees as more than a friend, almost as if he were the leader of an undeclared resistance.

They descended a steep hill, the pebbly brown plain stretching out before them. Solace noticed a darker coloration of the soil—she was fairly certain that a water source lay ahead —and she estimated they were two days' ride from Urhl. Rhees pulled up his horse and waved his uninjured arm at a narrow valley nestled between two hills in the distance. She pulled up next to him and looked where he was pointing.

"See those scraggly-looking trees at the base of those two hills? That's where we'll be staying the night."

"Another settlement?"

He shook his head. "A widow named Peka and her two sons farm the land in that valley. They're better off than most. They have a secret water supply."

"Enough perhaps for a bath?" Solace asked eagerly. Her hair and clothes were coated in dusty grit from their days on the road.

Rhees squinted as the sun dropped behind the hills,

backlighting them in an orange glow. "Afraid not, but at least we won't need to pay for extra water."

"Don't tell me we're going to ride all the way into Urhl looking like this, covered in sand and grime?"

Glancing over at her, he smirked. "You *are* looking more and more like a mercenary every day."

Solace shook her head. "Seriously, aren't we going to arouse suspicion riding up to the gatekeeper looking like two dusty thieves?"

"I can promise you a hot bath and a good night's rest at our final stop." Neither one of them slept well most nights, since they bunked down in poorly-insulated shacks with large, noisy families.

Solace wished she could bypass the farm and ride through the night, if it meant a nice bath at the end of the journey and uninterrupted sleep. "How do you know Peka?"

"Peka and her husband were close friends of Fenwith and Chelyss when they all lived in Urhl, and later on, her son Behn and I trained together as pages, along with Wilhm. When Peka inherited her father's farm, her husband retired from the king's service and moved the family here. Unfortunately he happened to be visiting his eldest son, who was a knight and member of the king's elite riders, during Neuss's rampage, and—"

"Let me guess, Peka's husband and eldest son were killed?"

Rhees nodded. "I suppose the pattern's becoming obvious?"

"Everyone we've met along the route has a grudge against Neuss, with good reason. And they all seem to think you're going to help them somehow, as if you're their savior."

"They don't think I'm their savior," Rhees grumbled.

"If not their savior, then certainly their leader, a man with secrets and plans and one very crazy scheme."

Rhees scowled at her. "What crazy scheme?"

"Kidnap a water diviner from Yelosha; force her to secretly

73

search for water under Neuss's nose, and then incite a rebellion in the Toreszan hills." Solace looked at Rhees, whose scowl had deepened, and added, "*That* crazy scheme."

CHAPTER 8

Solace knew she'd hit a nerve, because Rhees's mouth compressed and he squinted at the darkening sky. "Remember when I said that I had to show you why I brought you to Toresz? You can see for yourself how much these people need the services of a diviner."

Solace tossed her head, her long black braid swishing across her back. "But why didn't you simply *ask* me for help back in Yelosha? Why did you have to *kidnap* me?" Solace noticed that Rhees never used the word "kidnap" to describe his own actions, which made her all the more determined to call it out.

Rhees's voice rose in frustration. "Do you really think that if I'd waltzed up to your father and asked him whether I could borrow you for a year, he'd have agreed? He'd have been more likely to kill me than listen to me."

Solace knew there was truth in what he said. "He might have let me help these poor families after the harvest, when he could have ridden along with me to Toresz. Or he might have sent Arik to accompany me here."

"Who's Arik? Your brother?"

Solace shook her head. "My best friend. He would have married me if—"

"If I hadn't taken you from Yelosha." Rhees squared his jaw. "I've wronged more people than I realized—you, your father, and some poor chap named Arik—and I'm sorry for it. But what's done is done, and the only way out of this is to see it through."

Solace didn't bother explaining about her and Arik. It was complicated and not any of his business. "You haven't denied the other part of your scheme."

"What are you talking about?"

"Are you really planning a rebellion?"

Rhees flicked the reins and Zirott took off at a gallop toward the scraggly trees. *So much for honest communication*, thought Solace as she and Jenx followed behind them.

They took a worn path through stubbly fields recently sown with winter wheat, trotting into a tidy yard where several chickens pecked at the dirt. The horses made a beeline for the stable behind the old stone cottage. One of Peka's sons greeted them and took their reins.

The snug cottage, which looked about the size of Fenwith and Chelyss's, was sparsely but comfortably furnished, with a front room that served as the parlor, a large eat-in kitchen behind the parlor, and several bedrooms down the hall. The house smelled of home cooking, making Solace yearn for her father and her own home.

She felt immediately at ease with Peka, who reminded her of her mother before her illness—a kindly yet strong-willed hill woman, entirely capable of running her farm and her household. Peka wore a pale blue chambray dress that had been patched at the elbows. Her salt-and-pepper hair was twisted into a simple bun at the nape of her neck. She and her sons shared the same large gray eyes, tawny complexions, and welcoming smiles.

Peka greeted them and fussed over Rhees; actually, all the women fussed over Rhees. She hugged Solace and congratulated Rhees on his "lovely fiancé, Lace." Rhees had carefully introduced her as Lace everywhere they'd traveled, explaining each time how they'd met during his recent trip to Yelosha. While it had gotten easier for Solace to play along, acting like a young woman traveling with her fiancé to Urhl, she hated pretending to be in love with Rhees. She felt slightly nauseated after each performance.

Peka's simple chicken stew and fresh bread were a welcome change of pace from the meager meals Solace had been eating all week. Behn, Peka's older son, seemed about Rhees's age, and his brother Bray was several years younger. During dinner, the three men discussed horses, farming, and the latest news from the capital.

"Have you heard that Neuss executed three men for treason because they dug an unauthorized well?" Bray asked.

Rhees avoided eye contact with Solace and sipped from his mug. "That so? Where were they from?" Bray described a location in the northwest corner of Toresz.

"They've suffered from severe drought these past three years up north, and Neuss's men still extort payment for every liter of water," said Behn, shaking his head.

"We have to be very careful not to let anyone know we have our own water supply. Bray still goes every other day to purchase water from the guards at the town well," said Peka.

Rhees nodded. "So long as Neuss is in power, you must keep up the pretense. It's the only way to stay safe."

"Rhees has tried explaining it to me, but I still don't

understand how Neuss wound up controlling all of the water. It couldn't have happened overnight, given the size of Toresz. What happened here?" asked Solace.

"Neuss was a sly one," said Peka. She stared absently into her cup of tea, lost in her memories. "Ten years it's been now. Behn here was fourteen and Bray was ten when their father and older brother were taken from us.

"But we lost more than our loved ones that day. We lost our freedom too. Neuss had planted his henchmen in all the major cities. As soon as they received word King Meade was dead— murdered by Neuss—they killed the governors of each province, declared themselves in charge, and placed guards over all the wells.

"After that, it was easy for them to overcome what little resistance remained in the rural towns and mining settlements. In less than a month, we lost our water privileges, and anyone who complained saw their sons and daughters taken away and forced to work in the mines."

Rhees picked up the story. "A lucky few, like Peka and Chelyss, had recently dug new wells on their property, before their old wells had run completely dry. They were able to camouflage their new wells and keep them hidden. Of course, they run the risk of being charged with treason every time their property is inspected by Neuss's guards."

"It's worth it, just the same," said Peka. "Gives me peace of mind to know we'll not go thirsty during a drought."

Rhees nodded. "Fenwith says the same thing."

Solace felt a twinge of guilt for the hot bath she'd enjoyed while visiting Chelyss and Fenwith. She didn't know whether they'd purchased that water or secretly drew from their own well, but in either case they'd taken pains to supply the water for her and Rhees.

They were up before dawn the next morning, as Rhees was anxious to reach their final stop before nightfall. Solace thanked Peka for her hospitality, and Peka winked at her, saying it had been a pleasure to meet the young woman who'd finally tamed Rhees. Solace shifted uncomfortably and mumbled her goodbyes.

Solace knew their last stop was not a mining settlement or a farm, but a monastery tucked into the side of the Tor Mountain near the capital city of Urhl. She noticed Rhees became more impatient the closer they drew to the mountain. Their path took them around the base of the mountain, and as they rounded the bend, the monastery came into view.

Solace gasped. "How are we going to get there? I don't see anything resembling a path up the mountain." The ancient building, hewn from the sand-colored rocks and stones of the Tor, was constructed in tiers, with each tier progressively smaller than the one below, like the multi-layered cake Solace had seen in the marketplace back home. Each tier was topped with a red clay-tiled roof and surrounded by a balcony on three sides.

"Look to your left, over there," Rhees pointed with his good arm. "There's a path behind those boulders that'll take us inside."

"Inside the mountain?"

The pounding of hooves heading their way swallowed up Solace's question. A small unit of mounted men, wearing navy hooded robes and carrying short swords, emerged from behind the boulders and surrounded the pair. Their leader pulled back his hood to reveal a bald head and long beard. He broke into a crooked grin when he recognized Rhees.

Sheathing his sword, he turned and shouted to his men, "Stand down! They're expected!"

Smiling at Rhees he said, "Well met, Rhees! You're overdue and Brother Tomyss has been fretting more than usual. Who travels with you?"

"Lace Blusari, my fiancé. She is also expected by Brother Tomyss."

The long-bearded man nodded soberly at Solace and said, "Well met, Lace Blusari." Solace returned his greeting, wondering what kind of religious order required mounted guards to patrol its entrance. But then she thought about the various stops she and Rhees had made on their journey to Urhl and realized these monks must not be on friendly terms with Neuss. And yet they were powerful enough, or respected enough, to have survived ten years under his rule.

Solace and Rhees followed their hooded escort behind the boulders and up a narrow, rock-strewn path that wound around the mountain. Before they reached the monastery, the monks turned their horses abruptly to the left and they seemed to melt into the mountain itself. Next, the mountain swallowed Rhees and Zirott, with Caya and Jenx following blithely behind them. They trotted into a slender chasm that opened into a large cavern, big enough to fit all of their horses easily. As Rhees dismounted, several more hooded monks emerged from the shadows and began leading the horses away. One of them approached Solace and waited expectantly for her to dismount.

The long-bearded man, whom Rhees introduced as Brother Evryst, motioned two of the hooded monks over to him and said, "Please take our guest, Lace Blusari, to the hot baths and then have her join Brother Tomyss for dinner."

The monks bowed and started to lead Solace away, but she asked them to wait. She bowed to Evryst, the lead monk. "You should know that Rhees was injured during our journey. He should be seen by a healer as soon as possible." Rhees grumbled that he was fine but didn't argue when Evryst offered to examine Rhees himself.

The monks led Solace down a dim passageway lit periodically by oil lamps, which hung from iron hooks hammered into the hard bedrock of the cave. The passage smelled vaguely sulfurous, the smell growing stronger the deeper into the cave they traveled. They finally emerged next to an underground spring; a valuable source of water controlled by the brothers that Solace figured must be a well-kept secret. The taller of the two monks pointed to a roped off area behind a privacy screen. "That is designated for our female guests. You will find soap, towels, and robes on a ledge beyond the screen. Please leave your travel clothes behind; we will launder and return them." The monks bowed and left her alone.

Solace slipped behind the ropes and exhaled in relief. Here was plenty of water for a bath, in fact more water than she'd ever seen in her life, since she'd never visited the seaside. Her father had always promised to take her and her mother to the coast, but they never got the chance.

The water gently lapped against the sides of the stone walls of the small grotto reserved for women. She pulled off her traveling cloak, peeled off her tunic and leggings, and tested the temperature of the water with her toes. Smiling, because the water was perfect for bathing, she grabbed a piece of soap and plunged in. She scrubbed until her skin was tingling and shampooed her hair five times to ensure it was truly clean.

Leaning back against the stone wall, she closed her eyes, her senses alive to the water all around her and below her, where this water source connected with others across the hills. Solace caught her breath, as the map of water sources nearby snapped into focus in her mind, and she could *see* where the water flowed closer to the surface, perfect for digging a well, and where it ran deep below the earth, a hidden reservoir for future generations. And she knew, with the certainty that came with her gift, there was more than enough water for Maysel's children, and all the other children she'd met along the way to Urhl. Anger bubbled up inside her, as she thought of Neuss and his henchmen, allowing children to go to bed thirsty.

She rose from the water, toweled off, and found a strange

linen undergarment to wear, over which she layered a navy hooded robe that she tied at the waist with a simple white rope. Slipping her feet into brown, shearling-lined boots, Solace grabbed another towel and continued drying her hair. She finger-combed it and not having anything to tie it back with, left it loose around her shoulders.

Solace heard someone clear his throat and stepped around the screen. A man with silver hair and beard that reached halfway to his waist sat on a large rock nearby, his hands folded and his chin on his chest. His darker coloring reminded Solace of the hills after a winter rain, their rich brown hues foreshadowing the spring to come. He wore the same hooded robe as the rest, although he used a red rope for a belt. She thought he might be napping, but at the sound of her footsteps, he raised his head, his black eyes examining her in a not unfriendly way. Solace felt she must have passed the test, because he rose, bowed deeply and said, "Welcome to Tor Monastery. I'm Brother Tomyss."

"Thank you," she returned his bow and hesitated, not sure how much he knew about her true identity. "I'm grateful for your hospitality."

"Shall we?" he indicated a different passage than the one she'd taken earlier, and they walked for several minutes along the stone hallway, the swooshing sound of their soft-soled brown boots echoing in the silent corridor. The walls inside the monastery were whitewashed and unadorned.

"I fear you must hate Rhees for taking you from your people." Solace started, surprised he knew she'd been taken by Rhees but didn't reply. He continued, "And yet, Brother Evryst tells me you insisted Rhees be seen by a healer immediately. And Rhees himself has told me that you could have left him for dead after he was wounded but you did not. I would like to understand why."

Solace blew out a puff of air, uncertain how to respond.

Tomyss misread her hesitancy for reluctance. "I have a good reason for asking."

Solace opted for the truth, as best as she could explain it. "Of course I hated Rhees at first and some days I still do. He snatched me from my father's farm, where I have always felt safe, and despite his assurances that he'll take me back home, I wonder every day whether I'll ever see my father again.

"Rhees is stubborn and demanding, which makes it even easier to hate him. But he's never hurt me, or even tried to touch me, and somewhere along the way I began to realize he wasn't an ordinary kidnapper. After I met Chelyss and Fenwith, I saw that people actually did care about him and he cared for them in return.

"Later, when he was injured saving my life, I felt it was my duty to see to his wounds and give him a fighting chance. I nursed him through the first night and planned to leave later. But the next morning there were carrion birds circling in the distance, and I couldn't leave him to that fate. So I stayed."

Tomyss led her to a quiet alcove off the main corridor, where several benches were scattered about, and he invited her to take a seat. Sitting down next to her, he said, "Rhees tells me you've seen for yourself the devastation wrought by King Neuss, and you've guessed the reason why he brought you here."

Solace was surprised at how much the elderly monk knew of Rhees's travels and true intentions. She nodded soberly. "I understand how someone with my gift for divining water can help your people, but I can't imagine how we'd get away with it."

"It's dangerous, to be sure, but the plan has a good chance of succeeding."

A small line formed on Solace's brow. *Brother Tomyss thinks Rhees's plan might succeed? What could this old monk know of water diviners and rebellions?* "Which part of the plan? Secretly divining for water? Or what comes later?"

"What do you think comes later?"

"Another rebellion. I'm certain that's Rhees's ultimate goal."

"Ah, I see. So is that what really concerns you? The rebellion to come?"

Solace's frown deepened. "Wait a minute, it sounds as if you agree with Rhees."

"Aye, I do. In fact, Rhees and I have been working on this plan for more than a year."

"So *you* were behind my kidnapping?" Solace wasn't sure she'd heard the old monk correctly.

Tomyss nodded sadly. "Aye, I'm afraid I'm as guilty as Rhees."

Solace jumped up and blurted out angrily, "But you're a monk, you're supposed to be one of the good guys! How could you be part of such a plan?" She struggled to control the fury building inside her against this silver-haired monk, against Rhees, and most of all, against Neuss for fostering such misery across Toresz.

Tomyss waited for Solace to sit back down. He held up three fingers and counted down his reasons. "First, I can't bear to see my people continue to suffer from lack of clean water, when we both know there is an abundant supply. We need a water diviner, and you are our only option, however much we've wronged you.

"Second, Neuss took the throne unlawfully, murdering our king, his family, and many of his most loyal subjects. And despite the fact he's King Meade's younger brother, he's not the rightful heir."

Tomyss hesitated. Solace felt certain she was about to hear a crucial detail, something to do with Rhees and his involvement. "And your third reason?"

"We must restore the kingdom to King Meade's one true heir, his only surviving son."

Solace blinked fast a few times, trying to understand what she realized he must be trying to tell her. But she wanted Tomyss to say it out loud. "And who would that be?"

"Rhees Demore."

CHAPTER 9

"**B**ut how can that be? The king's family was killed, as you said," Solace sputtered as certain pieces of the puzzle fell into place: Fenwith telling her Rhees was a much better man than she gave him credit for. Wilhm, Peka, and the others treating Rhees with a certain deference—had any of them guessed at the truth? And Rhees himself, as the sword-wielding, girl-snatching librarian, never added up.

"Ellanora, Rhees's mother, had been the royal healer for a number of years, and a trusted friend to both the king and queen. After the queen's untimely death, King Meade turned more and more to Ellanora for advice, support, and ultimately, love. Meade asked her to marry him, and she accepted, but on one condition: that their marriage remained a secret."

"But why so secretive?" Solace canted her head to the side, not understanding why Rhees's mother would want to hide the truth about her royal marriage.

Tomyss rose from the bench with a sigh and paced around the alcove, pausing occasionally to glance down at Solace, who remained seated, too stunned to move. "Although Ellanora's family were minor nobles, and her brother Chelyss ran the royal training school for the king's knights, without either great wealth or a royal title, she knew she'd never be accepted at court. And she didn't want to raise any future children at the palace. She wanted them to have the same carefree childhood she'd had. Since King Meade already had two heirs, and he loved Ellanora deeply, he agreed. I performed the marriage ceremony in secret, here at Tor Monastery, twenty-five years ago. Rhees was born a year later."

"And who did Ellanora say was the father?"

"She never said anything about the father, letting people think what they would of her. Naturally she returned home to live with Chelyss and Fenwith once she realized she was with child."

"Did Rhees ever get to see his father?"

"The king visited each of his provinces annually, but he always found a way to visit a certain cottage in the Shulamorn Province several times a year, staying a week each time. His personal guards assumed Ellanora was his mistress."

That explained the huge mahogany bed, thought Solace. "And so Rhees lost both his parents on the same day?"

Tomyss nodded. "He went from being a spoiled boy of fourteen to the grieving heir to the throne, in the span of one day. And he was so filled with rage against Neuss that he wanted to ride into Urhl and demand a duel. Chelyss asked for my help with the boy, and for a time, Rhees lived here, where he was treated like one of the brothers, always as a servant, never as a prince. I like to think we taught him some humility."

"Humility?" Solace sputtered.

Tomyss arched one silver eyebrow. "Well, under the circumstances, perhaps you've not seen him at his best."

"Why have you told me this?"

Tomyss sat back down. "You've been honest with me, and I felt I owed you the truth."

Solace took a deep breath, trying to sort through

everything she'd just learned. If she helped Rhees and Tomyss by divining for water—and what choice did she have, other than to pretend she didn't know where the water sources were —then she'd be planting the seeds of a rebellion against a ruthless leader, and she'd be aiding the future king of Toresz, who also happened to be her kidnapper. She rubbed her temples, which were beginning to throb.

"I wonder, Brother Tomyss, whether I could have a cup of tea?"

Tomyss laughed. "How about joining me for dinner *and* a cup of tea?"

As they left the alcove, Tomyss explained they'd be eating in his private study while she visited, as women did not eat in the main dining area with the other monks. He led her down another hallway, their boots falling softly on the stone floors. Everywhere she looked, Solace saw whitewashed walls and minimal furnishings, cast in a soft glow by flickering candles set in sconces along the walls.

Tomyss paused before a row of full-length glazed windows that faced east toward Urhl. She'd heard of windows enclosed with sheets of glass but neither her cottage at home nor any she'd seen in the hills on either side of the border had glass windows. Hill people pulled their shutters closed when the weather was harsh; otherwise they left their windows open to the night air when they slept.

She pressed her nose against the glass to have a closer look. The sun had set behind them, and the first stars were appearing in the night sky. The light from a thousand candles and torches and fires below made the capital city look like a necklace of jewels, tossed casually across the foothills of the Tor. Its beauty made her heart ache.

"It's quite a sight, isn't it?" Rhees entered the hall, joining them in front of the windows.

Solace didn't look up at him, but continued staring down at

the twinkling city of Urhl. "It's beautiful, like looking at a constellation that's fallen from the sky to the hills."

"It's best that your first view of Urhl is at night then," Rhees said bitterly. "Under the full glare of the sun, there's no hiding the deprivation and suffering of my people."

Solace turned around to face Rhees, who was attired like the rest of them in a blue robe, although she noticed his rope belt was gold. *Gold for royalty?* She wondered. His dark hair and beard were neatly trimmed and his eyes glittered in the candlelight. She noticed he looked thinner; his injury and the constant travel had taken its toll.

She took a deep breath, her mind made up. "I'll help you divine the water sources needed to help your people. There's more than enough water in these hills. I have the map up here." She tapped the side of her head. "But promise that you'll take me home before the rebellion begins. I want no part in it, and I want to see my father once more before...before he dies of heartbreak." Her voice wavered whenever she mentioned her father.

Rhees turned away from the window and took her hands in his. "I promise. And thank you." He continued holding her hands and Solace nodded, feeling suddenly exposed, as if she'd said yes to something more than divining for water. She took a step back, slipping her hands from his.

Tomyss coughed. "Now that's settled, let's have dinner and that cup of tea I promised this young lady."

They stayed four days at the monastery. Evryst, who was both a master healer and led the warrior monks guarding the Tor, insisted that Rhees needed the extra healing time. Solace didn't mind. She remained as a guest in Tomyss's private wing and had her own tiny bedroom with just enough room for a cot and a shelf, which reminded her of her own room back home. Best of all, Tomyss gave her a key to his private library, inviting her to explore and read anything she liked.

When Tomyss showed her the library for the first time, on the morning after their arrival, her mouth opened in a silent *O*. Solace stepped reverently into the room and slowly walked past each wall filled floor to ceiling with books. She spun around and said, "How can you stand it?"

Confused, Tomyss asked her what she meant.

Waving her hand at the shelves of books, she said, "All these books. How can you stand not knowing whether you'll ever be able to read them all? And even if you do read them, how can you possibly remember them all?"

Tomyss threw his head back and laughed. Solace frowned, thinking he was mocking her, but he quickly sobered when he saw her face. "My dear girl, there are more books in the world than any man or woman could ever hope to read! And this library is but a small collection. Wait until you see the Great Library, where you'll be working."

Solace couldn't imagine a library as massive as Tomyss described, and for the first time since Rhees had told her she'd be a catalog assistant, she began to worry whether a simple Yeloshan hill girl could ever work in a library. She told Tomyss her concerns.

Smiling, Tomyss took her arm and led her to a narrow wooden cabinet tucked between two desks in the center of the room. The cabinet was filled with little drawers. Opening one of the drawers, he asked Solace to pick out a card. She reached in and withdrew the card. He then patiently explained the cataloguing system that he used, the same system used at the Great Library where she'd be working.

Tomyss then withdrew several cards at random and asked her to find the books. After she'd mastered that task, he asked her to close her eyes while he plucked some books off the shelves and placed them on one of the desks. When she opened her eyes, he instructed Solace to re-shelve the books, using the card catalog to point her to the correct shelf and section. She made some mistakes in the beginning, but by the second day, she'd learned how to catalog and felt more confident about her new "job."

That's when Solace stopped feeling overwhelmed by the library and began to enjoy it. She started reading right after breakfast, took lunch in her own room, and read right up until dinner. She'd never experienced the luxury of reading a good book, uninterrupted by the need to do her chores. She thought if she stayed much longer, she might forget how to work altogether.

The afternoon before their departure, she asked for permission to bathe once more, and one of the hooded monks led her back to the secluded grotto. When she returned to Tomyss's private wing, she found Rhees standing in front of the windows that overlooked the capital. He carried a package wrapped with string under his arm. She walked over to the windows and joined him. The sun was setting behind the Tor Mountain, bathing Urhl in a wash of golden light.

"Tomyss tells me you've mastered cataloging," he said.

"It's so logical, almost like a map."

"Ah yes, you and your mental maps. Good, that will make it easier for you to assume your new identity when we depart in the morning."

"Why do we need to go into Urhl? Don't I need to divine for water in the hills and plains of Toresz?"

"Aye, you do. And what better cover for your trips to the countryside than to be traveling with your fiancé, who visits the smaller libraries and book sellers across Toresz, searching for books to add to the king's collection?"

"So my job at the library will be my cover story. That's a good idea."

Rhees smiled. "You sound surprised. I've been planning this for a long time, thinking through every detail." Pointing to a watchtower in the distance, he said, "That's our first official stop in your new life as my fiancé. The guards will check your papers and question you. They may ask how we met, when we became engaged, and when we plan to get married. They'll also be examining your face and your clothes and even your saddlebags, trying to make you nervous. I thought that we might spend a little time before dinner rehearsing our story."

Since Solace had a Yeloshan hill country accent, Rhees recommended they keep their story as close to the truth as possible. They would tell everyone that they'd met while Rhees was traveling in Yelosha, searching marketplaces for rare books for the Great Library. They fell in love—Rhees actually used the phrase "it was love at first sight"—at which point Solace hooted in laughter.

Rhees scowled at her. "You're not taking this seriously! Having our stories straight is especially important for you. It's essential everyone believes you're my fiancé and under my protection."

Solace laughed so hard that tears streamed down her face. Rhees shook his head at her. "What's *wrong* with you? I've never seen you like this. You're always so self-contained."

Solace stopped laughing long enough to catch her breath. "I couldn't help myself. Your story of 'love at first sight' was right out of one of my mother's books. It's not real life, and the idea of saying that about you just made me laugh."

Rhees's scowl deepened. "What's that supposed to mean? I'll have you know that any number of mothers would give their front teeth to have me propose to their daughters."

Solace's eyes flashed as she crossed her arms. "Is that so? They might look elsewhere for a son-in-law if they knew you kidnapped young women from their homes and carried them off over the back of your horse!"

Rhees ran his free hand through his hair and spoke through gritted teeth. "Fine. I'm a kidnapper, guilty as charged. I knew it was wrong, but I did it anyway. There, I've said it. Now can you leave it alone? We have work to do!"

"And you're a thief."

Rhees seemed confused until he remembered the three silver coins. "And I'm also a thief, although I do intend to pay you back."

"When?"

Rhees shifted his gaze back to the window. "There's plenty of money in the royal treasury."

"I don't believe it! You expect me to wait for my money until you've overthrown Neuss—which could fail, since most rebellions do—and you've ascended to the throne, if you survive long enough to become king?"

Rhees set his jaw. "Thanks for the healthy dose of reality. That about sums it up." He shook his head and said, "Look, can we get past my crimes and finish our story? I'll strike the part about love at first sight. I wouldn't want you to have a giggling fit when someone asks how we met."

Solace bit her bottom lip to keep from smiling. "By all means, let's finish our story."

Rhees seemed to enjoy spinning the tale, so she let him carry on. Shortly after they'd met, Rhees asked her father for her hand in marriage. Her father agreed and they signed the official betrothal papers, a formal contract that any responsible father would have required before permitting his daughter to travel with her future husband. Her dowry was three silver coins, two of which they'd used during their journey. They planned to marry next summer, in Urhl.

After Solace recited the story several times, Rhees finally nodded his approval. "We're ready to discuss your appearance."

A line formed between Solace's eyebrows. "What's wrong with my appearance?"

"Nothing. You're a pretty Yeloshan hill girl. But you're not in Yelosha anymore."

It surprised her to be called pretty. Solace didn't think anyone, including Arik, had ever told her that before. "What's so different about the way city girls in Toresz look?"

"For one thing, your hair's too long."

Solace touched her slightly damp hair, which reached past her waist. Her mother used to trim it for her once a year, but Solace hadn't bothered to cut it since her mother passed. "How much shorter do they wear it in Urhl?"

Rhees pointed to a spot halfway between her shoulder and her elbow. "That's the longest any city girl would wear her hair."

"That short? Really?"

Rhees nodded. "At least that short, if you want to blend in."

"What else about city girls do I need to know?" Solace asked.

"Well there's a lot, and I can't teach you all at once. But the only other thing the guards will care about is how you're dressed. Now I know Fenwith packed custom-made dresses and tunics and so forth for you, but you're going to need a riding habit when we enter Urhl tomorrow. And well, here." Rhees handed her the package. "Go on, open it."

Solace removed the string, tore off the paper, and gasped. "These are beautiful! City girls wear clothes like this just to go riding? I can't imagine!" She pulled out a long dark green and gold brocade jacket that gathered at the waist and then flared, a gold long-sleeved top, dark green breeches, and a pair of black-leather riding boots. Caught up in the wrapping paper was a gold clasp. Holding it up, she asked, "What's this? Some kind of brooch?"

Rhees laughed. "No, it's called a hair barrette. It's to hold back some of your hair."

Solace examined the scrollwork. "It sure is lovely, but take look at my head of hair. Even shorter, there's no way this will hold my hair back."

"It's not supposed to hold back all of your hair. You use it to hold back some of your hair."

"Doesn't sound very practical to me. I prefer a braid." Solace looked at Rhees, who shook his head. "But I guess city girls don't wear braids either, huh?"

"Only servants wear braids down their backs, and you're not a servant. Here, let me show you how this works." Rhees grabbed a hunk of his own thick, wavy hair and clipped it back with the barrette. "See, the idea is to hold back the hair that gets in your eyes."

Tomyss walked into the room, took one look at Rhees wearing a gold barrette in his hair, and grinned broadly. "Looks like you're busy right now. Perhaps I'll ask Jenleah to return later."

Rhees hastily pulled the barrette from his head, wincing because he pulled a few hairs out with it. "Please, ask Jenleah to join us." Turning to Solace he said, "Jenleah is Tomyss's niece. She's offered to trim and style your hair."

Rhees and Tomyss left after introducing Jenleah, who looked to be Rhees's age, with Tomyss's darker coloring and twinkling, mischievous eyes. She took one look at Solace's hair and expelled a puff of air. "My, my. That might be more hair than I've ever seen on one head before. Here lass, let's get you settled." She took charge, instructing Solace to carry her new clothes into her bedroom and meet her in Tomyss's study in five minutes. When Solace arrived, Jenleah had already commandeered one of Tomyss's chairs, covered it with a sheet, and spread out her scissors, brush, comb, and mirror on the table.

"Please don't cut it shorter than here," Solace pointed to the same spot on her arm that Rhees had indicated.

Jenleah arched an eyebrow at Solace. "I cut and style for the finest ladies in the capital. Trust these hands!" She held up both hands and wriggled her fingers.

Ninety minutes later, Jenleah handed Solace the mirror. "You look positively stunning. *Never* let your hair grow that long again!"

Solace picked up the mirror and opened her mouth, unable to believe the transformation. She hardly recognized herself. Not only had Jenleah trimmed her hair to shoulder-length—a bit shorter than Rhees had indicated, but Jenleah said it was the latest style—she'd used the gold barrette to capture some of Solace's hair and artfully arrange it on one side. Jenleah also showed Solace how to put a touch of rouge on her cheeks and lips and gave her a small pot of rouge to take with her.

"I love it! No wonder all of the ladies want you to do their hair."

Jenleah smiled. "I'm glad you like it. Call on me anytime. No charge for a friend of Rhees."

Solace hugged Jenleah. "Thank you."

There was a knock at the door and Solace went over to answer it. Rhees stared at her as if she'd sprouted a beard. Tomyss, on the other hand, bowed as if they were meeting for the first time. "And who might you be? A wealthy landowner's daughter perhaps? Or a baronet?"

Solace smiled. "Your niece is the miracle worker." She looked at Rhees, who was still staring. "Well, what do you think?"

"You'll pass well enough," mumbled Rhees.

Tomyss rolled his eyes. "Don't listen to him. You'll be brilliant. In fact, we may have created another problem for ourselves."

"How so?" asked Rhees.

"Such a lovely young lady, betrothed or not, is going to attract an awful lot of attention, and too much attention could get her in trouble."

CHAPTER 10

They left after breakfast the next morning, Solace wearing her new riding clothes under her leather traveling cloak, which the monks had managed to clean and polish until it looked new. Rhees made her pack her slings and dagger away in one of the saddlebags, explaining that proper young city ladies didn't ride into town with a sling on their saddle and a dagger in their pocket. She replied that proper young city ladies had never been called upon to defend their sheep from rabid jackals. Rhees had raised both eyebrows and said she was probably right about that.

Solace enjoyed the ride from Tor Mountain to the gates of Urhl, whose outer walls and city buildings were constructed from golden sandstone and topped with clay-tiled roofs. She thought the city looked just as enchanting by daylight as it did at night, despite what Rhees had said.

But as they approached the outer walls, she began to see the other side of Urhl, the impoverished families camped outside the city, living in makeshift lean-tos that offered no protection from the stiff winds sweeping through the brown hills. Rail-thin children pawed through heaps of trash for scraps, fending off stray dogs when they found something edible. The smells of their encampment turned her stomach; they weren't the normal odors of farmyard animals and unwashed bodies, but of raw sewage and illness and decay. It was far worse than the mining settlements she'd visited with Rhees, and when she couldn't bear it anymore she focused her eyes on the tiled roofs instead.

When they reached the watchtower, they lined up behind everyone else waiting to be processed through the main gate: a small unit of soldiers returning from one of the provinces, a row of merchants' wagons that rattled and jangled when they moved, and three fine-looking carriages drawn by stallions with tall feathers woven into their manes. Solace thought the carriages looked like something out of a storybook and wondered if a foreign dignitary were visiting the city. When she asked Rhees, he'd laughed and told her they were a traveling theater troupe heading to the palace to entertain the king.

When it was their turn, she and Rhees dismounted and he tossed copper coins to two of the street urchins who offered to stay with their horses while they entered the watchtower. "You'll get two more coins when we return. Keep a close eye."

The older of the two boys nodded and said, "Aye, we'll be here waitin' on ye."

Solace whispered to Rhees, "Aren't you concerned they'll steal from you?"

"Not at all." Tilting his head in the direction of the guards who paraded in front of the gate and watchtower, he added, "I'm paying the boys to keep an eye out so the guards don't steal from me, and the guards will ensure the boys keep their hands in their pockets. It's a system that works quite well. When no one trusts anyone else, everyone is a snitch."

Rhees guided Solace into the tower, removed her traveling cloak and then his own, and hung them on a hook by the door.

Solace realized he'd been through this routine dozens of times. Even so, she could sense his tension and realized he was more worried than he wanted to let on. Maybe she wouldn't pass this inspection after all. *Then what? A trip to the dungeon?*

A sour-faced guard squinted at the papers Rhees thrust in his hand and then scowled at Solace, his eyes raking over her face and jacket, resting on the swell of her bosom beneath her clothes. He spit a plug of tobacco on the floor and she heard him mutter, "Yeloshan scum."

Her stomach felt jangly and her throat went dry when the guard asked for her name. Rhees answered for her, "Lace Blusari, my fiancé, as the papers state."

The guard growled at Rhees. "Is she mute?"

"Not at all."

"Then let her answer for herself." Rhees fell silent and Solace's hands felt clammy inside her leather gloves.

"State your name, occupation, reason for visiting Urhl."

Solace stammered through the answers. Then the guard asked when she'd met Rhees and when they'd become engaged. She provided the same answers she'd rehearsed with Rhees the day before.

The guard turned to Rhees. "Where's the betrothal contract?"

Without skipping a beat, Rhees said, "It's back in Yelosha with her father, where it rightfully belongs."

"Date of the wedding?"

"Sometime in the summer," said Rhees curtly.

"Dowry?"

"What's it to you? I'm not marrying you, I'm marrying her!" Rhees bellowed, and several of the guards moved in closer, their hands on the hilts of their swords.

Solace took a deep breath to steady her quaking knees; Rhees's temper was going to land them both in the dungeon if she didn't do something fast. Placing a gloved hand on Rhees's arm, she said as sweetly as possible, "Dearest, let's answer this gentleman's questions so we can proceed. He's only doing his job, after all." She tossed her hair and smiled at the guard, "My dowry was three silver coins, but we've spent two during our journey here. And of course, I needed some new clothes." She shrugged her shoulders and winked.

The guard cleared his throat. "Aye, well, move along then." He nodded at Solace, scowled again at Rhees, and stamped both their papers.

Solace didn't breathe normally until Rhees had collected their horses, paid the two urchins, and they were riding past the tower and down a side street. Rhees put out his hand and grabbed her reins, bringing them both to a stop. "What was that?"

"What was what?"

"Your performance in there. Do you realize you could have gotten us both arrested? Don't embellish and don't ever wink at a guard!"

"If you hadn't lost your temper, I wouldn't have had to step in."

"I didn't lose my temper."

"Then why did the other guards have their hands on their hilts?"

"Let's just forget it." Rhees grumbled and released her reins. "It's a short ride to our quarters."

Rhees led the way down cobblestone streets, past shops and inns and open air markets, until they arrived in a residential neighborhood where two- and three-story homes lined both sides of the street, one house running right into the next. Rhees told her later they were called row homes. Growing up as she did in the hill country where the smallest homestead was forty acres, Solace wondered why anyone would want to live on top of their neighbors. They turned into the mews that ran behind a block of yellow brick row homes, and

Rhees showed her the stable for Jenx, Zirott, and Caya. After they removed the bags, gear, and saddles, they worked side-by-side, brushing down the horses and then feeding and watering them.

Rhees picked up her saddlebags. "You'll be sharing living quarters with two other women who work at the library. I'll get you settled and then will show you around."

Solace followed Rhees around to the front stoop of one of the row homes. He reached to the lintel above the white clapboard door, pulled down a key, and unlocked the door. Rhees ushered her inside the narrow foyer, which smelled like wood smoke and lemon oil. Hooks for cloaks and hats and scarves lined the wall to the left. Solace removed her leather traveling cloak and hung it on one of the hooks. A door to the right opened into a sitting room with two upright chairs and faded sofa. Beyond the sitting room was a kitchen with a large table and fireplace for cooking and keeping warm. Rhees led her up a set of creaking wooden stairs behind the kitchen.

The second floor opened directly into a large bedroom with a sloped ceiling. Three beds formed a neat row across the room. At the foot of each bed stood a trunk for storing personal effects, and above each bed was a small shelf with a candleholder. Rhees dropped her saddlebags on the floor next to the empty trunk and told her he'd be back after he unloaded the other bags.

Solace sat on the bed and squeezed her eyes shut, recalling her cramped bedroom back home, the scarred kitchen table and winter pantry, the old sofa and her father's pipe smoke. She wondered, not for the first time, whether Arik had moved on and found someone else. She hoped so. She wanted at least one of them to be happy. Her lower lip quivered, and she snapped her eyes open. She would not give in to tears and sadness.

Solace unpacked quickly and changed into a burgundy and gray paisley blouse and gray wool skirt. After she carried the empty saddlebags back downstairs, she explored the kitchen, hoping to find a crust of bread or scrap of cheese. The pantry contained a handful of dried beans, some herbs, and a sack of flour. *What do these women eat?*

Rhees returned half an hour later and found her sitting at the kitchen table with a book. "What are you reading?"

Solace turned the thick volume over so he could read the title. He blinked in surprise. "*The Kings and Queens of Toresz.* Where on earth did you get that?"

"Tomyss let me pick out three books from his collection as a parting gift."

"What are the other two?"

"*A Healer's Book of Cures* and an atlas with maps of every province in Toresz and Yelosha."

"History, healing, and maps. Three good, practical choices. I'm impressed."

Solace shrugged. "Wouldn't any proper young city lady choose something similar?"

"I think you might be able to teach proper young city ladies a thing or two about common sense."

Solace quoted an old Yeloshan saying. " 'The hill country is a practical teacher.' "

Rhees smiled. "My mother used to say that all the time." He reached into his pocket and brought out a half-shriveled apple and a moldy hunk of wrapped cheese. "This was the only food in my pantry." He sliced the apple and cut the cheese, sharing half with Solace, who'd eaten worse during the dark Yeloshan winters.

Solace pointed behind her. "This one's not much better."

"We'll replenish our supplies later. But first, we've got to report in at the library. I'm long overdue and Neuss will have my neck if I'm not careful."

❧

They walked several blocks uphill toward a sand-colored building that soared above them. Four graceful towers, one at each corner, stood like sentries around the building, and the red clay-tiled roof gleamed in the midday sun. Fluted columns lined the front entrance, with two fierce-looking stone lions guarding either side of the double door, painted the same red as the roof. A grand staircase, worn in places from the number of boots and shoes climbing its steps through the years, ascended from the street to the doors.

"Is that the palace?" Solace arched her neck to take in the entire building, which encompassed several city blocks.

"Actually, it's the former palace. The new one was built about two-hundred years ago," said Rhees.

"Why build a new palace when you've already got one?"

"As the story goes, old King Ulyss was an avid collector of books and scrolls, and when they finally spilled into every room of the palace, his queen put her foot down and said, 'Ulyss, it's either me or the books.' Well King Ulyss loved his queen and his books, so he came up with an interesting solution. 'My dearest, why don't we donate this drafty old palace to the people as a library, and you can build yourself a new palace?' The queen thought it was a marvelous idea and designed a new palace, smaller than the first, but more elegant and a lot less drafty. Since then, the Great Library of Toresz has been a place for everyone to enjoy, from kings to clerks."

Solace waved her hand at the imposing building. "And you're in charge of this whole library?"

"The king's in charge; I just work here."

The Great Library earned its reputation on the inside, as well. The main entrance opened into a four-story atrium, with balustrades running around each of the levels, and row upon row of books running at right angles to the atrium, so it seemed the rows of books never ended. A statue of one of the Toreszan kings dominated the center of the atrium. When Solace walked up for a closer inspection, Rhees nodded at the statue. "That's King Meade. The people raised the funds and commissioned the sculpture themselves. It was completed last year." Lowering his voice, he added bitterly, "And King Neuss made a little speech praising his murdered brother at its unveiling."

Solace noticed the strong family resemblance between the stone face of Meade and his flesh-and-blood son, and she wondered whether anyone had guessed Rhees's parentage. She glanced at Rhees and whispered, "It's uncanny."

"What?"

"The resemblance."

Rhees's eyebrows shot up. "Really? I never noticed."

"Let's hope no one else notices either."

A harried-looking woman with gray-streaked hair spotted Rhees and hurried to his side. "You're late, really, really late! We've been worried sick about you. Even the king's been asking for you." She glanced behind her and said softly, "You'd better have an air-tight excuse, because he's furious with you."

"Didn't Tomyss send word I'd arrived at the monastery four days ago?"

The woman nodded. "But you're two weeks late, Rhees. And you know how the king feels about Tomyss." She noticed Solace standing behind Rhees and added, "Where are my manners?"

Rhees waved his hand between the two women. "Lizbet Een, may I introduce you to Lace Blusari."

Lizbet bowed. "Welcome to the Great Library, Lace Blusari."

Solace returned the bow. "Thank you. I've never seen anything quite like it."

When Rhees put his arm around Solace's waist and drew her closer, she steeled herself not to squirm out of his reach. Solace understood the importance of playacting, but sometimes Rhees overdid it. "Lace and I are betrothed. We met while I was traveling in Yelosha. She's been assisting Tomyss with his collection and is going to help you with the cataloging. Lace will be staying with you and Halys at the house." He explained to Solace, "Lizbet runs the catalog department and oversees the other assistants."

"I'm so pleased to be working with you." Solace extended her right hand and placed her left hand under her right elbow. This was a formal sign of respect in the hill country of Yelosha and Toresz, and she hoped it translated well in the capital. Smiling, Lizbet extended her right arm in the same fashion and they shook hands.

"Welcome to the Great Library—and congratulations on your betrothal. Let me show you around and introduce you to the other staff." Lizbet smiled kindly at Solace, whose stomach was twisted in knots at the thought of working in such a place, and under false pretenses.

Lizbet started to lead her away and called back to Rhees over her shoulder. "You'd better call at the palace immediately. Bring the books or scrolls or whatever you've acquired for the king's inspection, and make sure you can explain your extended absence."

Rhees patted a large leather pouch slung over his shoulder. "Got 'em right here. And my lovely fiancé is the reason for my delay. See you both shortly...I hope."

Lizbet compressed her lips as she watched him leave. "I hope you can talk some sense into that young man. He takes risks he shouldn't."

Solace nodded, thinking that Lizbet didn't know even half the risks Rhees took, including kidnapping a water diviner and planning a rebellion.

Lizbet introduced Solace to the other employees, beginning with the library guards who patrolled each level. Their chief responsibility was to ensure none of the king's books or scrolls were damaged or stolen.

Halys, the other catalog assistant, was betrothed to a soldier and shared the house with Lizbet. She welcomed Solace with a friendly smile and said she wanted to hear all about how she met Rhees, since no one thought he'd ever get married. Lizbet put Solace to work cataloging books on the second floor, and she became so absorbed she didn't realize how late it was until Lizbet told her the library was closing.

Solace looked up from the books she was sorting and frowned. "Rhees hasn't returned?"

Lizbet shook her head. "No, but I'm sure nothing's wrong. The king probably kept him waiting all afternoon for an audience."

Solace joined Lizbet and Halys for the walk back to their row house, after a detour to the grocer's shop on the way. Lizbet paid the grocer for their food and seemed in charge of their finances. They passed several well-guarded public wells and Solace asked if they needed water.

Lizbet shook her head. "We paid to fill our urns last night, enough to last us a few days. At the end of the week we'll purchase extra water so we can bathe." Lizbet unlocked the door to their house and Solace followed her inside.

She noticed the home next door where Rhees lived was completely dark and she wondered whether something had happened to him. *Wait a minute,* she thought, *why am I worrying? He can take care of himself.*

"Could you please help me with dinner?" Halys asked Solace after they'd hung up their cloaks.

"Of course." They decided to fix a stew, and Solace showed Halys how she used to prepare it "back home." Solace hadn't cooked with another woman since before her mother's final illness and found it oddly comforting.

There was a knock at their front door during dinner, and

Halys went to answer it. Rhees followed her into the small sitting room, tossed his cloak on the sofa, and said, "Smells wonderful."

"Come join us," said Lizbet, who set another plate at the table.

After Rhees had a spoonful, he said, "Delicious. And different...is that cinnamon in the stew?"

"Aye, and cardamom," said Solace.

"Your fiancé can catalog *and* cook!" said Lizbet with a smile. Everyone laughed and then she added, "How did your audience with the king go?"

"Fine. He complained about how long I'd been gone but was pleased with the scrolls I'd acquired. Then he complained again, and so I told him I'd brought back something else from my travels, but it wasn't for him."

"You didn't!" Lizbet looked horrified and Solace shook her head, wondering why Rhees provoked the king unnecessarily.

"Aye, I did. Of course his face turned red and he roared at me, demanding to see 'it' immediately but I said that I'd need to check with 'her' first. I explained I'd become betrothed while in Yelosha, and Neuss sat back and had a good laugh. Then he insisted on meeting you, Lace, tomorrow night." Rhees directed the last part at Solace. "Remember that traveling troupe we saw on the way into Urhl? Neuss invited us to attend their performance tomorrow night, with forty of his closest 'friends and advisors' as he calls them."

The knots in Solace's stomach had loosened somewhat during the afternoon, as she settled into her new routines at the library, and they'd nearly disappeared while she made dinner with Halys. Now her stomach tightened painfully and Solace wished she hadn't eaten any stew. "Tomorrow night? At the palace? But how will I..."

Halys interrupted and told Solace not to worry. "I'll help you get ready—it will be fun! You're so lucky to be invited to the palace on your first night in Urhl." Solace glanced at Lizbet, who nodded sympathetically at her and patted her arm.

Lizbet said, "We'll leave the library a little early tomorrow, and we'll all help you get ready."

Rhees stood up. "Thank you, ladies, for dinner and for offering to help Lace tomorrow." He went over to Solace's chair and pulled it away from the table. "Lace, come join me for a walk around the block. I could use some fresh air."

Solace rose wordlessly, furious that Rhees had mentioned their fake betrothal to Neuss; they needed to attract less attention to themselves, not more. She wondered whether Rhees really understood the dangers of trying to divine for water in a country where the crown owned everything, even the water supply. She grabbed her cloak from the hook in the foyer and followed Rhees. Once they were outside, she punched him in his good arm.

"Ouch! What was that for?"

"For provoking the king," she hissed. "For thinking only of yourself and forgetting that one false step on your part could mean death for us both. And for playacting so well you almost had *me* convinced I'm your happy little fiancé."

Solace picked up her skirt and ran blindly ahead, her vision blurred. *No tears, Solace!* She told herself, but she couldn't hold them back any longer. She hated Rhees, hated this horrible city, and hated having to pretend she was in love with her kidnapper. Her heart ached with longing to be home with her father and her sheep and her dog.

She ran around a corner into a darkened alley just as Rhees caught up with her. Grabbing her arm, he said gruffly, "Don't ever walk down dark streets alone. Ever!"

He pulled her along and they walked down another side street, where candles and oil lamps glowed in front windows, providing enough light to see by. She swiped at her eyes and he sighed. Reaching into his cloak, he handed her a handkerchief.

"We have to pretend we're happy together. You know that as well as I do."

Solace sniffed into the handkerchief and didn't answer him.

"But I'll admit that I provoked Neuss and unnecessarily placed you in greater danger than you're already in. And for that I'm sorry. I promise to do better."

Solace wiped her tears and wadded up his handkerchief in her pocket. "How much does Lizbet know about your plans? She seems to know you very well, by the way."

"Lizbet is Tomyss's younger sister and Jenleah's mother."

Solace exhaled, her breath visible in the chilly air. "Good, then I don't have to pretend quite so much around her."

Rhees spun her around and gripped both her arms. "You have to pretend all the time. You can't ever stop pretending. Your life and the lives of every thirsty child you're going to save depend on it. Can't you understand that?" He released her and said more softly, "You're worried about meeting Neuss tomorrow night, aren't you?"

Solace thought about Maysel's twin boys with the enormous brown eyes, and the stick-thin children pawing through the trash outside of Urhl. Her voice caught in her throat as she whispered, "I'd be a fool not to be worried."

"He knows you're from the Yeloshan hill country. He's not expecting a Toreszan city girl. You can be yourself."

"With my false name, my false papers, and my false betrothal, you mean?" Solace grumbled.

"Precisely."

CHAPTER 11

H alys was waiting in the bedroom for Solace to return so they could pounce on her trunk together. She asked Solace to try on each of the evening dresses Fenwith had altered for her, finally selecting a simple green velvet dress with a low-cut scalloped neckline, which Solace kept tugging until Halys scolded her for being silly. Solace had never worn anything below her collarbone before and felt exposed. Halys went to her own trunk and pulled out a set of glass beads for Solace to borrow.

"What about evening shoes?" asked Halys. Solace rummaged through her trunk and found a pair of black satin shoes and long black gloves. Halys nodded her approval.

Lizbet closed the library an hour early the next day and hurried everyone home so they could help Solace get ready. After she'd freshened up and changed into the green velvet dress, Lizbet sat her down at the kitchen table, fixed her hair, and applied a bit of rouge to her lips. When Lizbet was finished, she handed Solace a mirror and said, "Take a look."

Solace touched the back of her hair, which Lizbet had managed to suspend above her neck in some kind of a twisted bun. Solace found it hard to believe that city women chose to wear their hair off their necks like that, especially in colder weather, but she trusted Lizbet's judgment and thanked her.

Halys heard Rhees knocking at the front door and invited him into the tiny sitting room. Solace's stomach churned when she heard his voice, knowing she had to put on her best performance yet that evening, and she took a deep breath before following Lizbet into the room. Everyone waited for Rhees to say something.

He was sitting in one of the straight-backed chairs but he jumped up when Solace entered. She glanced at Rhees's fitted, gray and black silk jacket, crisp linen shirt, charcoal waistcoat, and pale gray cravat, and she wanted to turn right around, her insides quivering at the thought of pretending to be his fiancé in front of the king of Toresz. *There's no way we're going to pull this off,* she thought, wondering whether it was too late to decline the invitation.

Rhees stared at her with a quizzical expression on his face, as if he'd asked a question and was waiting expectantly for an answer. "Lace, you look beautiful, fit for a king." Then he helped Solace into the matching green velvet overcoat that Fenwith insisted she bring, tucked her arm in his, and escorted her outside.

A black and silver horse-drawn carriage sat waiting outside the row home, and a footman hopped down to open the door for them. Solace turned to Rhees, a question on her lips. "I wanted us to arrive in style at the palace, so I rented this for the evening. Besides, you'll never be able to walk all the way there in those satin shoes." Rhees helped her climb into the carriage and sat down across from her. "I meant what I said inside. You'll charm everyone tonight."

Solace twisted the strap of a beaded black reticule Lizbet had lent to her. "I don't know how you do this."

"Do what?"

"Live two such separate lives—the one inside Urhl, where you have to report to Neuss and behave as if this life is normal, when you know it's not—and your life outside the city, where you see people suffering everywhere you look. How do you do it?"

"I focus on the future, on a new Toresz where everyone has enough clean water to drink." Rhees grasped her hands to stop her fidgeting. "And I focus on keeping the most important person in Toresz safe, so she can use her amazing gift to save my people."

Solace bit her bottom lip and nodded. It was a good reminder that she was there for one purpose: to divine for water so Maysel's children, and so many others, would not have to grovel for a cup of Neuss's overtaxed water. And when her work was done, she could go back home to the hills she loved.

Rhees leaned back and peeked through the privacy curtain. "We're almost there. Are you ready?"

Solace swallowed hard. "Can't be worse than facing down an angry bear or a rabid wolf or jackal."

Rhees snapped his head around. "You've done all that?"

"Of course. Never lost a single sheep."

"Old Neuss is part bear and part rabid beast, so perhaps he's finally met his match."

The carriage jolted to a stop and the footman opened the door. Rhees hopped out first and then helped her down. He slipped his arm through hers and escorted her up the staircase. Solace's legs felt shaky as she climbed the stairs. She glanced around at the palace designed by King Ulyss's queen. It was smaller than the library but every bit as imposing, with tall columns, an arched entrance, and rows of glazed windows, all lit up from the inside. Solace calculated that hundreds of oil lamps and candles were illuminating the palace.

Rhees handed his invitation to the uniformed guard who

admitted them to a circular foyer that rose three stories above them, where a huge chandelier floated from the ceiling, its candles flickering brightly. One of the liveried servants took Solace's velvet overcoat and guided them to the king's drawing room, set up as a small theatre with a raised dais and rows of cushioned chairs.

After they were seated Rhees leaned over and whispered, "We've been invited to join the king and his guests for dinner following the entertainment."

"Can't we just slip away after the performance?" Solace asked softly.

"No, we can't. It would be considered an affront to the king."

Solace rolled her eyes. "We wouldn't want to do that."

"No, we wouldn't." Rhees noticed her hand was shaking as it rested on the arm of the chair. He reached over and grasped her hand firmly in his. "Just breathe."

Solace's mouth turned up at the corners. "I think I can remember that."

Everyone stood when the king entered the room and waited until he adjusted the folds of his burgundy robe and sat down before retaking their seats. He was tall like Rhees, with the same aquiline nose, but that's where the resemblance ended. Where Rhees was lean and quick, always ready to spring into action, Neuss was rounder and moved with a languid grace. *Here is a man who enjoys food and drink in abundance, while his people shiver and starve.*

A quartet of musicians began tuning their stringed instruments and the audience fell silent. A man with a ridiculously large belly, wearing a red robe that dragged behind him and a crown propped at a rakish angle on his head, walked onto the stage, followed by two men in oversized uniforms they kept tripping over, and a man and a woman wearing tattered rags, their hands out for crumbs. The actor-king behaved like a buffoon, ordering the guards to rid the kingdom of the beggars.

Solace sat up straighter and noticed Rhees tensing up next to her. There was no missing the resemblance, however comical, to the real king. "What the devil are they playing at?" he muttered.

The play continued, with the actor-king banishing the beggars and punishing everyone else, including his own guards, with imprisonment, until a beautiful woman, dressed in a gauzy blue gown and covered in a long veil, visited him. She touched his heart with a long wand and he fell to his knees, begging for forgiveness. He freed the prisoners and welcomed the poor back into his kingdom.

Everyone held their breath and their applause, waiting to see how the king would respond. Finally Neuss clapped, declaring it an amusing performance, and the audience clapped and smiled. Solace whispered, "What was that all about?"

"I'm not sure, but I want to meet the leader of that troupe. He's either a fool or the bravest man in Toresz!"

They followed the king into the formal dining room, where floor-to-ceiling tapestries depicting various scenes from Toreszan history draped the walls. A long table covered in fine linens and set with plates that seemed to have been dipped in gold occupied the center of the room. The king sat down at the head of the table in an elaborately carved chair. Liveried servants wearing garnet-colored jackets and white gloves stood along the perimeter, waiting to begin serving the first course.

Rhees looked for their name cards near the far end of the table and kept moving forward until he found their places. Solace was horrified to see she'd been placed next to the king. Rhees sat on her other side and kept glancing at her, a worried look on his face. *Just breathe!* She thought, looking blindly at all the dishes and glasses and flatware in front of her. *How does anyone know where to begin?*

The first course was hot soup, and Solace waited for the king to pick up his spoon so she could see which one to use. There was very little talk at their end of the table; it seemed the king was hungry. After they finished the soup, there was a brief lull while the servants cleared away the dishes, and Neuss looked at Rhees.

"Well, are you going to introduce me to this lovely young woman, or keep her all to yourself?"

Rhees cleared his throat. "I beg your pardon, Your Majesty. May I present my fiancé, Lace Blusari."

The king nodded at Solace, leering at the neckline of her dress. Resisting the urge to tug her dress up or push her bosom down, she bowed her head respectfully. "Your Majesty. Thank you for your kind invitation." Her heart was racing and she didn't know what else to say, so she stopped there.

The second course, some sort of meat pie, was placed before them, and the king dug in. When he was finished, he said, "Tell me, Lace Blusari, what did you think of the performance?"

"Since this is my first play, Your Majesty, I have nothing to compare it with."

"So you didn't like it?"

"Oh, I liked it well enough, although it seemed rather silly, don't you think? With the guards tripping over their pants and the king's heart being changed at the touch of a wand?"

The king looked at Solace through hooded eyes. "And what would you prefer? Something more serious, say a historical drama?"

"Do they produce those sorts of plays?" Solace asked.

The king threw back his head and laughed. "I can see why my Chief Librarian couldn't tear himself away from Yelosha. Who could resist a beautiful hill girl with no guile?" Still chuckling, the king turned to his third course, roasted duck, and Solace's heart rate gradually returned to normal as she picked at the food.

The king rose after dessert and went to his chambers. Solace couldn't wait to leave as well, but first they had to collect her coat, and then they stood in line to wait for their carriage to be brought around. While they were waiting, one of the servants handed Rhees a note.

Frowning, he broke the wax seal and read the note. He refolded it, placed it in his pocket, and stood in stony silence next to Solace until the carriage pulled up. Once they were inside, she asked, "What was in that note?"

Rhees didn't answer right away. Rubbing his beard he said, "As usual, Tomyss was right."

"About what?"

"About you attracting attention, perhaps too much attention."

"Did I do something wrong?"

Rhees shook his head. "Not at all."

"Then I don't understand."

Reaching into his pocket, he said, "Here, why don't you read this and tell me what you think." Solace unfolded the note, scrawled on the king's personal stationery.

Rhees,

You have done well on your recent travels. I am pleased with the scrolls you secured. Although you were gone overlong, I find that your stay in Yelosha was not without merit. In fact, I quite approve. I give you leave to travel in a fortnight to Xenyss, as I have my eye on several rare manuscripts. Take your fiancé with you. Such a fresh young thing must not be left unattended.

Neuss Orillya
His Majesty, King of Toresz

. . .

Solace grimaced at being called a "fresh young thing" by Neuss. She handed the note back to Rhees. "I'm not sure what he means about being left unattended. It feels almost like a threat."

Rhees squared his jaw. "My thoughts exactly. I don't like that he's taken notice of you. It'll make it that much harder for us to do our real work."

And that much harder for me to get back home, thought Solace.

CHAPTER 12

S olace lay awake for hours as scenes from the evening replayed in her head. She waited until dawn to dress and go downstairs and was sipping coffee when Lizbet and Halys joined her in the kitchen. They wanted to know about the palace, the play, the food, and the other ladies and what they'd been wearing. She answered all of their questions as honestly as she could, until Halys asked her opinion of the king. Solace pursed her lips, not sure how to respond. She opted to say as little as possible. "Not what I expected."

Lizbet's dark eyes twinkled. "That's a diplomatic answer if I ever heard one. You must have formed some impression of the king."

Solace shrugged. "The king behaves like a typical monarch. He commands with one wave of his hand and enjoys watching everyone snap to attention. I found the whole evening completely unnerving—I'm relieved it's over." Solace didn't say anything about the note Neuss penned to Rhees, or the vague-sounding threat, or how much she hated being in the same room with the king.

Solace's cataloging work at the library helped her focus on

something other than Neuss's note and Rhees's plans. As she was carrying a stack of books to be shelved after lunch, she noticed a man who looked somewhat familiar walk out of Lizbet's small office. Their eyes met, and her mouth opened in recognition. *The actor-king from last night!*

Solace closed the office door behind her, which had just enough space for a narrow desk and two chairs, and said to Lizbet. "That man was at the palace last night. He's one of the actors."

"Aye, I know."

"Who is he?"

"Jenleah's brother-in-law. Her husband's older brother."

"He took an enormous risk last night, playing the king. Rhees said he's either a fool or the bravest man in Toresz."

"Well, he's no fool. Brave, perhaps. Mostly, he's desperate. Desperate for change, for hope. He uses the stage to hammer home his message."

Solace went back to work, thinking about the play, which wasn't comical or silly, as she'd originally thought. The play was subversive, and Solace was glad to have been there, applauding Jenleah's brother-in-law.

The next two weeks passed quickly for Solace, who surprised herself by learning to enjoy her work at the library. Not that she didn't miss her father and her home, but she began to recognize there were different ways of living, and while she'd always love the hill ways best, she could understand why someone like Lizbet, with her love of books and plays and shops, might prefer the city ways.

Solace certainly preferred winter in the hills, which amounted to several weeks of hard rain followed by a dry spring, summer, and autumn. She loved the rain-soaked smell of the soil in winter and the greening of the hills that never lasted for long. City winters, on the other hand, were messy and depressing, with the rain turning everything into muck for weeks.

She'd seen very little of Rhees since their trip to the palace, except for a quick head nod while they were at work or several short visits to the house she shared with Lizbet and Halys. In fact, Solace thought he might be avoiding her altogether, and instead of feeling relieved at not having to play her role whenever he was around, she found herself annoyed by his absence. She felt certain he was making plans that included water divining during their trip to Xenyss, which she'd learned was in the northern province, and she thought the least he could do was include her in the planning.

The night before their departure, Rhees stopped by the house after dinner and suggested they go for a stroll. Even though the rain had stopped, every surface glistened with a fine sheen of moisture, and little rivulets of water ran down the streets. They walked for several blocks, their boots clacking hollowly on the damp cobblestones.

"Pack lightly for the trip, as we won't be taking Caya along. We'll leave after breakfast."

"How long will we be gone?"

"A couple of weeks." Rhees lowered his voice. "Some of that time will be spent retrieving manuscripts for Neuss, and some of it will be for you to do your work."

"How safe will we be while I 'do my work?' "

Rhees shrugged, "Safe enough."

Solace's temper flared at his cavalier attitude toward her safety. "What are your plans? What precautions have you taken?"

"I'm not in the habit of discussing plans and precautions while walking on the streets of Urhl." Rhees hunched his shoulders. "Why, are you afraid all of a sudden?"

"No. I want to get this over with as quickly, and safely, as possible. The sooner I'm done, the sooner I can go home."

"I'm moving things along as quickly as I can," Rhees growled. "If we move too fast, we'll be exposed."

"Well, keep things moving along. I want to be home by spring. I don't think I can bear to be away much longer," Solace snapped.

"Aye, I've heard it before, you miss your father and your 'special friend' Arik."

"And my sheep and my dog. I miss my home!"

"You'll go home when your work is finished, and there's no way it'll be done by spring," Rhees said mulishly.

Solace started walking faster, curling and uncurling her fists, but Rhees's long strides easily kept pace. She stopped suddenly and turned to face him. "You really are a hard, unfeeling man."

"A young hill girl from Yelosha can't possibly understand me or my feelings," he said through gritted teeth.

"I'm good enough to snatch from my home and use for your 'plans,' but I'm not good enough for an honest conversation." Solace thrust her hands, which were numb from the damp cold, deeper into the pockets of her cloak. She didn't want to stand outside arguing with Rhees. Her breath formed misty puffs in the chilly air as she asked her next question. "Could you *please* explain how I'll be able to divine for water without Neuss's henchmen finding out?"

Rhees folded his arms and thrust his bottom lip out, refusing to answer her.

"I hate you," she hissed. She thought of her mother, who'd taught her it was wrong to hate anyone. Then again, her mother had never been kidnapped so she could divine for water in a foreign land run by a crazy king.

Rhees compressed his lips and closed the gap between them. Drawing himself to his full height, he glowered down at her. "I can live with that."

When Rhees knocked at the front door the following morning, Solace slipped on her traveling cloak and hastily said goodbye to Halys and Lizbet, who gave her a fierce hug. "Peace go with you, lass," she whispered in her ear. Solace had a feeling Lizbet knew more than she was letting on about their trip to Xenyss.

Solace and Jenx followed Rhees and Zirott out of the barn. Since they were both traveling under the king's written orders, which Rhees provided to the guards at the gate, they were waved through without any fuss.

They stopped at midday so the horses could graze while they shared some bread and cheese. Rhees commented on the weather, which was clear but cold, and the hills, which had greened with the winter rains, and asked if she was warm enough. Solace nodded a few times but was in no mood for small talk.

Sighing, he mounted Zirott and she vaulted onto Jenx's back. They traveled in silence until the moon was up, when Rhees pointed to a rocky outcropping and said, "We'll be out of the wind over there."

After they unloaded, rubbed down the horses, and set up camp, Rhees started a fire with damp wood and brush, which sputtered and smoked. Solace's eyes burned from the cloud of sooty smoke and she coughed.

"Are you feeling ill?" Rhees asked solicitously.

She shook her head.

Rhees threw down the wood he was carrying and yelled, "Then what's wrong with you? You haven't said a single word to me all day. It's like traveling with a ghost."

Solace shrugged and handed him a bowl of gruel. She found a rock to lean against that was close enough to the fire to keep her warm, but allowed her to turn her back on Rhees, and she took her gruel with her.

She heard Rhees muttering under his breath, something about "women" and "moody" but she ignored him. When she finished her gruel, she wiped out her bowl and returned it to the saddlebag.

"I know what you're doing," Rhees said. "You think by not speaking to me that I'll feel bad about last night and will open up, tell you anything you want to know."

Solace yawned, picked up her bedroll, and went into the tent. She fell asleep almost instantly and woke up to Rhees shaking her shoulder the next morning. She smelled the rich aroma of coffee somewhere nearby and opened her eyes. Rolling over, she saw Rhees squatting next to her with one of the tin cups in his hands, which he handed to her after she'd hoisted herself into a sitting position.

He left the tent and returned a moment later with a mug for himself. He sat cross-legged on top of his bedroll. Staring down into his coffee, he said, "I'm sorry. You have a right to know my plans, since you'll be in as much danger as I'll be. It's just that...it takes me a long time to open up to anyone. And you're not just anyone."

"What's that supposed to mean?"

A half-smile formed on Rhees's lips. "You said something."

Solace rolled her eyes and waited for him to answer her question.

"As you often remind me, I took you from your home by force and I'm keeping you here until you've divined enough water to see us through a rebellion. Sometimes when I look at you, I can't believe that I've sunk so low, that I've actually kidnapped a young woman. Then I'm ashamed all over again and don't want to talk to you or acknowledge what I've done."

"So, instead, you glower and growl and refuse to answer even a simple question."

Now it was Rhees's turn to shrug. "Pretty much."

Solace sipped from her mug. "Tell me how we're going to get away with divining for water in these hills."

"We have a lot of allies in these hills, here in the north as well as the south. In fact, I've been standing up a small army."

Solace almost spilled her coffee. "You've *what?* How do you know they can be trusted?"

"They're men and women like Peka and her sons, and Wilhm and Maysel. People who are looking for something to spark the rebellion, and you're that spark."

"*Me?* But I want nothing to do with armies and rebellions. I've told you that."

Rhees reached across the small space that separated their bedrolls and gently removed the empty mug from her hands. He picked up both her hands and turned them over, palms up. "You have a gift, perhaps the greatest gift any man or woman can possess, the gift of water, which is the gift of life in these dry hills. You are that spark whether you choose to be or not."

Solace looked down at her hands and wished, for the hundredth time at least, that she'd never inherited her mother's gift. She'd still be home in her beloved hills. If she closed her eyes, she could see herself there still, walking with Barley and her sheep along the ridge, or harvesting tomatoes in the vegetable garden outside her cramped cottage, or reading one of her mother's books by candlelight on her narrow bed.

Rhees picked up their cups and said, "We need to leave now if we're going to reach Xenyss by nightfall."

As they prepped their horses for departure, the sun rose over their right shoulders and burnished the hills in gold. Solace breathed in the fresh air, relieved to be out of the city and in the hills again, even if they were Toreszan hills. In truth, they looked very similar to her hills back home. Glancing about, Solace gasped out loud.

"What's wrong?" Rhees asked.

Solace frowned as she looked into the valley below them. "With the recent rains, it's going to be harder for me to divine for water. The soil is a uniform shade, and it'll contain enough moisture for a while to disguise the presence of a water source."

Worry lines creased Rhees's brow. "Can you still do it?"

"I've never tried divining immediately after the winter rains before, so I'm not sure. I'll have to rely much more on my sense of hearing. We'll have to be walking rather than riding, which will take longer."

"I believe you'll be able to do this for us. I have faith in you."

"*You* have faith in *me*? Why?"

"I was there, in the hills above that desperate farmer and his family, watching you divine for water. I've only observed one other person with that same single-minded focus."

"And who was that?"

"My mother, when she was diagnosing a patient." Rhees glanced at the sun. "At least we have clear weather ahead. Perhaps a week or so of solid sunshine will help. We'll purchase the manuscripts first, and then we'll search for water."

As they rode, Solace kept searching for any signs of a subterranean water source in the color variations of the soil, but it was impossible. Everything looked the same shade of brown.

They arrived at Xenyss's city gate as the sun was setting and seemed to be the only visitors. When Rhees commented on it, the guard looked at him with surprise. "We're under curfew. Come full nightfall, I wouldn't be opening that gate for anyone but the king himself."

"Since when? I've been through here several months past, and there was no curfew in place."

"Since those three men were hung for treason." The guard handed the papers back to Rhees and nodding at Solace, he said, "Best to get your lady inside soon, and stay put until morning. The streets aren't safe for any who travel under the king's orders."

Rhees thanked him and guided Solace and the horses toward the inn at the center of town. Xenyss was a rugged mountain town, with neither the elegance of Urhl nor the quaintness of a Yeloshan village. Neuss's guards were everywhere, and the few men on the streets kept their eyes averted as they scurried past. Solace sensed their fear, which hardened her resolve against Neuss. She'd turn over every rock if she had to, but she'd find water in these northern hills.

They rode up to a weather-beaten building that sagged slightly in the middle. A worn sign out front confirmed it was the inn. After Rhees paid for the horses to be stabled and unloaded their bags, he ushered Solace into the inn, which smelled of candle wax and lye soap. He booked them two rooms on the second floor.

"Will ye be wanting dinner then?" asked an old woman, so stooped over that her body formed an *L*. Her face hardened when she noticed Rhees's traveling papers stamped with the king's insignia.

"Aye, and a bottle of ale for me. And be quick about it," Rhees grunted.

After the woman shuffled to the kitchen, Solace said softly, "Why were you so rude to that poor woman?"

Rhees leaned over and whispered in her ear. "Playing the part of the king's Chief Librarian."

"Tone it down a bit. Otherwise, you may wind up with a knife in your back."

Rhees's dark eyebrows shot up. "Good point."

They climbed the creaking stairs after dinner and found their rooms. As Solace opened the door to her room, Rhees said, "I have three different book dealers I'll be haggling with over the next few days, which means I'll be out early and returning mid-afternoon. Stay inside. It's not safe for you to be walking about alone, even during the day."

"Can't I join you?" Solace hated being stuck indoors with nothing to do.

Rhees shook his head. "You're too distracting. The dealers will spend all their time flirting with you instead of haggling with me."

Solace snorted. "That's a backhanded compliment."

"That's the truth."

By the time Solace had dressed and descended the stairs the next morning, Rhees had already left the inn. The old woman nodded at Solace as she sat down at one of the tables in the inn's lobby, which also served as parlor and dining room. Solace thanked her as she set down two poached eggs, toast, and coffee.

The woman paused and squinted at Solace. "It's my job. No need to say thanks."

Solace smiled. "I've been fixing breakfast most of my life. When someone else fixes it for me, I'll gladly thank them." She asked, "What's your name?"

The woman's bird-like eyes bore into Solace's, as if to assess her sincerity. She shrugged. "Valira. Been working here since I was twelve."

"You're not the owner?" Solace asked as she sipped her coffee.

A cloud passed over Valira's features and her voice shook with emotion. "My nephew, Del, inherited this place from my brother. But after Del's death, the crown seized it. So I guess Neuss now owns it." She looked like she wanted to spit but swallowed instead.

Solace reached out and squeezed the old woman's arm. "I'm so sorry for your loss. Was it an accident?"

Valira exhaled in a huff. "If ye call being hung for digging a well an accident, then I suppose."

Solace's eyes grew moist and she shook her head. Valira

looked at her and said, "You're a good lass. Too good for that bossy man of yours."

For some strange reason, Solace felt compelled to defend Rhees's reputation. "Oh, he's a better man than he seems." Now she sounded just like Fenwith.

"Perhaps." Valira left to wait on another guest, but she returned a short time later and handed Solace a package wrapped in brown paper. "He left this for you."

Solace lifted the package. It was surprisingly heavy. She carefully removed the paper, gasping in surprise: a book of Toreszan fairy tales, with enough stories to last until she returned to Urhl.

She'd been looking through the library's copy one day, and Rhees had peeked over her shoulder to see what she was reading. He must have remembered and purchased the book for her. She opened the book's cover and found a folded note:

Lace,

I hope this book will help keep you occupied while we're in Xenyss. It belonged to my mother and was one of my favorites as a boy.

Rhees

Valira said, "When he handed me that package, he also ordered me to be sure you don't set foot outside these doors." She added, "He cares for you, and that's something anyway."

Solace shook her head. "He cares for what I can bring to our marriage, but he doesn't care for me. Not really."

"I've seen how he looks at you. He'd move mountains to keep you safe."

He has one purpose for keeping me safe, and that's so I can find water for his people.

CHAPTER 13

It took Rhees four days to secure the manuscripts the king wanted, at the price Neuss was willing to pay. In truth, Toreszan book dealers knew they had to sell their manuscripts to the king, unless they wanted his guards to seize their shops under a false pretense. But hill people everywhere enjoyed a good haggle, so in the end all parties were satisfied.

Valira kissed Solace as they were leaving the inn and repeated the same hill blessing as Fenwith. Solace gripped the old woman's hands and thanked her for her hospitality. Rhees looked at the two women, strangers a few days earlier, and scratched his head.

As they were riding toward the city gate, Rhees said, "What was that all about? She was barely civil to me."

Solace shrugged. "You represent the crown, and her nephew was one of the men convicted of treason and hung for digging a well. You're not going to be very popular around here."

"I understand that, but what is it about *you*, that causes Fenwith and Lizbet and that old woman in there to embrace you after a brief acquaintance? I don't get it."

"Jealous?"

Rhees waited until they'd cleared the last of the guards and were walking their horses through the city gate. "Curious, I guess."

"It's simple. I treat them with respect, I appreciate how hard they work, and I listen to their stories."

"And I do none of that?"

"When was the last time you sat down at Fenwith's table and asked about her arthritis? And maybe offered to help her chop an onion or wash the pot after she cooks for you?"

Rhees looked away at the hills in the distance and was silent. Shaking his head, he said, "I can't remember the last time. I used to be more like that, as a boy, but everything changed when my mother and father were killed. Everything. I've been consumed by their deaths. First, by the desire for revenge, but Tomyss managed to turn me away from that, and now, by the desire to help my people." He paused. "I guess I've lost sight of the simple things that people need."

After they'd mounted, he pointed to the ridge of hills behind Xenyss. "We're heading to the caves tucked inside those hills."

Solace brought her hand up to shield her eyes. The top layer of soil was starting to dry out across the plain, but she still couldn't see the color variations she needed for her divining. She knit her brows together, trying to extend the mental map of water sources from the Tor monastery, where she'd "seen" the water, to the northern hills. So far, she had nothing.

They approached the ridge while there was still an hour of daylight left and Rhees led them to a deserted cave entrance. He dismounted and said, "Wait here. I've never approached with another rider before." He entered the cave and was gone long enough that Jenx started pawing the soil. When Rhees returned, two other men accompanied him. The men quickly unloaded Jenx and Zirott and led the horses away to a separate cave entrance that served as a stable.

Rhees took Solace by the elbow and guided her inside the cave. He paused long enough to grab a charred hunk of wood from a stack on the ground and thrust it into the flames of a large, battered oil lamp hanging near the entrance. Handing the torch to Solace, Rhees leaned his shoulder into what appeared to be a large boulder, but was actually a door that opened onto a narrow passage. They walked single file, following a twisting path, with Rhees stooping over to avoid bumping his head.

The passage opened into a huge chamber that was lit with at least a dozen torches. A group of about forty men and women were assembled there, gathered around a campfire. They had enough dry wood and oxygen for a lively fire, so Solace figured there must be an opening in the rocky ceiling above them to let out the smoke.

A burly man, with long salt-and-pepper hair and a beard to match, left the fire to join them. Rhees introduced him as Kryss, the leader of the band of rebels that met in the cave to train and prepare for the day they could overthrow Neuss.

"Well met, Lace Blusari! Welcome to our humble rebellion."

Rhees said, "Perhaps the three of us could discuss our plans for tomorrow?"

Kryss nodded, "Aye, of course. Follow me." He turned around and shouted, "Keep practicing your sword fighting. I need to see better blocking!"

Solace and Rhees followed Kryss down a different passage to a small room that served as a makeshift office. There were a few bedrolls stacked in one corner. Kryss unrolled them and invited Solace to sit down on top of them. Rhees and Kryss sat on the ground across from her.

Kryss smiled at Solace. "I understand you've got the gift."

Solace didn't know how to answer him. Rhees replied, "It's

alright, Lace. I've told Kryss about you. We need to have a couple of people in each province who can serve as lookouts for us while you're divining, and who will dig and hide the wells later."

Solace felt better knowing she could speak freely with Kryss. "I've been divining for water on my own since I was fourteen, and before that I helped my mother."

"When were you first aware you had the gift?" asked Kryss.

"My father told me I started making maps of water sources when I was five. I used to scratch them out in the sand. The first time my mother realized what they were, she thought something was wrong with me. Apparently her gift didn't manifest until she was fifteen."

Kryss laughed. "My mother had the gift, and her mother before her. They divined the locations of many of the wells in our province. Of course, after Neuss came into power, all our diviners disappeared, my mother included."

"What do you mean, disappeared?" Solace asked, feeling a pit opening up in the bottom of her stomach. She hadn't heard about any disappearances.

Kryss glanced at Rhees. "You didn't tell her?"

Rhees wouldn't meet Solace's eyes. "She knows the dangers, we've discussed them. But we never discussed what Toresz was like before Neuss overthrew King Meade, back when we had our own water diviners."

"What happened to them?" Solace wasn't sure she really wanted to know.

"They vanished," Kryss replied. "My mother left for a divining and never made it there. Same thing happened to the others. Shortly after the disappearances, Neuss proclaimed the crown 'owned' all water rights in Toresz."

Certain pieces of the puzzle behind her kidnapping fell into place, like the fact she was the last living water diviner in Toresz. Although water divining was a rare gift, Solace knew of at least two other women in Yelosha who divined for water on the other side of the Hawxhurss Mountains.

Crossing her arms, she glared at Rhees. "Why is this the first time I'm hearing about this?"

Rhees finally met her gaze. "I didn't think it mattered at this point. You knew digging for wells was illegal. And I didn't want to frighten you needlessly."

Solace arched an eyebrow. "That would be a first."

Kryss ran a hand through his long salt-and-pepper beard and seemed to be weighing his next words carefully. He turned his head, glancing between the two of them. "Sounds like an interesting courtship."

"Very," they replied simultaneously.

Kryss wisely didn't pursue the matter any further, and he rose in Solace's estimation. *Perhaps Rhees's trust in this burly man of the northern province is not misplaced,* she thought.

After a restless night of worrying about whether she'd be able to find any water because of the recent rains, Solace woke up, temporarily confused about where she'd bedded down. She was lying in a bedroll in one of the rooms that connected with the main chamber, curled next to six other women, all part of Kryss's band of rebels. She yawned and sat up, not even sure whether the sun was up because of the gloom inside the cave.

She dressed as quietly as possible, stowed her bedroll, and headed into the main chamber, where she found Rhees and Kryss hunched over mugs of coffee. Rhees handed her a mug and some dried jerky, explaining they'd be leaving as soon as their horses, which would be carrying extra water skins for their journey, were saddled and ready. Solace's stomach tightened at the prospect of succeeding and inviting Neuss's punishment, or failing and inviting Rhees's scorn.

They mounted their horses as the sun edged above the horizon, painting the hills a burnished copper, and rode several hours farther north. As they rode, Solace noticed abandoned homesteads, where poor Toreszan farmers had tried and failed to scratch out a subsistence living. They passed mining settlements, where Neuss's men guarded the silver ore and the water supply, ignoring the malnourished children begging for food. A cloud of misery hung about the Toreszan hills, and it sliced through Solace's heart, hardening her resolve to help Rhees find water for these people, despite her fear of being caught.

Kryss reined in his horse near an abandoned mining settlement tucked at the base of a range of hills, facing a broad valley. Rhees and Solace slowed to a walk and followed Kryss to a patch of grasses and low brush. Dismounting, they took one water skin each and enough food for the day and left their horses to graze, since they'd be spending the rest of the day on foot. They entered the settlement, the weathered shacks leaning over precariously, some already collapsed in gray heaps on the ground.

Kryss led them to the only well, which he explained had run dry several years earlier. Solace walked over and closed her eyes, listening. She heard nothing, no trace murmurings of water nearby, nothing but the wind in the grasses and the cawing of blackbirds overhead.

Rhees turned and waved his hand across the valley and hills, which the winter rains had greened. Solace knew after several weeks of sunshine, the hills would return to their normal shades of tan and beige and brown, just like the hills back home. "Go ahead, Lace, we'll follow you," he said.

Solace inhaled and exhaled slowly, clearing her mind of everything except her sense of water. She walked out of the settlement and surveyed the valley. The recent rains had soaked the ground to a uniform brown, although she could see areas that were beginning to lighten. She walked on, pausing periodically to pick up a handful of soil and first sniff, and then sift it through her fingers. She even tasted the soil, but the amount of moisture in the surface areas still masked the water sources running beneath them.

She continued on in this way, zigzagging across the valley, trying to find even a trickle of water that could help her map the water sources. As she began to climb another hill in the range running along the western edge of the valley, Kryss offered to return to the horses and set up camp for the night in the abandoned mine.

Solace and Rhees climbed the hill and stood on a ridge that overlooked the next valley, farther west. She put up her hand to shield her eyes from the sun, which would be setting in another hour. Closing her eyes, she swayed slightly, waiting for her gift to tell her where to go.

She dropped to her knees and then stretched herself out on the ground. Placing her ear against the pebbly soil, she listened. *Maybe,* she thought, *maybe that's a murmur, but I can't be sure until the soil dries out, or I hear the water running.*

Solace rose and wiped off the front of her cloak. Frowning, she bit her bottom lip. She took her water divining seriously, and her gift had never failed her before. Why was it failing her now, when the stakes were so high?

A tear escaped and rolled down her cheek. She swiped at it with her hand, realizing too late she'd probably smeared dirt on her face. "I'm sorry; truly, I am. This has never happened before. I've always been able to find water." She looked at Rhees, "You believe me, don't you?"

Rhees pulled out a handkerchief and gently wiped the dirty smear off her cheek. Then he took her hands, one at a time, and wiped them as well. He put the soiled handkerchief back in his pocket and placing his hands on her shoulders, he said, "Of course I believe you. It's the rains; they've camouflaged the water sources. We'll come back in spring and try again."

Solace took a shaky breath and nodded. Then Rhees took her hand and helped her climb back down the hill and cross the valley. Her legs felt leaden and she wondered how many miles she'd walked that day.

When Kryss saw them, his face fell. "No luck?"

Rhees explained about the winter rains and Kryss nodded, disappointed, but Rhees assured him they'd return in spring and find water. After a simple meal of bread and cheese, Solace spread out her bedroll inside the entrance to the mine, rolled on her side, and fell immediately asleep.

As she slept she dreamt of a stream with clear running water, which she scooped up in her hands. She smiled as the sunlight glinted on the water she held cupped in her palms. Raising her hands high, she poured the water over her head and let it run in tiny rivulets down her face. Solace woke up feeling refreshed and lighter somehow. Her mother used to talk about the lightness of water and how her gift would replenish itself— and her—when she most needed it.

She blinked, trying to figure out whether she was still sleeping, because she thought she heard the whisper of water deep down inside the mine, running beneath the hill and outward into the valley. She rolled onto her other side and listened intently. *Aye, there it is. I can hear it and see it!* The mental map snapped into place, and she knew where to search for the best well locations.

She reached for her cloak, tossed it over her shoulders, and stepped across Rhees, who was sleeping nearby. The sun hadn't risen yet, and the sky was an inky dark blue, but Solace didn't need to see the soil now. She climbed the hill directly behind the mining settlement, stumbling a few times in the dark. Sitting cross-legged near the hilltop, she faced east and waited for the sun to rise and the sky to lighten from dark blue to light blue and then to gold.

Once the sun had risen high enough to brighten the valley, she could see where some of the soil was a shade darker than other places, and it lined up with her mental map of the water sources. She stood up and stretched, and then decided she'd lead Rhees and Kryss toward the eastern side of the valley, where the water ran closer to the surface.

Solace started back down the hill, kicking up stones as she went. As she walked around a large boulder, she collided into Rhees, who was running up the hill. He threw his arms around her, drawing her into a bear hug. The hard edge of her anger, which she'd been carrying around since Rhees had taken her, collapsed and her heart softened toward him. She still believed he'd wronged her and her father, whom she missed every day, but she no longer hated Rhees. In fact, Solace realized she'd stopped hating him weeks ago.

Rhees pulled himself away to examine her, deep lines etched in his brow. "When I woke up and saw you were gone, I thought maybe—"

"Maybe I'd hiked back to Yelosha?" she quipped.

His frown deepened. "No, not that. You were so down last night, so defeated, I was concerned, that's all." Then he noticed she was smiling and arched an eyebrow. "What?"

"I've found water, or at least, I know where we can search for it. Let's go get Kryss and head back out across the valley."

Rhees's face relaxed into a smile. "I knew you'd find us water. But first, can I grab a mug of coffee? It's exhausting, following behind you. We must have walked twenty miles yesterday, maybe more."

After all three of them had coffee and porridge, they rode across the valley with Solace leading the way. Rhees and Kryss quietly watched as Solace used all of her senses—sight, smell, hearing, touch, and finally taste—to divine the precise location for the new well. "Here, you'll only have to dig fifty feet to find your water!" she said.

Kryss let out a whoop and clapped Rhees on the back. Then Kryss returned to his horse and brought out a jar of inky black dye and a rag. He surveyed the area and then paced off the number of steps from the water source to a gnarled tree that stood like a sentry in the center of the valley. Kryss dipped the rag into the dye and began sketching a series of symbols into the bole of the tree.

As Solace watched him work, Rhees asked her, "Do you recognize those symbols?"

She shook her head and smiled. "No, but you're using your Chief Librarian's voice, so I'm sure you're going to tell me."

"I don't have a Chief Librarian's voice. Do I?"

Kryss paused and said over his shoulder, "You most certainly do."

Rhees looked about to object, but Solace reached over and tapped his shoulder. "Never mind, tell me about the symbols, please."

"Our ancestors, the hill people who lived in Yelosha and Toresz over a thousand years ago, used symbolic language to make maps, record important events, even identify water sources."

Kryss rolled up the rag and carefully sealed the jar of dye. Joining them, he said, "Rhees taught the symbols to those of us who are interested in fighting Neuss and saving our country, so we could communicate in secret."

"Don't you run the risk of someone, a scholar perhaps on Neuss's payroll, being able to read the symbols?"

Rhees said, "It's possible, so instead of using the symbol for 'water,' we use the symbol for 'life.' We've made several other adjustments as well."

"Rhees thinks of everything," Kryss said. Solace tilted her head at Rhees, who looked away, embarrassed.

They mounted their horses, and as Kryss turned to lead them back toward his cave hideout, Solace said, "Not yet. We're going to find several more before we leave."

Solace rode for another hour farther north, where she located a second well for them to dig. Kryss scouted around until he found several boulders that he could use as a marker. After pacing off the distance to the new water source, he expertly sketched the well location onto the largest of the boulders.

When he was finished they set up camp inside the ring of boulders, shielding themselves somewhat from the wind. Kryss went hunting and came back with a dead snake, which he cooked for their dinner. Solace had never eaten snake meat before but was so hungry she thought it might become her favorite meal, but only if cooked over a campfire.

They rose early the next morning because Solace was determined to continue divining. She led them to three more water locations in the next valley before they turned their horses around and rode back to Kryss's cave hideout, arriving after nightfall.

Kryss invited Solace to join him, Rhees, and several of their most trusted rebels in his "office" for a private celebration, which Solace suspected would involve watching the others drink large amounts of ale and tell stories about people she'd never met. She politely declined, claiming exhaustion. Spreading out her bedroll in one of the cave's chambers reserved for women, she felt content for the first time since she'd been taken from her home. She realized her mother had been right: divining for water made her feel lighter somehow, more like her real self. And even though she was hundreds of miles from home and still technically a captive, she felt strangely free.

CHAPTER 14

Rhees suggested they stay at the monastery for a night on their return trip to Urhl and Solace readily agreed. She looked forward to seeing Tomyss and discussing the books he'd given her, and she longed to bathe again in the small grotto. Water divining was a messy business, and she didn't want to ride into Urhl covered in layers of dirt.

When Evryst came forward with his guards to greet them, his eyebrows peaked in surprise at their disheveled state. Evryst asked several of the brothers to escort Rhees and Solace to the springs for bathing, after which they went to Tomyss's office, where he had a hot meal waiting for them.

"What news from the capital?" Rhees asked after taking a sip of Tomyss's best wine.

"They say that Neuss is more cheerful than usual, even taken to humming."

"What could be the cause of his good cheer?" Rhees asked, frowning.

Tomyss picked up his glass of wine and swirled the contents before taking a swallow. "We're not certain, but it seems to have started the day after the king invited a small party to the palace for theater and dinner. Our friends tell us he's been bathing more frequently and has ordered the dead queen's chambers redecorated." Tomyss paused and locked eyes with Rhees. "Tell me, did he seem to pay particular attention to any of the young ladies that evening?"

Rhees shifted uncomfortably in his seat. "He took uncommon interest in our Lace here."

Solace's stomach lurched and she put down her fork. "What are you saying? And do I even want to know?"

Tomyss looked at her, his brown eyes filled with compassion and something else—sadness—as if her fate were already sealed. "Don't worry just yet. Even if Neuss has taken an interest in you, you're still betrothed to Rhees, which offers some protection. I'm sharing this as a precaution to you both, and especially to you, Rhees. You must take extra care with Lace, and try to accelerate our plans."

Rhees's mouth formed a thin line and he nodded. "Understood."

Solace didn't really understand but decided not to ask more questions. The mood around the table had grown somber, and she was tired from the long ride back from the northern province. Tomyss noticed her hiding a yawn and suggested she get some rest. Solace thanked him and returned to the small, whitewashed bedroom where she'd stayed previously. She undressed, got under the covers, and despite the thoughts and fears swirling in her head, fell into a dreamless sleep.

When she entered Tomyss's office early the next morning, Rhees and Tomyss were already hunched over mugs of coffee, speaking in low voices. The two men seemed so companionable—despite the differences in their age and appearance—with Rhees's tall, muscular build and dark, unruly waves contrasting with Tomyss's wiry frame and neatly-combed, silver hair. Then Solace recalled Tomyss had mentored Rhees through his emotional crisis following the deaths of

King Meade and Ellanora. It seemed the elderly monk had become almost a second father to Rhees. They heard her footsteps and leaned back in their chairs.

"You look lovely, my dear," Tomyss said as he stood and pulled out a chair for her. Solace had carefully packed the riding habit Rhees had purchased for her first trip into Urhl; she'd brought it along to wear on her return to the capital. She glanced at Rhees, who seemed oddly flustered.

Rhees cleared his throat. "We'll leave soon after breakfast. Tomyss and I need to meet with Evryst first."

They shared a light breakfast of coffee, buttered scones, and dried fruit. Solace couldn't help feeling something had changed overnight and the stakes were higher, for Rhees and Tomyss and especially for her.

She rose from the small dining table in Tomyss's office to give the two men some privacy, since they clearly had unfinished business. "I'll be in Tomyss's library, curled up with a good book."

"Very good, lass. I won't keep Rhees much longer." Tomyss smiled gently as Rhees nodded at her. Both men seemed distracted.

When the guard at the watchtower examined their papers, he asked them to wait while he walked over to the desk and picked up a note. Handing it to Rhees, he said, "From the king. Orders are that you ride immediately to the palace."

Rhees looked at the note, which had been addressed to the guards, and he nodded. When they were out of earshot, Solace asked, "What's that all about?"

Rhees shrugged. "Neuss writes to say he wants to see his manuscripts immediately, and that we're to present them upon our arrival in the capital."

"Why do I have to go?"

"Because we rode out under his orders, and we're riding back under his orders. We've no choice here."

They remounted and rode through the streets of Urhl. It was still early by city standards, with servants sweeping front stoops, shopkeepers opening up for business, and street peddlers calling out their wares. Rhees and Solace led their horses up the steep incline toward the palace, where they handed their reins to palace attendants and were escorted immediately to one of the opulent parlors. Rhees carried the manuscripts he'd purchased in Xenyss in a leather messenger bag. One of the servants brought them glasses of lemon-infused water in heavy mugs, while another offered them a variety of finger foods, which they declined.

The servants bowed and withdrew from the room, leaving Rhees and Solace sitting awkwardly in stiff-backed chairs, waiting for the king. Solace shifted in her chair a few times, deciding that riding on top of Jenx was far more comfortable than sitting in one of the king's chairs.

They heard heavy footsteps and looked up as Neuss, resplendent in burgundy robes, entered the room. They rose, bowed, and the king inclined his head to indicate they should retake their seats. Solace's nerves were already on edge, but her stomach twisted in tight knots when she saw Neuss lean back in his chair, which was larger and set higher than theirs, and look down at her through hooded eyes. In fact, he only looked at Rhees once, when he asked him for the manuscripts. Rhees removed them from the messenger bag and handed them to the king.

Neuss examined them quickly, nodding his approval. "Well done, and what did I pay for these?" As Rhees explained, the king continued to stare unabashedly at Solace. Finally he addressed her. "And what did you think of Xenyss?"

Solace hesitated, not sure how to respond, but she opted for candor. "At first, I didn't like Xenyss. It's a rough, frontier town with nothing to recommend it. But as I got to know some of the people, I found the city had grown on me."

The king took a sip from a jewel-encrusted goblet. "Tell me, Lace Blusari, do you always answer with such frankness?"

"That's the way of my people, Your Majesty. We're known for our candor."

The king chuckled and didn't take his eyes off the swell of her bosom inside her riding habit. Solace felt like a mouse cornered by a hungry cat. Neuss nodded at her, placed his goblet on a side table and rose. Rhees and Solace stood up and bowed once again as he left the room.

A servant escorted them back outside, where their horses were brought around for them. Solace glanced at Rhees a few times, but he was grinding his teeth and muttering under his breath.

Solace followed Rhees through the city streets, back to the stable behind their row homes, where they removed the saddles from Jenx and Zirott and brushed them down, neither of them breaking the silence. Caya neighed in her stall, and Solace went over to rub her nose and whisper, "I missed you, milady!"

Rhees came up behind Solace and scratched Caya's ears. "There's a good girl."

He cleared his throat and waited for Solace to look up. She noticed his worry lines were back. "I hated the way Neuss looked at you. I'd hoped Tomyss was exaggerating, but it's clear the king is besotted."

"But he believes I'm your fiancé, so what can he really do?"

"Legally, he can do nothing. But he's crafty, and he's the king, so we have to watch our backs."

"Aren't you in more danger from Neuss than me? Couldn't he just decide to arrest you, or do something even worse?"

Rhees shrugged. "Let's not get ahead of ourselves. We'll both be careful for the time being, at least until Neuss finds another young woman to occupy his thoughts. He's a fickle man."

"How fickle?"

"Six wives and countless mistresses."

Solace wanted to know what had happened to the other wives, but Rhees's mouth was set in a firm line, and she knew he wouldn't tell her. She'd ask Lizbet when she had the chance.

They resumed their normal working routines, with Solace leaving for the library each morning with Lizbet and Halys, and returning each evening to their modest home. Rhees kept his distance again, stopping in occasionally after dinner for a visit in the sitting room, and then leaving early, without once suggesting they go for a walk. Solace decided that her life was much more stable and even sedate this way, which was fine with her.

A few weeks later, Solace found herself working late at the library. Rhees had left to attend the monthly meeting of all the guilds, including the Library Guild. Halys's fiancé had an unexpected leave from the army, and Lizbet had given Halys the week off to visit her parents. So when a special request arrived at the library from the king's secretary, Lizbet asked Solace to stay late cataloging a set of forty books, a gift to the king from one of the provincial governors. The king's secretary planned to visit the library first thing in the morning to inspect the collection. Lizbet explained she had to join Rhees at the guild meeting and was already running late.

Solace didn't mind and she wasn't entirely alone either. The library guards were still on duty, and she got down to work, finishing the cataloging late in the evening. She said good-bye to the guards, locked up the library's main doors using Lizbet's key, and began walking home. The streets were largely deserted, the shops and markets closed hours earlier.

As she rounded a corner, she thought she heard footsteps falling in behind her and turned around, but no one was there. She picked up her pace and walked another block. She heard footsteps again, and whipped her head around. She thought she saw a shadow lean against one of the buildings, but she couldn't be sure. Solace decided to jog the rest of the way home, her heart beating in rhythm with her feet, and she heard the footsteps quicken behind her. She broke into a run, and so did whoever was following her.

Panicking, Solace ran down a darkened side alley, only to realize it was a dead-end. She turned around to run back out, but an enormous man, the lower part of his face covered with a scarf, grabbed her, and threw her roughly against the stone wall of a building. Clapping a hand over her mouth, he pressed his body against hers and then grabbed the top button of her cloak, which he unbuttoned. She tried biting his hand, but he clamped down harder on her mouth and covered her nose, so she struggled to breathe. He ripped open her cloak and tore her blouse, her buttons falling to the ground like discarded pearls. She tried kicking him, and he brought both of his hands to her throat and squeezed. Solace gagged, tears springing to her eyes. She managed to free one of her legs and stomped down hard on his foot with the heel of her boot.

The man howled, breaking his grip on her neck. He smacked her across her mouth, causing her to bite the inside of her lip, and he raked his nails down her neck and chest. Throwing her down to the ground, he kicked Solace in the stomach and ran out of the alley.

Solace curled up on the ground, trying to catch her breath. She listened anxiously for returning footsteps, but the man was gone. Solace pushed herself off the pavement and leaned against the wall for support. She stood up shakily, terrified the man might reappear. Moving cautiously down the alley toward the street, she paused to pull her hood up over her head and grip the top of her cloak so it wouldn't flap open, and then she ran the rest of the way home, tears streaming down her face.

Solace fumbled with the key but managed to open the front door and dash inside, slamming it behind her. She slid down onto the floor, safe at last, sobbing tears of relief. She heard footsteps again, and gave an involuntary shudder, but it was Lizbet, who cried out when she saw Solace on the floor.

Lizbet didn't ask what happened but gently helped her up off the floor. The older woman wrapped an arm around Solace's waist and spoke in dulcet tones, guiding her out of the foyer. There was a commotion at the front door, someone pounding on it and then turning the doorknob, and Solace screamed out, realizing she'd forgotten to lock it.

Rhees stormed into the sitting room, and Solace realized he must have been searching for her. When he saw her leaning on Lizbet, he stopped in his tracks. The expression on Rhees's face told Solace how awful she must look. The blood from her mouth had dripped down her neck and chest, which had angry red welts from the man's nails scoring her skin. Her cloak and blouse sagged open, revealing the tops of her breasts, which she quickly tried to cover with her hands.

Rhees roared, "Who did this to you? Why were you walking home alone at this hour? Tell me who did this, and I'll run the man through with my sword, I'll..."

Solace started sobbing harder, and Lizbet grabbed a throw from one of the chairs and wrapped her in it. "There, there, now, you're safe," said Lizbet. She helped Solace into the kitchen and started heating water to cleanse Solace's injuries.

Rhees followed them into the kitchen, pacing around the table and yelling at Lizbet for asking Solace to work late, and at Solace for not having one of the library guards escort her home. Lizbet finally said, "That's enough Rhees. All you're doing is upsetting her. Now leave us for an hour, while I clean her wounds. You can join us for tea if you promise not to yell anymore."

Rhees started to object, but Lizbet stared him down. He closed his mouth and nodded, then walked over to where Solace sat huddled in the throw and brushed the top of her head lightly with his fingers. After he'd closed and locked the front door, Lizbet pulled off the throw and removed Solace's cloak to reveal her bloodstained blouse beneath. Lizbet spoke quietly to Solace, and later she couldn't recall a thing Lizbet had said, only that she'd felt soothed by her.

After Lizbet washed Solace's face, neck, and chest, she helped her up the stairs. Still shaking from her attack, Solace changed into a pale blue satin nightgown and matching robe, which she belted firmly around her waist. Lizbet rolled up the torn blouse because it was beyond repair, and she told Solace she'd find new buttons for her cloak tomorrow. Solace nodded, numb and exhausted. Lizbet took her by the hand, guided her back downstairs to the kitchen, and made tea for the three of them, because by then Rhees had let himself into the house.

Rhees didn't ask Solace any more questions and he didn't yell. He sat across from her, his dark brows knit together and his brown-black eyes moist, almost as if he'd been chopping onions, which made no sense to her, so she didn't say anything. Instead Solace sipped her tea while Rhees asked Lizbet about her injuries. They discussed her as if she weren't right there, which didn't bother her. In fact, the sound of their voices, speaking barely above a whisper, reminded her that she wasn't alone.

After a while, Rhees stood up to leave. "Stay home tomorrow, both of you. Solace needs her rest, and I don't want to leave her here alone after her ordeal. I'll get to the library early and will be there to greet the king's secretary."

Lizbet nodded and followed him out to the foyer, and they spoke in hushed whispers for several more minutes. Solace yawned and climbed the stairs slowly to the bedroom, where she curled up in her bed and tried to forget the feel of the man's hands on her body.

Solace stayed in bed until nearly noon. She heard Lizbet climb the stairs several times to check on her, but Solace felt weak as a newborn lamb. When she heard Lizbet start up the stairs again, she slid her legs out of the covers and put her feet on the floor. She tossed her robe around her shoulders and stood up unsteadily.

"I don't know what's wrong with me. I'm moving like an old woman."

Lizbet put an arm around her shoulders. "When Rhees said you'd been through an ordeal, he was right. Some of your injuries are visible and some aren't, but they hurt just the same. I've fixed you bone meal broth, which will help with your healing."

Solace held onto Lizbet and descended the stairs slowly, each step jarring her insides. Then she remembered the kick to her stomach.

"He tried to choke me, and then he kicked me before he ran away," Solace said as she sat down.

"Where did he kick you?"

Solace touched her abdomen and winced, "Here."

"He did that to knock the air out of you so you couldn't scream as he escaped." Lizbet paused. "Did he hurt you elsewhere?"

Solace shook her head and pointed to the red welts on her neck and chest. "Other than these, no. He came upon me quickly and left just as quickly. Maybe he heard something that startled him."

"We have to be thankful for whatever it was that startled him away." Lizbet placed a large bowl of broth in front of Solace and waited until she'd finished before asking, "When did you know you were being followed?"

"I heard footsteps behind me almost immediately." Solace described how she'd kept turning around, finally realizing someone was following her, and that's when she'd panicked and run into the alley. Tears sprang to her eyes when she described how the man had attacked her. Lizbet listened without saying a word, and then patted Solace's hand.

"You're safe now, and you'll not be walking around alone again, or Rhees will have both our heads. That man went berserk when we returned from the guild meeting, and you weren't home yet."

Solace sipped her tea. "He's a bit of a worrier, isn't he?"

"Where you're concerned, aye."

He's not worried about me, but about my skills as a water diviner. He can't afford to lose the only water diviner in Toresz. She couldn't exactly say that to Lizbet, so she took another sip of tea.

Lizbet suggested Solace bring her tea into the sitting room and stretch out on the sofa. Lizbet brought down the collection of Toreszan stories Rhees had given Solace during their stay in Xenyss, and she spent a lazy afternoon, reading and sipping tea. Lizbet drew a bath for Solace and checked her injuries, including the nasty bruise that had spread across her abdomen.

Solace knew Rhees planned to join them for dinner and decided she felt well enough to slip into a tunic, leggings, and slippers. She'd returned to her spot on the sofa and was absorbed in her book when Rhees showed up at the front door. Lizbet let him in and returned to the kitchen to finish preparing meat pie with root vegetables. Rhees sat in one of the chairs near Solace and glared at the red welts showing above her neckline, as if they offended him somehow.

When Lizbet called out that dinner was ready, Rhees hovered until Solace rose from the sofa and walked into the kitchen. He trailed behind, pulled out her chair, and sat down across from her.

Solace asked him about the visit from the king's secretary. Rhees finished his helping of meat pie before answering. "He was quite pleased with the collection and how quickly you cataloged it. He even asked to thank you personally, but I explained you were unwell and resting at home today."

"Which reminds me," Rhees added after helping himself to more meat pie. "I received a note from Neuss as I was leaving the library."

"What did it say?" Solace asked.

"I haven't read it yet."

Lizbet exhaled loudly. "What if it's a summons? Or an invitation? Why wouldn't you read a note from the king immediately?"

"I was in a hurry and tucked it in my pocket." Lizbet frowned at him. "Fine. I'll go get it."

Rhees left the kitchen to retrieve the note from his cloak, which was hanging in the foyer, and returned to the table. He placed it next to his plate and said, "Neuss can wait until after I've finished my dinner." He ate slowly, occasionally glancing over at Solace's neck and then looking back down at his plate. When he finished, he wiped his mouth on a cloth napkin, picked up the note, and broke the seal.

Rhees's expression darkened as he skimmed the note, which he crumpled into a tight ball. Slamming his fist on the table, he shouted, "That murderous, conniving scoundrel!" Rhees jumped up from his chair, knocking it over, and ran a hand through his dark, wavy hair. "I won't let him get away with this!"

Solace's heart beat faster. There was something in the way Rhees refused to meet her eyes that scared her.

Lizbet put down her cup and asked, "Rhees, what's wrong?"

Rhees didn't answer right away. He picked up his chair and gripped it tightly, holding it in front of him like a shield. "Neuss has reprimanded me for inadequately protecting my fiancé from harm. Somehow, he's heard about the attack on Lace, and he's decided to place her under *his* protection."

"Good heavens!" Lizbet gasped.

"But what does that mean?" asked Solace. Even Lizbet wouldn't meet her eyes now, and a cold wave of fear washed over Solace.

Rhees said through gritted teeth, "It means the king has claimed you for himself."

CHAPTER 15

Solace brought her hand to her mouth. She wanted to retch but forced herself to swallow the bile rising in her throat. "I won't. I can't. I'd rather die first."

Rhees's eyes flashed darkly. "You won't have to marry him. If it comes to that, I'll kill him myself."

"Then his guards will kill you. That's a terrible idea." Solace twisted her napkin in her lap, feeling completing unmoored.

"I'll go see Tomyss in the morning. He knows every law and by-law and proclamation in the kingdom. And he knows Neuss. Tomyss might be able to think of something," said Rhees.

"Let me come with you. Please don't leave me behind in the city."

Rhees hesitated and then shook his head. "I can't take you with me without bringing all the king's guards down on our heads. You're under his protection now, not mine."

"It can happen that quickly?" asked Solace, her voice raising a decibel. *What will become of me? How can I possibly escape from the king himself?*

Rhees dropped his gaze to the floor and spat out his words. "He's the king. Of course it can happen that quickly."

"How much time before...?" Solace choked out the question, but Rhees knew what she was asking.

"Two days. But I promise I won't let him take you away from—"

"Two days? What can we possibly do in two days?" Solace dropped her face in her hands.

Lizbet got up and put her arms around Solace. "Don't give up. Tomyss and Rhees are smarter than Neuss. They'll think of something."

Solace raised her head, which had begun to throb. She rubbed her temples. "But what should I do in the meantime?"

Rhees pulled out his chair and sat down heavily. "Do you think you can go to the library tomorrow with Lizbet?"

Lizbet looked shocked. "Why are you sending this poor girl back to work?"

Rhees set his mouth in a firm line. "Because I want all the king's spies to see her back at the library, looking as if nothing's wrong. Although she'll have to put a scarf around her neck to hide what that brute did to her." He reached across the table and gripped Solace's hand. "I'm convinced Neuss was behind the attack on you. There were too many coincidences."

"He would stoop that low?" Solace whispered.

"He murdered his own brother and nephew and niece. What do you think?"

Solace dressed in a simple gray knit dress and Lizbet artfully arranged a burgundy scarf around her neck. They walked a bit more slowly than usual, as Solace felt even more bruised and sore than she had the day before. When they arrived at the library, Lizbet brought Solace into her office. Solace sat down in one of the chairs and Lizbet sat in the other.

"I'm going to find some light work for you today. I don't

want you carrying stacks of books or stretching to reach the higher shelves."

Solace nodded. Lizbet squinted at her. "How are you feeling about what we learned last night?"

"I'd rather be dead than have to marry that horrible man."

Lizbet's brow furrowed. "No matter what, we have to find a way out of this. None of the king's wives live longer than a year or two."

"What happened to them?"

"Most of them died in bed, likely from poison. One wound up hanging herself, and another was tried for treason and beheaded."

"What about the children?" Solace swallowed hard to keep her breakfast down.

"That's the worst part. There aren't any, although several of the women who died were with child. It seems the king doesn't want any heirs."

Solace shivered. "No wonder Rhees wants to accelerate his plans."

Lizbet looked at her curiously. "Rhees is cooking up another plan?"

"What do you mean, another plan?" asked Solace.

"That young man has been planning a rebellion for the past three years, at least. I can't believe he hasn't been found out before now." Lizbet shook her head.

Solace stood up and walked in circles around the small office. "Maybe he has."

"What are you saying?"

"Maybe the king is toying with him—with us. If he believes Rhees is planning a rebellion, then he may think I'm involved somehow. This could be a test."

Lizbet waved at Solace. "Please sit down; you're making me dizzy. I need to think." Solace sat down and waited, trying hard not to fidget.

At last Lizbet said, "You could be right. This has all the earmarks of one of the king's twisted plots, especially because Rhees is obviously smitten with you."

Solace snorted. "Smitten with me? I don't think so."

"I've been around long enough to recognize all the signs when I see them. I'm telling you he's smitten. Whatever part you may be playing in his plans for rebellion—and I don't want to know; it's safer that way for all of us—Rhees will do anything to keep you safe. And Neuss knows it too."

Solace shook her head, refusing to believe it. "Look, Rhees is very good at playacting, and that's all he's doing. He's pretending that he cares for me."

"Why would he do that?"

"You said you didn't want to hear about his latest plan."

Lizbet put up her hand, palm outward. "True enough. But there's pretending, and there's the real thing. Rhees might even be telling himself that he's pretending, but he's fallen for you, and that crafty old Neuss knows it."

"What should we do?" Solace's head was spinning as she tried to ferret out the truth. She didn't for a moment believe Rhees was smitten, but he *was* a good actor. If Lizbet thought so, it stood to reason so did the king.

"I'm going to get a message to Tomyss and Rhees and warn them this could be a trap."

Solace kept losing her place and had to re-catalog a set of history books. As she rubbed her back, which had been bothering her since the attack, she noticed a man who looked vaguely familiar walk into the office with Lizbet and walk out with a note he tucked away in his coat. Jenleah's brother-in-law, the actor, bowed to her, a smile on his lips, and was off.

~

Rhees returned after dinner and called at the house for Solace. She slipped into her cloak, with the new buttons sewn on by Lizbet, and went outside to join him. He said quietly, "I'm being watched. Let's go for a walk and talk about the weather, the library, anything but the king. When we get back, we'll slip inside my house so we can talk without being overheard."

Solace played along, chatting about how much she enjoyed her job at the library. She told Rhees she'd started cataloging the ancient historical texts. Whenever her work was caught up, Lizbet told her she could read one of the books. Right now she was working her way through *Ancient Urhl*, which was mostly about wars.

Rhees and Solace walked several blocks in one direction and then returned to their lane of row houses after twenty minutes or so. They casually walked past her door and opened the next door, entering Rhees's unlit foyer. She noticed Rhees's row home was a complete mirror image of hers, with the sitting room off to the left instead of the right.

"Did you get Lizbet's note?" Solace whispered, not trusting herself to speak out loud. Rhees removed her cloak and hung both of theirs on hooks nailed on the paneled walls of the entranceway.

"Aye, and Tomyss agrees with her. He thinks the king is onto us, or at least onto me, and this is some sort of test."

"But how do we pass this test?"

Rhees laughed bitterly. "We can't pass this test. We have to outfox him, instead."

"But how?"

"Tomyss says there's only one way to outfox him, and that's to beat him to the punch."

A small line creased Solace's brow. "What's that supposed to mean?"

"I need to marry you before the king does."

Solace backed away from Rhees and walked stiffly into his

darkened sitting room, which she noticed was an upgrade over hers. At least his sofa didn't sag. Solace sat down. "This complicated, crazy plan of yours has gotten way out of hand. I agreed to help you find water sources, not get married for real, not to you and certainly not to your mad king."

"He's not my mad king. My mad uncle, perhaps, but not my king."

Solace looked up at Rhees, who paced in front of the sofa, his face in shadows. "Do you think Neuss has figured it out?"

"Figured what out?"

"That you're his nephew?"

Rhees shook his head. "I'd be dead, my throat slit in my sleep, if he ever figures that out."

Solace shuddered. "Let's not even think about that. Tell me exactly what Tomyss said."

Rhees explained that according to the law, their engagement took legal precedence, even over the king, because the king and Solace were not formally betrothed, at least not yet. But if the king succeeded in forcing her into marriage, then the issue would be moot. Even if Rhees had a prior claim, it wouldn't matter. The only way to prevent the king from marrying Solace was for Rhees to marry her first.

Solace rubbed her eyes and yawned. She'd had too many late nights and far too much drama, all of which was Rhees's fault. She set her jaw and said, "I need some sleep. I can't think straight anymore." The idea of marrying Rhees in order to avoid marrying Neuss was out of the question; after all, if she didn't marry Arik, whom she actually liked, why on earth would she marry Rhees? They'd have to come up with another plan, but only after she'd had a good night's sleep.

"But there's not a minute to spare! Don't you realize Neuss could force you to move into the palace tomorrow, since he's placed you under his protection, and then what?"

Frustrated by the entire conversation, Solace threw up her

hands. "You're not making sense. Even if I agreed, which I'm not, how am I supposed to marry you tonight?"

Tomyss's voice said in the darkness. "I'm a monk, my dear. I can perform the ceremony."

Solace jumped off the sofa and then winced, bringing a hand to her bruised abdomen. "Tomyss, is that you?"

Tomyss walked out of the kitchen and stepped near the window, so Solace could make out his features by the soft glow of the moon.

She reached her hands out and Tomyss grasped them. "Is marrying Rhees really the only way?" She closed her eyes for a moment, willing him to give her another option, anything but this.

"It's the only way we can keep you safe from Neuss," said Tomyss gently.

"And we have to do this tonight?" she asked, a sinking feeling settling in her chest.

He nodded. "I intend to present the marriage contract to Neuss at the palace in the morning."

"But won't that put you in danger?"

Tomyss smiled. "I've been living for a long time on the Tor Mountain, praying for a chance to serve my king. My one true king, Rhees Demore Orillya."

"You've served me all my life, Tomyss." Rhees's voice shook with emotion.

"I've served from the safety of the monastery. It's time that I step out of the shadow of the mountain."

"What will happen after you present the contract? Please tell me the truth," said Solace.

Tomyss sighed. "Neuss will probably toss me in his dungeon while he mulls over what to do with me. But the full force of his anger will be aimed at the two of you. You'll need to flee —tonight."

"The horses are ready and waiting," Rhees added.

"But I'm not packed. And I haven't said good-bye to Lizbet."

"You can say good-bye to me on your way out of town," Lizbet said as she walked out of the kitchen.

Solace folded her arms and frowned at Rhees. "Who else is standing in your kitchen? I think I've had enough surprises for one day."

Evryst and another monk, whom Tomyss introduced as Alyn, stepped sheepishly into the sitting room. Unlike baldheaded Evryst, Alyn had a full head of black hair, which he pulled back into a tidy braid that trailed down his back. Alyn's beard was as long and dark as Evryst's.

Tomyss explained, "Evryst, Alyn, Rhees, and I rode into Urhl together, for several reasons. First, I need two witnesses to sign the marriage contract and make it binding. Evryst and Alyn volunteered. Second, we rode as three monks from Tor accompanying a man wearing a duster. When you ride out of here tonight, you will ride as three monks: Evryst, Rhees, and you. Of course you will have new papers identifying you as monks with the Tor order, and we've brought robes for you to wear."

Solace rubbed her head wearily as Rhees picked up the thread. "But before we ride out of here, we want to trick the men watching this house into thinking that I've escorted you back to your row house, where we plan to spend some quality time together, say until an hour or so before dawn. Alyn will be wearing my hat and duster when he walks next door."

"And I'll be dressed as you, wearing your cloak," added Lizbet.

"Just before dawn, Alyn will leave your house dressed once again as Rhees," said Tomyss. "And he'll ride through the main gate straight back to the monastery. He'll likely be questioned at the watchtower, but since he's committed no crime, they won't hold him for long. Finally, I'll remain here inside the house, hidden until mid-morning, when I'll go to the palace and present the marriage contract to the king."

Solace pursed her lips, assessing their plan for any flaws. She didn't like it one bit, but she had to admit they might be able to escape from Urhl without raising any alarms. On the other hand, she didn't think Neuss would give up that easily. He wasn't the type. "It sounds as if you've thought of everything to get us through tonight and out of Neuss's grasp, for now anyway. But there's something I need to understand about what happens later, about what happens to me."

She turned to Rhees. "Let's assume we survive all of this, which I think is a big assumption. After I've helped you find the water that your people need, what then? How can I go home, if I'm legally married to you?"

Rhees walked over to the window and peered outside while Tomyss answered her question. "If the marriage is not consummated, that is, if you and Rhees sleep apart from each other, then when this is all over, you'll be granted an annulment."

Solace felt herself turn beet-red. She was mortified she'd asked that question in front of three monks and grateful no one had bothered to light any candles in the sitting room.

"In other words," Rhees grumbled as he turned away from the window. "You'll be able to go home and marry your Arik."

Solace ignored the remark about Arik and nodded. "Alright."

Tomyss asked everyone to come into the kitchen, where he lit several candles and laid out two identical marriage contracts for them to sign. First Rhees and Solace signed the contracts, followed by Tomyss as the officiator, and Evryst and Alyn as the witnesses. Tomyss insisted that Solace sign using both her names: Solace Blu, also known as Lace Blusari. When she asked why they needed two copies of the contract, he explained Alyn would carry one of the marriage contracts back to the monastery for safekeeping, in case Neuss destroyed the other one.

Evryst and Alyn pushed aside the kitchen table and chairs to clear a space, and Tomyss asked Rhees and Solace to stand before him. Evryst held one of the candles so Tomyss could read the marriage ceremony from the book he'd carried from Tor. Lizbet stood on Solace's left side, and Alyn stood on Rhees's right side.

The ceremony went quickly, with each of them responding a number of times to Tomyss's questions by saying, "Aye, I will" or "Aye, I do."

When Tomyss reached the part of the ceremony where the bride and groom present rings to each other, he hesitated, preparing to skip the ring-gifting entirely, but Rhees pulled two silver bands out of his jacket. Tomyss arched an eyebrow but plunged ahead, and Rhees and Solace gifted the rings to each other. Solace wondered whether Rhees had purchased or borrowed the rings and was surprised to find the silver band fit the middle finger on her right hand—the ring placement indicating she was a married woman—perfectly, as if made for her.

Tomyss reached the end of the ceremony and closed the book. "By the authority vested in me as a brother of the Tor order, I now pronounce you husband and wife. At this point in the ceremony, it's usually customary to kiss the bride, but you could dispense with that, I suppose."

Solace opened her mouth to say that was fine with her, but Rhees leaned over and kissed her quickly on the lips. She'd never been kissed on the mouth before. Arik used to kiss her on the cheek, but the feel of Rhees's lips on hers made her feel lightheaded, which she attributed to hunger. She'd eaten very little dinner because every time she thought of being forced to marry Neuss, her stomach turned to lead.

Tomyss cleared his throat. "The two of you need to get

ready to leave with Evryst soon." Turning to Lizbet he said, "Can you help Lace change into the monk's habit? Use Rhees's bedroom upstairs while he changes down here."

Solace didn't know when—or whether—she would see Tomyss again. She'd grown very fond of him, despite the fact he'd helped Rhees hatch the plot that led to her kidnapping. She recognized sheer desperation had driven his actions then and now. Solace threw her arms around the elderly monk and gave him a teary good-bye before she left the room.

She followed Lizbet, who carried a candle, up the stairs. Someone had already laid out the clothes Solace needed to wear. Solace slipped on a pair of loose beige-colored pants with a drawstring belt, a long baggy tunic, and a monk's navy robe. Lizbet twisted Solace's hair into a topknot and then pulled up the pointed hood of the robe. Stepping back to examine Solace's transformation, she said, "Not bad, but we need to make you look more convincing. Do you trust me?"

"Completely."

Lizbet pulled a small jar from her left pocket and something that looked like a piece of fur from her right pocket. When she held the piece of fur up to the candlelight, Solace saw it was a fake moustache.

"Really?"

"Let's try it." Lizbet opened the jar, dipped a rag into the gooey substance inside, and applied it to the back of the mustache. She pushed the mustache onto Solace's upper lip. Nodding her approval, she said, "Much better. Now you look like one of the brothers."

"It itches."

"Look at it this way. So long as you're wearing that mustache, Rhees won't be kissing you."

Solace knew Lizbet was trying to make her feel better, but she was in no mood to be teased. "The last thing I wanted tonight was to be a married woman and on the run from Neuss. None of this was part of my plan."

Lizbet sighed and gave Solace a hug before picking up the candle and leading her back downstairs. "I know, lass, but there's nothing to be done for it now but see this thing through."

Rhees looked up as she came down. "Lace...ah, Brother Stihl, come, it's time for us to leave."

Could my life get any stranger? I'm dressed as a monk, married to my kidnapper, and on the run from the killing king of Toresz.

CHAPTER 16

Their first challenge was figuring out how Solace would mount Jenx wearing a monk's robe and nursing a badly bruised abdomen. Although Rhees gently lifted her onto Jenx's back in the privacy of their stable, they didn't want anyone wondering why one of the monks needed help mounting a horse. They decided to try the little-used western gate, where the guards had a reputation for laziness. Maybe they wouldn't have to dismount at all.

Another concern was Solace's voice. If anyone asked her even a simple question, she'd give herself away as a girl. Evryst suggested they explain to the guards that she'd taken a vow of silence.

They exited the mews in single file, first Evryst, then Solace, and finally Rhees, with Caya and Tomyss's horse bringing up the rear. Tomyss had asked that his beloved mare be delivered safely back to the monastery, as he wouldn't be needing his horse anymore.

Evryst carried the papers for all three of them, and they decided he'd handle any negotiations with the guards. And by negotiations, Solace knew they meant bribes. It was close to midnight, and the clip-clop of their horses' hooves echoed in the cobblestone streets.

Solace's heart thundered in her chest as they approached the western gate. A single guard lumbered out of the guard station, a low, squat building to the right of the gate. Evryst reined in his horse and dismounted. Bowing, Evryst handed the guard the papers for his party. The guard grunted and took the papers into the station for a closer examination, and he beckoned for Evryst to follow him. They were in the station for longer than necessary, and Jenx, sensing Solace's anxiety, began pawing the cobblestones and snorting. Solace leaned over to pat his neck, and Rhees came up beside her on Zirott.

"Remember what I said when you were going to meet Neuss the first time?"

Solace shook her head.

"Just breathe. Evryst is a cagey one, despite his robes and calling."

"I'll breathe easier once we're through that gate."

The door to the guard station opened, and Evryst emerged with the same guard, who now carried a torch in his right hand. As Evryst approached them, he winked. The guard held his torch high and examined their faces, lingering longer on Solace. She wanted to kick Jenx in the flank and take off at a gallop, but she took a deep breath and thought about Pawl, her least-obedient sheep, and how often she had to chase him down. She almost smiled at the memory, but caught herself in time.

Nodding, the guard waved them through the gate. Evryst mounted, and they followed him at a quick trot. Solace exhaled when they passed under the arched gate and they could break into a gallop. Her mustache blew off her upper lip, and she gratefully rubbed the remaining adhesive off with one hand.

When they approached the Tor Mountain an hour later, Rhees called a halt and dismounted. He approached Caya, running his hand along her back, and leaned in to whisper in her ear. Caya's ears flicked backward and then stood straight up. Rhees patted her neck, and then stepping back, nodded at Evryst. The monk waved and peeled away, with Caya and Tomyss's mare following in his wake.

"What did you tell her?" Solace asked as Rhees swung one long leg over Zirott's back.

"That what she carried had to be safely delivered to the monastery, so she had to follow the monk."

"What was she carrying?"

"Extra clothes and supplies, a few of my favorite books. My most important papers are already at the monastery."

"So in other words, you're just as sentimental about Caya as Tomyss is about his mare."

Rhees smiled. "Guilty as charged. I can't see the point of risking a horse if it's not necessary. Besides, we're traveling very light. I packed basic camp supplies, our water skins, and some food." What Rhees didn't say, but Solace understood, was that they didn't need to pack for an extended trip, because their freedom wouldn't last that long.

Rhees and Solace rode side by side, skirting the Tor and pointing their horses southwest, toward the hills near Peka's farm. As dawn approached, they found a narrow pass where they set up their tent. Solace slid off Jenx's back and sagged against him. Her abdomen and back ached, and the scratches along her neck and chest were itching beneath the baggy tunic.

Rhees glanced over, took her by the hand, and led her away from the horses. "Stay here and rest. I'll take care of the horses and set up our tent."

Solace didn't argue, but pulled her hood over her head and curled up on the ground. She woke up hours later to the smell of coffee somewhere nearby. *Dad must be up before me, boiling his coffee. I can't believe I overslept!*

Solace opened her eyes and cried out in disappointment. She'd had the loveliest dream of sleeping in her own bed in her tiny bedroom in her beloved Yeloshan cottage. The dream had felt so real she thought perhaps she was dreaming now, that she really wasn't lying inside a tent, the wind whistling all around her, shivering in a bedroll on the ground.

Then she remembered all of it, the brutish attack, her hasty marriage, the escape from Urhl, everything up until the moment she closed her eyes. Rhees must have carried her inside the tent and tucked her into the bedroll.

Rhees ran into the tent, stooping down to check on her. "I heard you call out. What's wrong?"

Solace sat up slowly and grimaced, every muscle revolting. "Nothing. I dreamt I was home and then woke up, startled."

Rhees's brown-black eyes softened. "Sometimes I dream that I'm still a boy, and my mother is calling me into the house for dinner. And then I wake up, realize she's gone, and I miss her more than ever."

Solace looked at Rhees, so tall he had to squat on his knees to fit inside the tent, and realized there was still a boy somewhere inside, a boy who'd lost himself the day his mother and father were murdered. A boy who'd become an orphan and a king on the same day, an exile in his own country.

"Did I smell coffee?"

Rhees nodded. "Stay put, I'll bring it to you." He returned a few minutes later with two mugs, and handing her one, he sat down cross-legged on his bedroll, balancing a mug on his knee.

Solace inhaled the rich coffee scent and took a sip. It was so hot it nearly burned her tongue, but that was how she and her father used to drink it back home. Arik preferred to let his coffee cool to room temperature, and he'd shake his head at them, wondering how they could swallow anything so hot.

Rhees picked up his mug and glanced at her over the rim. "I've completely upended your life, haven't I?"

"Pretty much." Solace answered honestly. "And when, or if, I get back home, I don't know what I'll find. I worry all the time about my father, and—"

"And your future husband, yes, I'm sure you're wondering whether Arik will still want to marry you." His eyes narrowed whenever he mentioned Arik.

"Not at all." She was tired of him bringing up Arik's name and making certain assumptions he knew nothing about. "Even though Arik wanted to marry *me*, I didn't want to marry *him*. I wouldn't have made him a good wife."

"Is that so?" Rhees seemed relieved, but the fact she didn't want to marry Arik didn't make her less homesick, and she told him that. Rhees asked, "Other than your father and your dog, what do you miss most about your old life?"

"The hills."

"Which we have here."

"My sheep."

"We have sheep all over Toresz."

"My mother's books."

Rhees conceded. "We don't have those."

"Why are you asking? You *are* going to take me home again, aren't you?"

Rhees uncrossed his legs and stretched them out across his bedroll. "I promised that I would, when our work is finished, and I keep my promises. I was wondering if I could do anything in the meantime to help you feel better."

"You could tell me more about what you're planning, instead of springing it on me at the last minute. That would be a good place to start."

Rhees scratched his dark beard and didn't answer right away. Nodding, he said, "You're right. You're on the run from Neuss and in just as much danger as the rest of us. You should be part of the planning."

Rhees reached out his hand and helped her up. They went outside and sat near the embers where Rhees had heated the coffee. "We need to eat and then ride out toward the next range of hills." Rhees handed her some jerky and bread, and explained there were small bands of rebels like Kryss's, training in caves and hills and valleys throughout the countryside. Peka, for example, led a small group of rebels who trained in the valley near her farm. "It's time we came out in the open."

"How?"

"We're going to visit each location where we have friends, and tell them you're here to help us find water. And you're going to begin divining for water, everywhere we go. "

"No more pretending we're engaged?" Solace asked, forgetting for a moment they were no longer engaged.

"No need. You're my wife, Lace Demore, the beautiful water diviner from Yelosha, and our saving grace."

Solace drew her brows together and thought about what he was saying. "Publicly divining for water is like spitting in Neuss's eye."

"True enough." Rhees added, "I'm telling you what I'm planning rather than springing it on you later. I hope you can appreciate my openness here."

Solace sighed. "I'll be part of the rebellion whether I want to be or not."

"I'm afraid so. I can't think of any other way at this point, now that we're outlaws."

Solace thought of her father and Gordo, and the other soldiers she'd known, and their war stories, some of victory and glory, others of pure misery and defeat. Rebellions were a risky business. Then she thought of Maysel and Wilhm, Peka and her sons, and so many others. They deserved something more than what they had under Neuss. They deserved to be able to drink freely from the abundant water that ran beneath the hills, to live and work and raise their families without fear.

Solace brushed the crumbs from her monk's robe and stood up. "Let's go start your rebellion."

CHAPTER 17

They rode past Peka's farm and through a slender valley tucked between rock-strewn hills. Rhees turned Zirott to the right and led them up a stony path that twisted around one of the hills. As the path narrowed, Solace and Rhees had to guide the horses up the hill in single file. Zirott's back legs slipped on the stones, but he quickly regained his footing. Solace blew out a puff of air when they'd rounded the hill and the path widened.

Although the hill's peak was still several hundred yards above them, they stepped off the path onto a swath of level ground that formed a plateau in the hillside. A group of men and women were training, some using swords and others practicing their archery. Rhees called out and Behn, Peka's eldest son, smiled and flagged down his mother, who was coaching the archers. Peka jogged over to greet them, a startled look on her face. Solace couldn't tell whether their visit or their monk's attire surprised Peka the most.

"Welcome to our training ground! We've made progress since your visit last summer, Rhees. And I see you've brought your lovely fiancé with you." Peka tucked a loose strand of gray-streaked black hair behind her ear and greeted them both with a kiss to the cheek.

"Lace is no longer my fiancé." Peka raised her eyebrows so Rhees hastened to add, "We were married these two days past."

Peka broke into a wide grin. "Congratulations to you both. So what are you doing here? And why the monk's robes? Shouldn't you be off somewhere, enjoying yourselves in private?"

Solace lowered her eyes, somewhat embarrassed by Peka's frankness. Rhees said, "Truth be told, we're on the run from Neuss." Rhees explained Neuss's interest in Solace, the attack on her, and Tomyss's recommendation they marry immediately and leave town, disguised as monks.

"So we're not staying long, because we're sure Neuss's men will be tracking us. But there's more, the real reason for our visit." Rhees paused and leaned in to whisper, "Our Lace here is a water diviner. We aim to divine several well locations here before we move on."

Peka's large gray eyes grew misty. "You'd take that risk for us?" she asked Solace.

Solace squared her shoulders and nodded. "I can't pretend I don't have this gift, and I can't bear not to use it to help all of you. It's...it's something I *want* to do for you and these other families." Solace realized she meant every word. Despite the fact she'd been brought to Toresz against her will, she couldn't ignore the suffering all around her. She wanted to divine for water in the Toreszan hills and find as many new water sources as possible, before Neuss's trackers caught up with her and Rhees. She refused to think about what came next.

Rhees said, "We need two of your most trustworthy people to travel with us as we search for water sources in this valley and in the hills to the south. We need them to serve as lookouts and to help us mark the locations with dye."

"Now?" asked Peka. "But you've just been married! Can't

you take a short holiday first?" She glanced with motherly concern at Solace. "Lace here looks as if she could do with a bit of rest, poor lamb."

Solace swallowed down a lump in her throat at Peka's sympathy and smiled at the older woman. "Thank you, but I'm fine. Just a bit weary from the long ride." Solace's muscles ached and her abdomen was still sore and bruised, but she also knew she and Rhees had a limited window for finding fresh water sources.

"Unfortunately there's no time to lose. We have to search for the water in daylight. We'll set up camp at night, but we won't spend more than one night in any one place. We have to keep moving."

Peka nodded and then called Behn and Bray over to her. "Take my sons with you." She sent Bray back to their farm to retrieve supplies for their trip. When he returned with the dye, as well as camping supplies for him and his brother, Peka hugged her sons, and then said the hill blessing over everyone.

"May you traverse these hills in safety, may you find rest when you are weary, and may your labors be honored and your water be plenty." Peka sniffed, swiped at her eyes quickly, and went back to yelling at her archers.

Behn and Bray led them and their horses across the training area, to where the plateau met the other side of the hill, and they began the descent to the valley below. Solace was relieved the path was broader and less steep; she didn't have to worry about Jenx or the other horses losing their footing.

Once they reached level ground, Solace pulled in front and rode ahead of the rest of the group, listening and looking for any water signs. After an hour of steady searching, following a pattern that only Solace could decipher, she flicked the reins and took off at a gallop on Jenx, with three obedient men trailing behind her. She pulled up Jenx near a patch of earth with the slightest discoloration, slid off his back, and tested the sandy soil, first with her fingers, and then with her tongue.

"Here!" She shouted triumphantly. "Sixty feet down is an abundant water source!" Behn and Bray clapped Rhees's back, and then they danced around Solace. She shook her head, laughing at their silliness, forgetting for a moment she and Rhees were fugitives, and what they were doing was punishable by death.

Rhees sent Bray in search of something they could use as a stake. When Bray returned a short time later with the stripped-clean bone of a desert animal, probably a wild boar or a jackal, Rhees pulled a piece of blue cloth from his pocket and secured it to one end of the bone. Bray walked to where Solace indicated and pushed the other end of the bone into the soil.

When they were finished, Behn looked at Rhees. "That little bit of cloth isn't going to last. We still need to paint location markers onto that boulder over there." He pointed to a prominent boulder that jutted from the hillside on their left, at the midway point of the range overlooking the valley.

Rhees smiled. "Agreed. But I like to think of it as our flag, our symbol for the rebellion."

Behn squinted at the flag flapping in the breeze. A golden lion's head, surrounded by a circlet of olive leaves, occupied the center of the blue cloth. Two swords crisscrossed beneath the lion's head. Behn's dark eyebrows rose in a peak. "That's King Meade's seal."

Rhees nodded. "I'm convinced he'd be a big supporter of *this* rebellion."

Bray grabbed the jar of indigo dye and a fresh rag and counted the number of paces to the boulder, where he used the same ancient symbols Kryss had used to paint a map showing the location of the water source.

"Should we continue looking for another well location or find a place to camp for the night?" asked Behn.

"Don't ask me, I'm not the diviner here." Turning to Solace, Rhees said softly, "I don't want to wear you out. You also need to rest. What do you want to do?"

Solace didn't answer right away. She walked deeper into the valley, listening for the whisper of water beneath their feet. Bending down to pick up a handful of soil, she let it sift through her fingers and fall to the ground. Rhees joined her as she rubbed her hands together to wipe off the excess sand. "We should press on," she said. "We'll find another good water source less than an hour's ride from here." Rhees lifted Solace into her saddle while the others mounted their horses, and Solace took the lead once again.

They found and marked two more water sources before they set up camp for the evening. Solace yawned as she rubbed down Jenx, who nuzzled her hair playfully. Rhees was grooming Zirott nearby and noticed Solace hiding another yawn. "Why are you pushing yourself so hard? I know you haven't recovered."

Solace paused, Jenx's brush in her hand. "We both know it's only a matter of time before Neuss tracks us down. If we're going to get caught anyway, I want to make sure it's really worth it."

"Worth what?"

"Worth going to prison for...or going to the gallows for. It's ridiculous to go to prison because we defied the king by getting married. But this—" She waved her hands to indicate the hills, so like her brown and gold Yeloshan hills, now washed in shades of copper and russet as the sun sank lower, finally dipping below the horizon. "This is about finding water for Maysel's children and all the other Toreszan children who go to bed thirsty every night."

Rhees helped her finish brushing down Jenx, and then Bray led the horses away to graze on the hillside below them. They'd set up camp out of the wind, on the lee side of a ridge that faced east, toward Urhl and Neuss. Behn and Bray waited until Rhees pitched his tent before setting up their tent, as far away as possible from Rhees and Solace. She realized they wanted to give her and Rhees—newlyweds in their eyes—a semblance of privacy. In other circumstances, Solace might have found their chivalry charming, even amusing, but not that night. If anything, she felt sadder.

The next morning they decided to alter their plans and avoid visiting any of the towns or mining settlements as they traveled south, even though they had friends who'd be anxious to help. Rhees and Behn were concerned they'd stand out and potentially raise suspicions. So they remained on the outskirts, searching for water near parched homesteads and mining communities, rejoicing quietly when Solace divined another location, waiting patiently for Bray to find a boulder or tree or cave entrance where he could sketch out the location.

On their third day, when their water skins were running low, Rhees visited an isolated farm, where he bartered three copper coins and one of his leather-bound books in exchange for four skins of water. After five days of traveling through the southern hills, they'd found eleven water sources and managed to avoid any search parties.

When their water skins ran dry again, Rhees said he would visit the mining settlement where Wilhm and Maysel lived to purchase water. Solace vetoed it and Behn agreed. "You are the one indispensable man, Rhees, and you know it. There will be no rebellion without you."

Rhees grunted, "Other than Lace, no one's indispensable, and I'll not have you risking your necks to beg for some water for us."

"There's a price on your head. And by now, every town and guard post knows it. You can't go." Solace crossed her arms and glared at Rhees, frustrated at his stubborn refusal to acknowledge the danger.

"I'll go," volunteered Bray. "I wouldn't mind a quick visit with Wilhm when he's off work." Solace knew Behn, Rhees, and Wilhm had been friends since they were boys. As Behn's younger brother, she figured Bray had formed an attachment to both Rhees and Wilhm.

"Fine," Rhees said. "But keep your head down, don't make eye contact unless someone orders you to, and don't overstay your welcome. Get in, get out."

"Got it," Bray said cheerfully, but Solace didn't think he was listening. He left mid afternoon and by the time the moon was up, Bray still hadn't returned. Behn muttered something about kid brothers, and Rhees paced in front of the cave where they'd stowed their bags and supplies. Solace got up every so often, climbed to the top of the hill where they were camping, and looked in the direction of the settlement. Even though it was dark, the moon illuminated the valley and main road.

Behn had decided to saddle up his horse when Solace climbed to the hilltop once more. "Behn, wait! I see something down below."

Rhees charged to the top, grabbed her by the waist, and pulled her out of sight from anyone below. "It's a full moon, and you're standing up there for all the world to see. I'll take a look."

Rhees crouched low, and when he reached the peak, dropped to the ground. "Two riders," he called out. "If it's Bray, he's bringing company." Rhees and Solace crept down from the overlook and hid in the tall grasses that sprouted in large clumps around the rim of the hill. Rhees's hand rested on the hilt of his sword, and Solace reached for her sling and several stones she'd tucked inside the pocket of her monk's robe. Behn brought their horses down the other side of the hill and then joined Rhees and Solace, the three of them belly down in the grass.

The two riders headed straight for their campsite and made

enough noise one of the horses—probably Jenx—neighed. "Behn, Rhees, where's everyone?" Bray's voice called out. Solace noticed his voice pitched higher than usual. He was scared. Whatever had spooked Peka's youngest son during his visit, at least he'd made it back safely.

"Show yourselves before Bray here breaks out in hives!" shouted the second man.

Rhees stood up abruptly. "Wilhm?"

"Well met, my friend."

"What took you so long?" Behn asked Bray. "Lace here has been worried sick, and I was about to saddle up and search for you." Solace knew Behn had been every bit as worried as she'd been, but he wasn't going to admit it in front of everyone.

"He's had a rough time," Wilhm said quietly. "Neuss's guards detained him for a few hours, simply because he was a stranger, and then they tried to scare him into confessing to trumped-up charges. They're getting meaner by the day." Wilhm spat on the ground.

"How did they come to release him?" asked Rhees.

"I was purchasing my water rations and saw a guard slapping someone around. When I realized it was Bray, I vouched for him, saying he was an old family friend come to visit. They'd had their fun with him at that point and let him go with a boot in his backside."

"But I did bring back fresh water," said Bray, holding up the water skins. "And Wilhm, who has some news to share."

"Aye," said Wilhm, sitting down on a low boulder. "Word from Urhl is that you're both wanted by Neuss, for acts of treason against the crown."

"What acts of treason?" asked Rhees.

"Neuss has learned that Lace is divining for water."

Rhees folded his arms across his chest. "But how? We've been careful to avoid the towns."

Wilhm shrugged. "Someone's seen Lace divining and sent

word back to Neuss. Oh, and one more thing," he added. "Apparently, Rhees has violated Neuss's rights to claim any unmarried woman in the kingdom, so Neuss plans to try you for treason *and* sedition."

Rhees snorted. "The punishment is the same in the end. He can only hang me once."

Solace's stomach twisted with fresh worry and she wondered how far they were from the Yeloshan border, and whether they could outrun the king's guards if they tried.

After sharing some bread and cheese, Wilhm stretched his long legs and slowly rose to his feet. "I'd best be going. I borrowed the undertaker's horse, and he'll be wanting it back."

Rhees clapped Wilhm on the shoulder and walked with him back to the undertaker's skinny horse. Solace sighed. Even the animals suffered under the brutish king's rule. She saw Rhees press something into Wilhm's hand. The other man resisted but Rhees pushed his hand away, saying, "For Maysel and the children." Wilhm looked away and nodded, mumbled his thanks, and mounted his horse.

After Wilhm left, Solace excused herself and crawled into her bedroll, every muscle stiff and aching. She'd never divined for five days straight before and felt drained, almost as if she'd broken off a piece of herself at every location where she found water.

Solace closed her eyes, yearning for the temporary release that came with sleep. She longed to forget she and Rhees were being hunted like outlaws, and if—when—they were caught, they'd be given a sham trial and executed. Restless, she forced herself to take deep breaths, trying to calm her mind enough to drift into an uneasy slumber. Solace must have dozed, because she woke to Rhees and Behn speaking quietly nearby.

"You mean to tell me you *kidnapped* Lace? That's just plain wrong, regardless of how much we needed a diviner," said Behn.

"Don't you think I know that?" Rhees growled. "Not a day goes by I don't regret taking her. I thought we could keep a low profile, have Lace help us find water, and then I'd take her back home."

"Then you should have kept her as far away from Neuss as possible."

Rhees exhaled loudly. "I've made a lot of mistakes, I'll grant you that. But the hardest part," Rhees's voice dropped to a whisper, and Solace missed whatever he said next.

Solace heard Behn shift and say, "I'm not surprised. In fact, I believed all along you were engaged for real. So did my mother. She even said you'd finally found a woman who could keep you on your toes."

"Peka is too smart for her own good," Rhees said with a soft chuckle.

"I'm sorry for you, for both of you. I'll do whatever I can to help."

"I'll not have you or Bray sacrifice yourselves. It's time the two of you head back to the farm."

"But we can serve as lookouts for you, visit the next town and report back what we hear."

"No, Behn. I want you to leave as soon as Bray's had a few hours of sleep. You need to get out of here before any of Neuss's men track us down. And that's an order."

Behn was silent for a minute and then said, "Alright, I'm not going to argue with you. We'll leave before the sun's up."

Solace tried to puzzle out what Rhees thought was "the hardest part." *Was it worrying the rebellion wouldn't take hold? Or that he'd not live long enough to lead the rebellion and overthrow Neuss?*

She gave up trying to get inside Rhees's head and fell back to sleep. She didn't dream of Yelosha and her father, but of Rhees, standing on a wooden platform with a hood over his head. Another man, dressed all in black and hooded as well, grasped a noose that hung loosely from a beam overhead and slipped it around Rhees's neck. The executioner stepped back several paces to a wooden railing, placed one gloved hand on a lever, and pulled hard. The part of the platform under Rhees's feet gave way. She heard a loud snap and saw Rhees briefly struggle, kicking out his legs. She reached out a hand toward him as his body went limp, swaying from the beam overhead.

Solace woke up screaming, tears streaming down her face. Rhees was next to her in an instant, his arms around her as he pulled her into his chest. She heard him say, "Shh, it's alright, you're safe."

She whispered, "But you're not, he's coming for us, but especially for you. He hates you."

Rhees pushed her hair out of her face and brushed away her tears with his thumb. "You're shaking. Are you feverish?" He felt her forehead like her father used to do and fresh tears rolled down her cheeks. After Rhees wiped away her tears again, Solace closed her eyes and rested her head in the hollow of his chest. She listened to the steady beat of his heart as she drifted to sleep. She had no more dreams, or at least, no dreams she could recall, only a sense of being held and soothed and safe.

When Solace woke up, she was surprised to see she was still nestled against Rhees's chest. She could tell by his steady breathing he was sleeping and tried not to move. In fact, she didn't want to shift herself away. She thought perhaps she liked sleeping with Rhees's arms around her. She frowned and wondered whether she was dreaming.

Rhees stirred, and she tried slipping out of his grasp, but he drew her closer. "Good morning," he said. "Feeling any better?"

"Much better." Then recalling the conversation she'd heard the previous night, she asked, "Behn and Bray?"

"Bray was too wound up to sleep for long. They packed and

left several hours ago. They said for me to tell you they'd gladly follow you anywhere you want to divine for water."

Solace smiled. "I can see why you enjoy spending time with them, and with Wilhm. Which reminds me, I saw you slip Wilhm something as he was leaving. What did you give him?"

Rhees hesitated and then tipped her face up to look at him. "Don't be angry with me, but I gave him your last silver coin. I'd been saving it for an emergency, and it occurred to me Wilhm and Maysel needed it more than we do."

"I'm glad you gave them the coin."

Rhees's brown-black eyes locked on hers, and he inclined his head. Solace leaned in, her pulse in her throat. His lips barely grazed hers when they heard a horse neighing outside and their tent collapsed on top of them. Rhees swore and felt around the ground for his sword. Solace tried wriggling free but the point of a sword pierced the tent fabric above them, jabbing Rhees's bedroll.

"Rhees Demore and Lace Blusari, you are under arrest by order of His Royal Majesty, King Neuss of Toresz!"

CHAPTER 18

R hees shielded Solace's body as another sword poked through, stabbing the ground next to her head. "Don't move, and don't resist arrest, if ye want to see another sunrise," growled a voice above them.

"Understood!" shouted Rhees. "We will cooperate."

Two king's guards lifted the tent and tossed it aside, while five others with swords drawn surrounded Solace and Rhees. The guard in charge, a stocky man with a shaved head and scraggly beard, grunted, "Stand up and keep yer hands where we can see 'em."

Rhees rolled away from Solace and sat up, grasping her hands in his and raising their hands high. As he stood, he pulled her up with him and held her hands tightly, almost as if he feared she'd do something foolish. Solace thought of her nightmare, of Rhees and the hangman, and fresh tears rolled down her cheeks. *Time has run out for King Meade's youngest son. There will be no rebellion, no water for Maysel's children, no second chances for any of us.*

Rhees noticed her tears. Furrowing his brow, he whispered, "Don't cry. I'll think of something—"

"Shut up! Hands on yer heads!" The stocky guard separated them, and two of the guards half-dragged, half-carried Solace toward Zirott and Jenx. "Saddle them horses." One of the guards dropped the saddles and bags at Solace's feet. She ran her hands down Zirott's back and then Jenx's, speaking softly. Rhees had left them untethered and no one attempted to tie them up. Neither stallion would have tolerated it.

She stole a glance at Rhees as she saddled up Jenx and noticed the guards had taken no chances. His hands were bound in front of him; chains crisscrossed his broad chest, wrapped around his neck, and then attached to the steel bands around his wrists. He managed to mount Zirott with difficulty and sat with his neck and shoulders hunched forward, but he couldn't sit up straight without choking himself. Solace couldn't bear to watch Rhees sitting with his neck bowed over his horse.

When she finished saddling Jenx, the stocky guard snapped a pair of manacles around her wrists and ordered her to mount her horse. Solace held up her manacles and said, "I can't mount him like this."

The guard slapped her across the face. "I don't want yer excuses."

Solace's cheek stung, but she didn't lower her gaze. She stared at the guard and waited. The man stared back. Finally he flicked his wrist and two guards jogged over. Pointing at Solace he said, "Get her on that horse." They came on either side of her, grabbed her under her arms, and tossed her into the saddle. Jenx pawed the ground uneasily, but Solace ran her fingers through his mane to calm him.

Guards rode in front and alongside her and Rhees, with the stocky guard called Yeln leading them. Instead of turning back toward Urhl, where Solace expected they'd be hauled in front of Neuss, Yeln pointed his horse south. She asked the guard riding next to her where they were headed.

"Shulamorn."

"Why there?"

"King's orders are to bring ye to the nearest province for yer trial and sentencing. Neuss likes things kept tidy." *And out of the public eye. But maybe we could see Chelyss and Fenwith one last time in Shulamorn.*

They rode all day and half the night, stopping several times to rest the horses, and arrived shortly after midnight at Shulamorn's main gate. Petr, the officious guard who had forced Rhees to pay a bribe the last time they passed through, emerged from a nearby hut and hurried over to greet the king's men. When he learned there were two prisoners of the crown in tow, he offered to guide them to the local prison.

Petr led them through the silent streets to a squat building, little more than a bungalow, with bars on its windows and a padlocked door. Petr withdrew a ring of keys, unlocked the door to the prison, and pulled it open. Guards surrounded Solace and Rhees after they dismounted and marched them into the dark interior. The building reeked of unwashed bodies, spoilt food, and overfull chamber pots. Most of the cells were occupied, the men grunting at having their sleep disturbed, but Petr opened another door and brought the group to the rear of the prison, where several cells sat empty.

Yeln removed their shackles and the extra chains on Rhees, and the guards shoved Solace and Rhees into neighboring cells. Petr locked their cell doors and guided the guards back outside. Solace could hear him fussing with the padlock on the outer door, and then the prison settled into the nighttime sounds of men snoring and rats skittering.

"I'll not let you hang for my crimes." Rhees whispered, his voice shaking. "I'll tell the governor I kidnapped you."

Solace crept closer to the cell door and hissed, "Whatever you say, don't tell the governor you kidnapped me. I know you regret it and you'd take me home if you could. But confessions to corrupt officials won't make a difference at this point."

"Then I'll tell him I forced you to divine for water. At knifepoint."

"You can't say that either. Don't you know it's impossible to coerce a diviner into using her gift? When all is said and done, a diviner must *want* to use her gift. She can't be threatened into divining for water."

"I don't care. I'll say anything to lighten your sentence. And Shulamorn's governor has known me since I was a boy. He might listen if I beg him to let you go. Then after...I'm gone, Chelyss will take you home and you can put all this behind you."

Solace gritted her teeth. "Rhees Demore, listen to me! I made my own decision to search for water, and I'd do it again to help the families we've met crisscrossing Toresz. Don't you dare say anything to lighten my sentence. I'll take my punishment same as you. After all we've been through together, do you think I can just leave here and forget everything?"

Rhees shifted in his cell. "When you were crying earlier, I thought you were scared." He added, "I know I'm scared."

"Of course I'm scared. But that's not why I was crying."

"Then why?"

"Remember when I was having my nightmare last night? I'd had a horrible dream of you being executed by a hangman. When we were captured a few hours later, it felt like my nightmare was coming true."

Rhees was silent for half a minute and then said, "I'm going to stop assuming I know what you're thinking, because nine times out of ten, I don't."

Solace yawned and her eyelids were heavy. As her head bobbed against her chest, she thought she heard Rhees say something about a remarkable woman and meeting under different circumstances. She didn't remember if she answered

Rhees or not, but she woke up hours later leaning up against the cell door. She shifted slightly and fell back to sleep.

The next morning, even before Solace was fully awake, she heard a familiar female voice speaking with authority to a prison guard. "I don't care how early it is. You know the rules as well as I do. Now let us in, Orno, or I'll speak with your father the next time I see him."

That could only be Fenwith! Solace rubbed the sleep out of her eyes and sat up straighter. The door separating their cells from the rest of the prison clanked open, and the guard called Orno ushered in Fenwith and Chelyss.

"How on earth did you find us?" Rhees asked with a yawn. "I don't think we've been here more than five or six hours."

"You know Fenwith," replied Chelyss, who set down a large, covered urn and an empty washing bowl on the floor while he waited for Orno to open their cell doors. "If she were a dog, she'd be a bloodhound. Practically sniffed her way here."

Fenwith shook her head. "I did nothing of the kind. When your horses arrived without their riders, we knew something was wrong." Fenwith paused and added delicately, "Given the current situation, I guessed the truth."

Orno said, "I'm only openin' up one cell at a time. T'other will just have to wait."

Fenwith frowned at Orno. "Fine. I think the young lady here is the needier of the two."

Orno nodded and opened up Solace's door. Chelyss carried the urn and washing bowl inside the cell and set them in the corner. Withdrawing a cup from his pocket, he set it down as well. He poured water from the urn into the bowl and cup. Stepping back, he said, "I'll give you two ladies some privacy while I visit with my nephew next door." Orno began to object and Chelyss added, "Through the cell door, of course."

Fenwith carried a satchel slung over her right shoulder and a hamper of food against her left hip. She wrinkled her nose, trying to determine where to put the hamper, and finally settled on a straw mat that Solace hadn't noticed the previous night.

"First, we're getting you cleaned up, although it'll have to be a sponge bath. I brought you a change of clothes, which I can see you sorely need."

Solace grinned. "I've gotten kind of used to dressing as a monk." She pulled off her robe, which Fenwith used to create a privacy screen. She held the robe up high enough so that Solace could sponge herself off and change into a simple gray tunic and leggings. It was impossible to do anything with her hair, but it had grown out enough she could braid it again. Fenwith withdrew a thick navy cardigan from her satchel and said, "Slip this on. There's a mighty draft in here. I'm going to burn these filthy monk's clothes."

Solace hugged Fenwith and sat down on the straw mat as Fenwith pulled out a large napkin, placed it beside her on the mat, and handed her the cup of water. Next came a hunk of fresh-baked bread, a slab of ham, a chunk of cheese, and an apple. Solace thanked her as she bit into the bread. She hadn't eaten since the evening before last and felt hollow inside. Fenwith patted Solace on the shoulder and called out to the guard. She and Chelyss transferred the urn, washing bowl, and hamper to Rhees's cell and waited for him to wash up and have some breakfast.

When they were leaving, Fenwith said, "We'll be back with your supper." Then she started to cry and Chelyss put his arm around her.

After they left, Rhees whispered, "Lace, can you hear me?"

Solace dragged the straw mat closer to her cell door and whispered, "Aye."

"Good. Chelyss says that hill folks are starting to arrive in Shulamorn and asking about the water diviner who's on trial."

"But why?"

"Folks have heard you've been divining for water and Neuss has arrested you for it."

Solace shook her head. "It never ceases to amaze me how quickly word spreads in the hills, despite the distances."

"Told you so."

"Told me what?"

"You'd be the spark that starts the rebellion."

"How strange that divining for water could be viewed as an act of treason." Solace yawned, despite her anxiety at their arrest. She'd never divined for so many water sources for so many days in a row—and she'd certainly never been on the run. She wound up napping on and off throughout the day.

When Chelyss and Fenwith returned with their supper, they told Rhees and Solace that Governor Ghrier had scheduled the trial for the end of the week. Solace's stomach churned at the thought of a public trial and hanging, but she pushed back against her fear. When Fenwith saw Solace's face pinched with worry, she said, "Don't give up hope. The governor is a better man than most."

Solace recalled Fenwith saying something similar about Rhees, when she'd first arrived in Shulamorn, and that had turned out to be true. She prayed Fenwith was right a second time. Their lives would be hanging, quite literally, on the fairness of one man.

CHAPTER 19

Rhees and Solace spent the next four days doing something they'd not had the time to do before. They told each other stories, about their childhoods, their friends and families, and the loss of their mothers.

"During the final months of my mother's illness," said Solace, "my father used to read aloud to her. He read all her favorite stories, except sometimes she would stop him and say, 'Oh no, Soren, not that one. Only stories with happy endings!'"

"What did your father say?"

Solace smiled at the memory. "My father's answer was always the same. 'Of course, my love.'"

One afternoon, Solace asked Rhees what it had been like to grow up knowing he was the son of a king, and yet never being publicly acknowledged.

"I'll not pretend it was easy, because it wasn't. From the time I can remember, my mother and I were called all sorts of names. I got into countless fights in the schoolyard defending my mother's honor. I wanted everyone to know my father was King Meade, and that he'd married my mother the year after the queen died. I used to beg my mother to let me tell the truth, but she absolutely forbade me."

Solace said, "And yet, the fact that only a few people knew your secret has kept you safe from Neuss all these years. Well, until now anyway. How often did you get to see your father?"

"He visited Shulamorn several times a year, spending a week or so each time." Rhees smiled. "I used to show off my sword fighting skills whenever he visited, and he'd encourage me to practice more. My father was a good man, a good king too."

"Did your father ever try to help you with the name calling and bullying?"

"In his way, yes, but never publicly—and not until I was ten and moved to Urhl to train as a royal page," said Rhees. "Behn, Wilhm, and I were in the same page's class. It was the first time I'd lived away from home. I was lonely and struggling to find my place.

"Prince Heris, who never knew I was his half-brother, was a squire by then. The squires used to tease the pages, ordering us to run extra errands for them and making us late for meals and classes, which then meant demerits and extra work assignments for us. Since I had no father, or at least none who claimed me, the squires saved all of the worst chores for me.

"One day Heris made me very late for class. He ordered me to polish his boots, and then he scuffed them up and insisted I hadn't done a good job. After I'd polished his boots for the third time, Heris put them on and proceeded to scrape the stone floor outside his room with the toes of his boots. Then he yelled at me, 'Page Demore, son of a whore, look at my boots! Can't you do anything right?'

"What Heris didn't realize was that the king and the royal trainer were inspecting the squires' rooms nearby and overheard everything. Father never acknowledged me, never let on that I was his son or that Heris was my half-brother. But he came up behind Heris, clapped a hand on his shoulder, and ordered the royal trainer to give the prince twenty demerits—which was a lot of demerits—for his disrespectful words toward my mother. Of course, Heris never knew my mother was actually his stepmother."

Rhees chuckled at the memory. "After that, the king showed more of an interest in all of us poor lowly pages. He showed up regularly to watch us train, inspected our report cards, and quietly ensured we were not being mistreated. I was still hazed like any other page, but no one insulted my mother after that day."

"If you were training to be a page at the palace, how did you come to be home in Shulamorn when Neuss overthrew King Meade?" asked Solace.

"I'd just completed the testing requirements to become a squire and was heading home for my midsummer school break. I couldn't wait to see my mother and show her the medal I'd won in swordsmanship! But you know the rest of the story. The king had asked her to travel to Urhl because Princess Nayla was very ill.

"In fact, I saw my mother just long enough for her to hug me, and for me to pretend that at fourteen, I was too big to be hugged. Then Chelyss, who'd traveled to Urhl with my mother, rode back to Shulamorn with me. And I never saw my mother or father again."

"What a horrible tragedy—for you and so many others." Solace could hear the pain in Rhees's voice, even after all these years. "I don't understand how Neuss was able to overthrow your father, since by all accounts your father was a highly respected king."

"My father's one flaw was entrusting his younger brother with more power than he could handle. Neuss commanded the Toreszan army, and over time, he developed a number of loyal army officers who were just as corrupt as he was. When Neuss decided the time had come for him to become king, a third of the army switched sides. Neuss took control of the country fairly easily after his 'army' killed my father, my half-brother and sister, most of the knights and palace guards, and anyone else known to be loyal to the crown."

Solace heard the lingering sadness in his voice and switched to less painful subjects. She talked about her favorite animals— her father's draft horses, Mirah and Mozrah, and the best sheep dog ever, Barley—and her strange yet wonderful gift for divining water. The one subject they never discussed was what happened in the tent moments before they were captured, their kiss and what it meant.

Solace wanted to talk about it, but the longer she waited for Rhees to say something, the more she realized he never would, which she decided was just as well. What was the use of starting something at the beginning of the week and then going to the gallows at the end of it?

On the morning of their trial, Fenwith and Chelyss arrived extra early with the washing bowl, urn of water, breakfast hamper, and fresh change of clothes, a dark gray sweater and black slacks for Rhees, and a blue wool dress for Solace that hung loosely on her, despite Fenwith's alterations. The past month had taken its toll on Solace's health—the attack in Urhl, the hasty marriage and escape from the capital, the race to divine water, and her arrest.

When Orno unlocked their cell doors, Solace took a deep breath and stepped out of the cell that had become something of a safe room, a temporary buffer, during the past week. She looked at Rhees, who took a step toward her, his brown-black eyes filled with compassion or tenderness or maybe even love. She wasn't sure it mattered any more, although if she were going to be completely honest, her heart beat faster whenever Rhees looked at her that way, as if they shared a bond beyond mere words.

Four guards and Orno surrounded them and prodded them

forward, through the small prison where cellmates shouted oaths, across the cobblestone street filled with curious townspeople, to the rear entrance of the provincial offices and courtroom.

Orno pulled open the heavy wooden door to the courtroom and a wave of sound crashed around them. Solace brushed a stray lock of hair from her face with a trembling hand. Rhees reached over, took her hand in his and squeezed. The guards led them to the defendant's box on one side of the room, where they were instructed to sit facing the witnesses, seated in the box opposite them.

The governor would be sitting on a raised platform along the wall to their right, giving him a good view of the witnesses and the defendants. Long benches filled with onlookers ran along the fourth wall, opposite the governor. Chelyss and Fenwith had secured a spot near the front.

Glancing at the number of witnesses sitting across from them, Solace whispered, "We were so careful to avoid farms and settlements when I was divining. How can there be that many witnesses?"

Rhees squinted at the witnesses and said softly, "You're looking at the witnesses for the defense, that's us! The witnesses for the prosecution are sitting on the other side of the box."

"How can you be so sure?"

Rhees nodded toward the larger group of witnesses. "Take a good closer look."

Solace gasped. "It can't be. Behn and Bray are here. Wilhelm too. And I think that's Kryss sitting behind him."

"And there are a couple of monks in the back. I'm guessing Evryst and Alyn have ridden here from Tor."

The bailiff opened a door behind the governor's seat and cried out, "All rise for His Honor, Governor Ghrier!"

Solace stood on her tiptoes to catch a glimpse of the man

who seemed about Chelyss's age, with a shock of white hair and a neatly trimmed white beard. He leaned heavily on a walking stick and seated himself with a grunt. Waving his stick at the crowded courtroom, his deep voice boomed, "Be seated!"

Chairs scraped the floor and skirts rustled as everyone sat back down. "Bailiff, please read the charges."

The bailiff unrolled a piece of parchment and said in a deep voice, "Rhees Demore and Lace Blusari are each charged with one count of treason, for conducting fresh water searches with the purpose of digging unauthorized wells. In addition, Rhees Demore is charged with one count of sedition, for marrying Lace Blusari, a woman under the king's protection. Signed His Royal Majesty, King Neuss of Toresz."

The bailiff rolled up the parchment and handed it to the governor. The governor reviewed the document, removed his spectacles, and asked Rhees and Solace, "Do you understand these charges?"

Solace nodded and Rhees answered. "Aye, your Honor."

"Very well. Bailiff, call up the first witness for the prosecution."

Yeln stood up and walked to the center of the room, facing Solace and Rhees in the defendant's box. He proceeded to repeat the charges against them, without adding anything new. When he was finished, Ghrier asked, "Did you find any shovels or digging implements when you arrested the defendants?"

"No, yer Honor."

"Do you have any eyewitnesses who wish to testify?"

Yeln nodded and called forward a grizzled farmer who carried a wide-brimmed hat in his hands. He stepped in front of the defendant's box and explained how a man, whom he identified as Rhees, arrived on his farm dressed like a monk and bartered for water with him. The farmer didn't think the man was a monk, but he agreed to provide him with water just to be rid of him, and then the farmer proceeded to follow Rhees until he met up with the rest of his group. The witness couldn't identify any one else in the group, but there appeared to be a small monk who was divining for water, and two others who seemed to be traveling with them.

Ghrier asked, "Since you were so far away, how could you be certain the small monk was divining for water?"

The farmer cleared his throat and said softly, "If truth be told, yer Honor, my grandmamma had the gift. I used t'follow behind her as a boy. It can look mighty strange if ye don't know what yer watching."

"Did you observe any of the group digging in the dirt?"

"No sir, the little monk was just lookin' at the soil and stoppin' periodically to test it."

The governor thanked the witness and called for the next one. Petr stepped forward and said, "Yer Honor, my guard patrol stopped these two prisoners when they was entering Shulamorn some months ago. I had my suspicions they was up to no good."

Ghrier waited for Petr to continue, and when he didn't, the governor prompted him. "Suspicions about what?"

"The girl looked like she'd been dragged through the mud. Not at all like someone's betrothed. Smelled fishy to me."

When Ghrier realized that was the sum total of Petr's testimony, the governor thanked him and glanced behind him for the next witness. Petr glared at Rhees and Solace as if they'd insulted him and returned to his seat. A few other prosecution witnesses testified, including several of Yeln's guards, but they repeated what Yeln had already said.

When the witnesses for the prosecution were finished, Governor Ghrier frowned at Rhees and Solace and asked them to confirm or deny the farmer's eyewitness account. Rhees said, "Your Honor, I acknowledge that I did approach that witness and bartered for water with him, after which I rejoined my wife."

"Who was actually divining for water, Mr. Demore?"

Solace spoke up quickly, hoping to distract the governor from questions about their traveling companions. "I was dressed like a monk, your Honor, and I was divining for water."

"I see. Tell me, Miss Blusari, once you've realized that a water source exists beneath the ground, can you pretend it's not there?"

"I'm not sure that I follow, Your Honor."

"Can you turn your gift for divining water on and off?" asked the governor.

"No sir, it doesn't work that way. Once I have a mental map of the water sources in an area, it stays with me. I can't pretend the map doesn't exist."

"So in other words, you carry around a map of water sources in your head, even when you're not actually divining?" Governor Ghrier leaned forward as he asked his question.

"Aye sir," Solace felt as if the governor was trying to gain a basic understanding of the principles of water divining, which she appreciated. "And besides, it would be wrong not to use my gift."

"What do you mean?"

"I've seen the abundance of water beneath the Toreszan soil. It runs freely in these hills! What right has the king or anyone else to control it?"

Chelyss and Fenwith began to clap and soon everyone, except for Yeln and the guards, were clapping and stomping their feet.

Ghrier banged his walking stick on the wooden floor until the clapping subsided. Ignoring the interruption, he asked, "Did you or Mr. Demore dig for wells in any of the locations where you thought you might have found water?"

Solace shook her head. "No, Your Honor. We did no digging."

"And what about the other companions identified by the eyewitness? Did they do any digging?"

Rhees interjected, "They were strangers to us, Your Honor. They happened to be passing through and we shared some of our food with them."

The governor looked skeptical. "Very well." Turning to the witnesses for the defense, he asked the first witness to step forward. One by one, Rhees's friends testified to their long association with him and to his character, as well as the fact that each of them, Behn, Bray, Wilhm, and Kryss, knew that Solace and Rhees were betrothed.

Ghrier turned to Rhees and asked, "Mr. Demore, for how long was Miss Blusari under your formal protection?"

Rhees answered, "For almost four months, Your Honor, and well before she was introduced to King Neuss."

"Miss Blusari, is that true?"

Solace didn't hesitate. "Aye, Your Honor."

"Very well. Mr. Demore, please describe the circumstances surrounding King Neuss taking the extraordinary step of placing your fiancé under his protection."

Rhees explained about the curious circumstances that led to Solace working alone in the library well after normal closing hours, and then he told how she was attacked after she left the library. The governor listened carefully and then asked him whether it was commonly known Rhees would be attending the guild meeting that evening. Rhees replied, "Aye, Your Honor. All of the guild leaders are expected to attend the monthly meeting."

Ghrier turned back to Solace and asked her to describe the special request from the king's secretary and how long it took her to catalog the collection. "And so after you completed the cataloging, you walked home alone?"

"Aye, Your Honor."

"And what happened next?"

Solace described how she'd been followed almost as soon as she left the library and attacked in a dark alley where no one heard her screaming. She blinked fast to keep from crying.

He asked Rhees, "How soon after the attack on Miss Blusari were you notified that King Neuss had placed her under his protection?"

"It was the next day, Your Honor."

The buzz of numerous conversations spread around the courtroom, and Governor Ghrier banged his walking stick again, waiting for the noise to die down. When the room quieted, he called for any remaining defense witnesses. Evryst and Alyn stepped forward.

"We wish to testify, Your Honor," said Evryst.

"Please proceed."

Evryst said, "Brother Alyn and I were present at the marriage of Mr. Demore and Miss Blusari. Brother Tomyss of the Tor Monastery performed the ceremony. We brought the marriage certificate here, Your Honor, as evidence."

The courtroom erupted at the mention of Tomyss's name. The news of his arrest had spread to the farthest outposts. Whacking the floor with his walking stick again, Governor Ghrier ordered everyone to be quiet, otherwise he'd close the courtroom. Evryst handed Ghrier the marriage certificate, which the governor examined carefully. He handed the document back to Evryst and thanked him for traveling to Shulamorn to provide the evidence.

Removing his spectacles, the governor frowned at Rhees and Solace. *This is it. He's going to find us guilty and send us to the hangman for sure.* They stood for their sentencing, Rhees gripping her hand hard.

"I'm a tidy man," said the governor. "And so we're going to carefully review each of the charges and the evidence presented. Regarding the charge of sedition against Mr. Demore, all of the evidence points to the fact that Mr. Demore and Miss Blusari were formally betrothed, and that Mr. Demore was not negligent in the matter of the attack on Miss Blusari. I find no evidence to support the charge of sedition, so that charge is dismissed." Solace heard Rhees heave a quick sigh. *Maybe they still had reason to hope.*

The governor continued. "The second charge, of treason for conducting fresh water searches with the purpose of digging unauthorized wells, demands that we first understand the intent and wording of the law upon which the charge is based.

"Ten years ago, King Neuss issued the following proclamation, 'Henceforth, all wells are the property of the Crown, and all revenues arising from the use of the wells or the sale of water will accrue to the Crown. Unauthorized digging for water sources is not permitted.' In laymen's terms, it's against the law to dig for a well, to own a private well, or to earn money by letting others use a private well.

"Nowhere does the law state that it is illegal for a diviner to have a mental map of water sources in her head, or to examine the soil for moisture, since these are natural activities for someone with the gift.

"I find no evidence that Mr. Demore and Miss Blusari were digging for wells or attempting to profit from the knowledge that water sources exist in these hills. The charge of treason is dismissed. The defendants are free to go."

Everyone stood up and started shouting at once. Most of the faces looked happy, even thrilled, but Yeln and his men wore sour expressions. Solace's mouth opened in surprise as Rhees hugged her.

"You mean we're really free?" she asked.

"We're really free." Gripping her elbow, Rhees guided her out of the defendant's box. "Let's get out of here and find

Chelyss and Fenwith." Their friends surged around them, clapping them on the back and laughing.

One man pushed his way through the happy crowd toward them. It was Petr, the surly guard. Solace couldn't understand why he wanted to join the throng of well-wishers, but he kept shoving his way forward.

Petr ran the last few steps and yelled at her, "Water witch, that's what you are!" Something flashed in his hand, and the point of a dagger pierced Solace in the side. Then she was falling, Rhees catching her in his arms and roaring, "No, no, no!!"

CHAPTER 20

Orno and his guards rushed in to disperse the crowd, while Behn and Wilhm wrestled Petr to the floor. The governor shouted at Rhees above the fray, "Bring her here!"

Rhees carried Solace to the rear of the courtroom, where the governor ushered them inside his office and closed the door. Clutching her side, she moaned as Rhees laid her on the governor's desk.

There was an abrupt knock on the door, and Fenwith pushed it open, with Chelyss, Evryst, and Alyn following her into the room. Rhees looked up and said, "Evryst, tell us what you need." Turning to Ghrier he added, "Brother Evryst is a master healer."

Rhees pressed his hands against Solace's wound to stem the blood flow, and Evryst hastily removed his outer robe and rolled up the sleeves of his tunic. He nodded at Rhees, who removed his hands briefly so the monk could take a look. Evryst grimaced and motioned for him to keep pressing on the wound. The monk whispered in Solace's ear, "Lace, I need to examine your wound now, so I'm going to cut away part of your dress. I know that every movement hurts you, but I'll do my best."

Solace's eyes were closed but her lips formed the word "aye." Her abdomen felt on fire, pain radiating out in every direction. She floated at the edges of consciousness, as Alyn helped Evryst cut away the fabric while Rhees continued to press down on her abdomen. Ghrier opened the door long enough to order the bailiff to bring water and clean rags for bandages.

Alyn took one of the rags, soaked it in a sweet-smelling solution, and held the rag up to Solace's nose. She turned her head to avoid the sickening odor but felt herself drifting away. Rhees stopped pressing on her abdomen long enough to allow Alyn to clean around the wound, while Evryst threaded a needle, dipped it in alcohol, and began the painstaking work of stitching the ragged hole made by Petr's dagger.

Solace wandered in and out of consciousness for days, living in a dark place where she was only dimly aware of her surroundings, often thrashing in her sleep and crying out in pain. Rhees was beside her every hour, smoothing her hair back from her forehead, checking for fever, and forcing her to take sips of water.

She often heard Rhees and Evryst speaking quietly, barely more than a whisper, and Fenwith's soft steps as she looked in on them. At some point, Solace noticed the voices seemed farther away, the dark place surrounding her more permanent. Once, she thought she heard someone whispering, "Lace, please. You have to live! Don't leave me here alone."

She found herself standing in a tunnel black as a cave, except for a pinprick of light at one end. She heard Evryst say, "Rhees, she's gone...I'm so sorry." Fenwith let out a sob and ran from the room, followed by Chelyss and Evryst. Only Rhees remained, kneeling next to a bed where a still form lay, weeping. *Who's gone? Why's everyone so upset?*

Solace turned away from the sad little room and saw a familiar figure standing in the bright light. Running toward the light, Solace cried out, "Mama! I'm so glad I found you!" Points of light radiated from her mother's hair and face and clothes, and all the ravages of her mother's illness were gone. She looked as healthy and lovely as a new bride.

Her mother held up her hand and said, "You've arrived too soon, my dear girl. You mustn't enter the light." The light withdrew farther back into the tunnel but Solace chased after it.

"Please, I want to stay here with you. I've missed you so much!"

"But your work isn't finished, Solace. You're needed elsewhere."

"Do I *have* to go back?"

Her mother cocked her head as if listening for instructions, her dark hair framing the perfect oval of her face. At last she said, "You've been granted a gift, Solace: the gift of choosing. However, before you decide, you must take one last look." Her mother pointed toward the other end of the tunnel.

When Solace turned, she saw Rhees kneeling next to *her* bed, weeping over *her* lifeless form. She couldn't bear to leave Rhees like that, so alone in his grief. Her heart, frozen in the still darkness of the tunnel, resumed beating, and the pain in her chest cut through her more deeply than any knife.

Solace opened her eyes and the room came into focus. She was lying in Ellanora's bed, with Rhees leaning across the coverlet, his forehead resting on top of his arms. It took all her strength to lift her hand and run her fingers through his dark waves. He jerked his head back, eyes wide, and then took her hand in his.

"Lace?" he whispered, as if afraid she might be a ghost.

"I saw my mother."

He carefully climbed onto the bed and lay on his side,

facing her. Still gripping her hand he asked, "What did your mother say?"

"She said I was needed elsewhere and showed me the way back."

Rhees kissed her on the tip of her nose. "I don't know who I love more at the moment—your mother, or you."

Solace smiled and went to sleep.

She slept for twenty hours before waking and asking for toast. Rhees stirred from the chair where he'd been napping to fetch her toast and Evryst, who'd been waiting to examine her.

Evryst placed a narrow silver tube over her chest and listened to her heart at the other end. He moved the tube around a bit, frowning. Then he checked her for fever, inspected the whites of her eyes, and changed the dressing on her wound. When Evryst was finished he said, "You're still running a fever, although it's come down, which means you're still fighting the infection that nearly took your life. You need plenty of rest and looking after." Turning to Rhees he added, "I'd like to stay a while longer, keep an eye on Lace, if you don't mind."

"Of course! Stay as long as you like."

Evryst nodded. "I'll send Alyn back to the Tor today, so the brothers don't become overly alarmed. Everyone's on edge with Tomyss sitting in the palace dungeon."

As Evryst and Rhees were leaving the room, Fenwith entered carrying a pot of tea and two cups. She handed Solace a cup and sat down in the chair next to the bed, sipping her tea and glancing up occasionally.

"Something's on your mind," said Solace softly.

Fenwith put her cup down on the mahogany nightstand.

"Rhees told me you saw your mother when you were...gone... and she helped you realize this is where you needed to be."

Solace nodded and repeated everything she could recall, stopping at times to try to put into words what she'd seen and felt. She described the tunnel, how her mother looked, what she said, and how in the end, Solace knew she had a choice to make.

"And so you came back for Rhees?" Fenwith asked quietly, her gray eyebrows drawn together.

"He looked so alone." Solace couldn't explain her feelings to Fenwith because she couldn't exactly explain them to herself. "You told me a long time ago he's a better man than I'd given him credit for, and I've come to realize you're right."

Fenwith stood up and kissed Solace on the forehead. "Bless you, lass, for coming back to him. Losing you would have crushed his spirit for good."

"Fenwith, please understand. Rhees still needs to take me home to my father. He's grieving as well."

"And so he shall, when you're recovered. Though it'll break Rhees's heart to leave you behind in Yelosha."

Solace thought about her father and Rhees, her familiar Yeloshan hills and the Toreszan hills and people she'd come to know. *How can I choose one over the other, when I love them both?*

CHAPTER 21

"We have a visitor," said Chelyss as he went outside to see who was riding up the path. Rhees was reading to Solace in the parlor, something he'd started doing during her convalescence. Solace discovered his flair for the dramatic the first time he used different voices and even props to tell a story. She was laughing at his imitation of an evil queen when Chelyss and his guest entered the room.

"It's good to hear you laughing," said Governor Ghrier. Rhees stood up and shook the governor's hand.

"Your Honor, we can never thank you enough for your fairness as a judge, and for what you did after, when Lace was injured."

The governor took a seat across from Solace and Rhees, who were side by side on the sofa. Fenwith left them to brew some coffee in the kitchen, where Evryst was writing letters, and Chelyss excused himself to see to the horses.

"I did what any decent man would have done," said Ghrier.

"You're more than decent, you're also brave, and I'm sorry for the trouble we've caused you," said Rhees.

Solace frowned, "What trouble?"

Waving his hand, the governor said, "Nothing for you to worry about, my dear. I've been recalled to the capital by the king, where he's sure to declare I'm no longer fit to serve as governor, and he'll appoint some hoodlum to take my place. It was bound to happen. I'm an old man, too old to put up with Neuss and his nonsense any longer. Which is why I'm here."

Ghrier withdrew a folded piece of parchment from inside his cloak and handed it to Rhees. Rhees broke the wax seal, scanned it, and handed the document to Solace. The Naming Day Certificate listed the names of the child and his birth parents: Rhees Demore Orillya, son of Ellanora Demore Orillya and Meade Rhees Orillya, King of Toresz. Governor Asher Ghrier had signed the certificate.

"I know who I am," Rhees shrugged. "Why are you giving this to me now?"

"Isn't it obvious?" Ghrier drew his bushy brows down into a *V*.

"He's reminding you of your duties," Solace said, resting her hand on Rhees's arm. "Your duties as the son of King Meade."

Rhees covered her hand with his. "My duties" —he looked at Ghrier— "drove me to take this young woman—against her will—and bring her to Toresz. We needed a water diviner and so I found us one."

Ghrier nodded. "I guessed as much. A Yeloshan water diviner suddenly showing up here with you, when we needed her most. But you can't force a diviner to use her gift. She wanted to help you, help us all."

"And she nearly died as a result." Rhees shook his head. "I've been scheming for years, trying to figure out how to break Neuss's hold on Toresz. And look what's happened, just when we were this close" —Rhees held up his thumb and forefinger — "we were discovered, arrested, and well, you know the rest. Our rebellion fizzled out even before it began."

"The people are frightened and weary. They need to be inspired, and for a short while they were, by you and Lace. But the longer you sit here, minding your own business instead of the people's, the more discouraged they become. You need to get back to the business of leading."

"Even if I could rally everyone of us with the will to fight, we're outnumbered twenty to one. I'd be responsible for slaughtering them and their families. We can't win, and I'll not risk any more lives needlessly. The price is too high." Rhees put his arm around Solace and tried pulling her closer, but she twisted around to look him in the eye.

"Rhees Demore Orillya. You're not just the son of a king—you *are* the king. You've never been cautious before. Don't start now!"

Rhees ran a hand through his wavy hair. "I've never had so much to lose before."

"You've never had so much to *gain* before."

Rhees folded his arms, waiting for her to continue.

"We can defeat Neuss, but not with swords and arrows," said Solace. "We need to outsmart him."

"How?"

"You have friends in the mining settlements, in the towns, on the farms, and in Urhl, right?"

Rhees waved his hand impatiently. "Aye, of course. You've met most of them—what can they do?"

"They can stop working."

Rhees looked at her as if she'd lost her mind. "A work stoppage? But the people will starve!"

Evryst followed Fenwith into the front room, carrying a tray laden with cakes, mugs, and a pot of coffee. He put the tray down on the low table in front of the sofa. "Not if we provide them food from our own supplies. We have enough stored in the Tor monastery to feed the neediest families. Most farmers have enough to tide them over. We had a good harvest and winter pantries are still stocked even this late in the season."

Rhees stood up and started pacing around the parlor. "What about water? Neuss will make sure the public wells are shut down if there's a work stoppage."

Ghrier said, "True, but some of us have private wells, and perhaps with some judicious digging a few more wells can be secured." Ghrier winked at Solace, who smiled.

Rhees frowned. "A work stoppage alone won't be enough. We need to draw Neuss out of the palace and into the open."

Chelyss had rejoined them and poured himself a mug of coffee. "If Neuss is angry enough, he'll come scurrying out of Urhl."

Solace looked at the governor. "What would happen if you refused to go to Urhl?"

Ghrier scratched his white beard. "I suppose the old assassin would send his goons to arrest me."

"But what if you sent him a message, telling him that Shulamorn is now an independent protectorate, and you are serving King Rhees, son of King Meade and the true ruler of Toresz?"

Rhees picked up the thread. "And just as the governor's message arrives at the palace, other messages would arrive, letting Neuss know of work stoppages across Toresz."

"And when he learns the source of all this unrest is in the least of all the Toreszan provinces? He just might ride out to Shulamorn to see what the fuss was all about," said Evryst.

"Especially if I tell him his guards are in jail and his wells now belong to the people. Free water for all!" Ghrier rubbed his hands together with a mischievous grin.

Rhees returned to the sofa and sat down next to Solace. This time when he put his arm around her, she nestled in closer. "Who knew that a warrior's heart beat inside our Lace?"

Solace said, "You forget I'm the daughter of an old Yeloshan soldier, raised on stories of our king's campaigns."

Rhees laughed. "Remind me to never underestimate our neighbors to the west."

They spent the next three days holed up in Fenwith's parlor, planning every last detail. Wells had to be dug and hidden, friends notified and recruited, and the work stoppage coordinated to coincide with Ghrier's message to Neuss. Rhees and Evryst agreed they needed forty days to set everything in motion, but Neuss expected Ghrier within the week.

Chelyss reminded them Neuss was a hypochondriac. He suggested Ghrier send Neuss a note, notifying the king he had a severe lung inflammation and would be delayed by several weeks.

Ghrier kissed Solace and Fenwith good-bye on their last evening together and whistled cheerfully as he limped out to his horse. Evryst, Rhees, and Chelyss would be leaving in the morning, each riding in a different direction but with the same end goal in mind—to bring down Neuss for good.

Fenwith and Chelyss headed to bed, and Evryst, yawning, padded down the hallway to the bedroom he shared with Rhees.

"I wish I could ride with you," Solace said. "I feel so useless."

"Don't even think of it. Evryst says you can't ride for another two weeks, at least."

"Evryst is over-protective," Solace grumbled.

"Evryst saved your life." Rhees drew her onto his lap and wrapped his arms around her. "Promise me you'll take care of yourself while I'm gone. This is your brilliant plan, so the least you can do is leave me with some peace of mind."

Solace leaned her head against his shoulder. "Fine. But don't be late, or I'll ride out after you."

Rhees cradled her against his chest, and then tipping her chin up, sealed his lips over hers. Solace inhaled and he gripped her harder, running his hands through her hair, down her back, holding her so tightly she could hardly breathe. She felt an odd ache in her chest and remembered the sharp pain she'd had in the tunnel, when she'd decided to come back.

Rhees drew a ragged breath and noticed Solace pressing a hand against her heart. Reaching for her hand, he said, "What is it? What's wrong?"

"Nothing. It just hurts sometimes."

Rhees didn't kiss her again, but wrapped his arms around Solace, who imprinted the memory of their bodies pressed together, of his heart beating a strong staccato and her weaker heart, echoing.

CHAPTER 22

Fenwith bustled around the next morning, getting the men breakfast, packing up lunches and water skins, and refusing all offers of help. Solace hoped for a private word with Rhees before he left, but it was Evryst who pulled her aside as Rhees and Chelyss saddled the horses. Streaks of orange and pink and gold lightened the eastern edge of the sky.

"Rhees told me you're having occasional chest pains," he said quietly as they walked into the yard.

It was the first time Solace had stepped outside since her injury, and she breathed the early spring air gratefully. Ignoring Evryst's question, she said, "Thank you for all you've done for me. I wouldn't be here without your healing skills."

"You're welcome, and you're changing the subject." Evryst continued, "The fever weakened your heart, which is why you're getting pains."

Solace looked up at the solemn monk whom she'd come to regard as another member of her strange, extended Toreszan family. "What does that mean for me...in the future?"

"It means you need to listen to your body and not push

yourself too hard while you're healing. If you're very careful, you should be able to lead a mostly normal life, although you'll tire more easily than in the past."

"And if not?"

"If you ignore the chest pains, they'll worsen, and the next time you enter that dark tunnel, you'll be heading toward the light. No turning back."

Solace nodded. "Alright, message delivered. You can let Rhees know I'll take care."

"Good. Now be sure you follow through."

Evryst left first, heading toward the Tor, and planning stops along the way to visit Wilhm and Peka and their other allies in the south. Several wells needed to be dug, and food had to be transported and hidden in caves and pantries and root cellars.

Chelyss was heading east, across the Orpash Plain to Urhl, where he planned to meet with Lizbet and key members of the various guilds who were loyal friends of Rhees and King Meade. Rhees's route was north, toward Kryss and his rebels, and then on to Xenyss and other northern towns.

Each of them carried certified copies of Rhees's Naming Day Certificate, signed by Governor Ghrier himself, to distribute as fliers in the towns and settlements they visited. Meanwhile, the governor was planning to lay low and send his servant out to the apothecary for herbs and potions that he really didn't need.

Rhees was the last to depart, lingering until the others had left. He strode to the front of the cottage where Solace and Fenwith waited. The old woman who'd helped raise him stood on her tiptoes to kiss his cheek, whispered a hill blessing over him, and reentered the house with damp eyes.

Solace smiled at Rhees and brushed the lapel of his old leather duster, which Evryst and Alyn had returned, along with Caya and their saddlebags, when the monks arrived to testify at the trial.

"What are you smiling at?" he asked.

"Although you made a handsome enough monk, I prefer you in the leather duster and wide-brimmed hat." Rhees had left his hat hooked over Zirott's saddle horn.

He shook his head. "Making jokes as I ride off to start an uprising?"

Solace bit her bottom lip and turned away. He gripped her arms firmly and turned her toward him. Cupping her face in his hands, Rhees kissed her gently at first, and then more urgently, pulling her into a tight embrace. Butterflies spun around in her stomach, danced across her injury, and fluttered up to her heart, which ached with desire. She knew this kind of chest pain wouldn't be healed by rest and herbs and potions.

Rhees said gruffly, "Make sure you're here when I return."

"Make sure you return—and do try to be on time!" Recalling her father never permitted long goodbyes, since they distracted his men, Solace stepped back and pointed to Zirott. "Now go!"

∼

Although Chelyss had hired Marek, a neighbor, to feed and exercise the horses while he was away, Solace missed Jenx and Caya and began to pay them regular visits in their stable. Caya immediately welcomed Solace by nuzzling her hair and blowing in her face. Jenx, on the other hand, remained aloof during her first few visits, pretending she was a complete stranger.

Solace tried wooing him with sweet talk and special treats, but nothing worked until she stood directly in front of his stall and said, "I'm sorry I didn't come sooner, Jenx. I've been really sick and couldn't leave the house." Jenx tossed his head, looked at her sideways, and then whickered. She patted his neck, laughing.

About a week after Rhees and Chelyss had left, Fenwith

found Solace searching through her dresser, pulling out every drawer. "Did you lose something?"

"I can't find my slings, which should have been in my saddlebag."

"I think I hung them up in the back of your wardrobe." Fenwith reached into the wardrobe and pulled out the slings Gordo had made. Putting her hands on her hips, Fenwith said, "You're under strict orders not to strain yourself. What're you planning to do with them?"

Solace grinned. "I'll take it easy. I just want to practice my aim for now. I won't try slinging very far." She picked up her drawstring bag filled with stones, which had been stuffed in the bottom drawer, and walked out the front door feeling more cheerful and free than she'd felt in a long time.

Her good mood quickly evaporated when she tried hitting the old targets used for archery and lance practice by Rhees and the other boys Chelyss used to tutor, after he'd officially "retired" as the king's royal trainer. She missed the first two targets completely and grazed the outer edge of the third.

Biting her bottom lip, Solace forced herself to slow down and focus on each phase of slinging: setting the stone in the cradle, gripping the knotted end of the sling, rotating her arm, and releasing the cord. Finally, she hit inside the target, but her aim was still off-center. She could never take down a rabid jackal in her current condition.

Solace walked slowly back to the house, her arm muscles aching and her chest tightening. Later that evening Fenwith caught Solace pressing her hand against her chest and said, "I knew it! You overdid it today, didn't you?"

"What do you mean?"

Fenwith pointed at Solace's hand. "You have chest pain."

Solace sighed. "Who told you to keep an eye on me, Rhees or Evryst?"

"Both of them."

"If I promise to take it easier, will you promise not to watch my every movement like a hawk?"

Fenwith smiled and patted Solace's shoulder. "Aye, lass, so long as you're promising me."

Solace paced herself after that, practicing with her sling and stopping as soon as she felt tired. Her accuracy improved more quickly than her ability to sling a deadly shot, but she continued to practice and build up her arm strength in a variety of ways, including brushing down Caya and Jenx after Marek exercised them each day.

Holding the brush in her hand, she glanced out the open doorway toward the stable yard and hills beyond. "Yer wanting to ride him again, ain't ye?" asked Marek, who was saddling Jenx for his daily ride.

Solace looked at the wiry old man, a fringe of gray hair peeking out beneath his wide-brimmed hat, and nodded. "I can hardly wait. But I'm still not able to mount him." Her wound was healed but her abdominal muscles needed strengthening.

Marek rubbed his scraggly gray whiskers and said, "Easy enough. Follow me." Marek led Jenx and Solace outside toward the hills behind the house. He stopped in front of a series of large flat rocks, each slightly larger than the last, which seemed to form a natural set of stepping-stones. When Solace commented on them, Marek laughed. "Ain't nothing natural about it. Chelyss and me moved them rocks around, t'help the young lads that he tutored learn how to mount a horse by their selves."

Marek led Jenx over to the row of stepping-stones and waited while Solace climbed up, starting at the bottom. When she reached the tallest rock, she was able to throw her leg over Jenx's back and plunk herself into the saddle. Marek adjusted the stirrups for her and gave her a nod.

She flicked the reins gently, guiding Jenx into a walk and then a trot and finally a canter through the fields and foothills connecting Chelyss and Fenwith's property with the Orpash Plain. A cluster of five towering boulders stood like silent sentries near the entrance to the plain. The boulders seemed to have been sculpted by nature to stand guard over the exit from Shulamorn province and were known by the locals as Stoneguard.

Solace galloped past the tall boulders, savoring the wind whipping around her face and hair. She slowed Jenx down to a walk and reluctantly turned him toward the stable. Marek was waiting for her when she returned, sliding off Jenx with a huge grin.

"Well?" prompted Marek.

"I haven't felt this good in a long time. I'd like to start taking Jenx out for his daily exercise, that is, if you don't mind."

Marek smiled. "'Course I don't mind."

Even though she woke up the next morning feeling stiff and sore from her ride, she felt no painful twinges in her chest, which she took as a good sign. Fenwith reminded her not to "overdo it" when Solace joined her for breakfast. Solace winked and headed first to the practice field with her sling and then to the stable for Jenx.

By the time Solace counted off thirty days from Rhees's departure, she'd started hunting small game again with her sling, supplying Fenwith with meat for her stews, and she could mount Jenx by standing on the lowest stepping-stone, stepping onto the stirrup, and pulling herself into the saddle.

On the fortieth day, Solace walked with Jenx toward the stepping-stones and paused as the memory of her vaulting onto the horse's broad back came to her. Facing Jenx, she rubbed his forehead. "Steady on," she whispered as she looped the reins around the saddle horn.

Stepping around to his left side and pacing off twelve long strides, she turned and began to run toward the horse. At the last possible moment she leapt in the air, using her left hand to grasp the saddle as her right leg soared over Jenx's back. She almost overshot him and grabbed a hunk of his mane in her right hand to steady herself. Jenx shifted slightly so that she managed to land firmly in the saddle. Patting his neck, she said, "Thanks!" and slipped her boots into the stirrups.

Marek walked toward her shaking his head. "That's the darnedest saddle mount I've ever seen. It's a beaut, though I don't think I'll try it me' self."

Solace laughed and flicking the reins, took Jenx for an extra long run, her thoughts flying to Rhees, wondering where he was at that moment and whether he'd been able to convince enough people in the northern provinces to pull off a work stoppage. She tried pushing away all thoughts of the two of them, and what they'd said to each other, and most importantly, what they meant to each other. Her mother always used to say that if she did what was right and stayed true to her heart, the future would take care of itself. The only problem was the enormous rift in her own heart, between her father's Yelosha and Rhees's Toresz—or more precisely—between her father and Rhees. She turned Jenx back toward the stable, knowing she couldn't outrun whatever the future would demand from her.

Evryst arrived after forty-four days with a posse of warrior monks led by Brother Alyn. Accompanying them were Peka, her sons, and their small army, and several dozen others who wanted to join the fight, including Wilhm and the old farmer who'd testified at the trial. Evryst led them past the farms and homesteads of Shulamorn, through the fields and hills behind Chelyss and Fenwith's land, to the flat, scrubby Orpash Plain that stretched for miles, connecting with the brown and beige Toreszan hills in every direction. They set up a campsite, pitching tents, combining food reserves, and assigning duties, everything from patrolling to cooking and cleanup.

Chelyss arrived the next day with an even larger group of willing fighters, including disaffected workers from every guild in the city, as well as a number of the former king's knights whom Chelyss had trained years earlier and who'd never supported Neuss. Chelyss's small army set up tents next to the warrior monks and others, more than doubling the size of the campsite.

Chelyss rode into his own yard and Fenwith ran out of the cottage to greet him. "I missed you, old man," she said softly. Solace followed her outside but waited by the front door, letting them have a private moment.

Chelyss grinned, dismounted, and planted a kiss on his wife's lips. "You're looking younger every day, wife. What's your secret?"

Fenwith chuckled and batted his arm. "Brother Evryst and Governor Ghrier have been waiting on you."

"What about Rhees?"

Fenwith shook her head. Chelyss caught Solace's eye and said, "Let's join Evryst and Ghrier inside. There's a lot of news and not much time."

Solace's stomach churned. "Bad news?"

"Come inside, lass," Chelyss said quietly.

Solace followed Chelyss and Fenwith into the parlor. Evryst and Ghrier stood up to greet Chelyss, but he waved them back to their seats. "Neuss and a legion of his goons are riding fast on our tails. They're two days behind me, more or less."

"That's good news, isn't it?" asked Ghrier. "We've drawn him out into the open."

"True, but without the northern provinces to help us, we're going to be hard pressed to win this fight," said Evryst.

"There's more." Chelyss hesitated. "Apparently Neuss flew into a rage when he received your note, Governor. And his rage intensified when he discovered that half the palace servants had abandoned their posts. Then messengers began arriving with news of work stoppages in various provinces.

"Neuss was so enraged he ordered the immediate execution of all prisoners." Chelyss put a hand on Evryst's shoulder. "I left Urhl shortly after hearing that news, but I expect by now Brother Tomyss is gone."

Evryst stood up and went to the window overlooking the front yard. He bowed his head in prayer. When he turned back to face them, he saw Solace's tears and nodded, his own eyes moist. "Tomyss knew he was walking into the lion's den when he delivered that marriage contract to Neuss. And he trusted us to carry out the work he started."

"So mote it be," said the governor, who pounded the floorboards with his walking stick for emphasis.

"So mote it be," echoed everyone else. A mournful silence descended on the room. Solace swiped at her eyes as she thought of Tomyss. She couldn't imagine visiting the Tor Monastery and not seeing the wise, kind monk in his library, sorting through a collection of manuscripts or showing her how to use the card catalog system.

"Any news from the north?" asked Fenwith. Solace knew Fenwith was as worried about Rhees as she was.

Chelyss sighed. "Rumors, mostly, of work stoppages and rioting, stories of Neuss's guards slaughtering not just the miners and laborers, but also the families of any who refused to work. I don't know what sort of support Rhees will be able to drum up." Ghrier asked about their preparations for Neuss's arrival, and he followed Evryst and Chelyss into the kitchen to draw their battle plans on a makeshift map.

Solace struggled to listen to anything after she heard "rioting" and "slaughtering." According to their plan, Chelyss, Evryst, Ghrier, and Rhees would rendezvous at the house by the forty-fifth day. They figured this would provide enough time to spread the word about Rhees's birthright, encourage the work stoppages, and observe the reactions of Neuss's men. Rhees was late, which was typical, but still worrisome.

Fenwith noticed the deep crease on Solace's brow. "I'm anxious about Rhees too. Even though he's rarely early or even timely, this is different. The stakes are life and death, and he would have been here on time if he could."

Solace's crease deepened. "My thoughts exactly."

"You're going to try to meet up with him, aren't you?"

"I can't sit around here any longer, wondering where he is or whether he needs help."

"But how can you possibly find him?" Fenwith waved her hand at the front door.

"I have the map with Rhees's route drawn out."

Fenwith arched one silver eyebrow. "How do you have a map with Rhees's route when no one else does?"

"He promised me he wouldn't be late and gave me the map as proof that I needn't worry, because the last thing he wanted was for me to ride out and search for him."

Fenwith shook her head. "He really didn't expect to be late, or he'd never have given you his route."

"Exactly. That's why I'm riding out at dawn to find Rhees, wherever he is on that route, and try to bring him and the others back before Neuss arrives."

"You can't be serious!" Evryst had reentered the parlor and overheard the conversation.

Chelyss said, "It's far too dangerous for you to search for Rhees on your own, and we can't spare anyone to ride alongside you." Ghrier agreed she mustn't take such a risk, pounding the floorboards with his walking stick to make his point.

Solace compressed her lips in a straight line. "Tell me, please, which king do you serve?"

Evryst's eyes widened in surprise and he glanced at Chelyss

and Ghrier. "We all acknowledge Rhees as the rightful heir and king, and we serve only him."

"And who is Rhees's wife?"

"You are, lass," said Fenwith with a wink.

"Then, gentlemen, what does that make me—legally, I mean?"

Ghrier cleared his throat and said with a courtly bow, "Our queen, milady."

CHAPTER 23

Solace waited to see if anyone disagreed. Nodding, she said, "I'm glad that's settled. I'm riding out at dawn tomorrow morning. I'm recovered and perfectly capable of traveling alone." Looking at Evryst she added, "And I haven't had any chest pain for several weeks now."

"I'll ride with you," said Fenwith.

Now it was Solace's turn to look surprised. "You will?"

Chelyss said, "Now wait just a minute, Fenwith. It's been a long time since you were a lady rider in the queen's guard."

"Aye, it's been a while, but I haven't forgotten how to ride a horse or hold a sword. And I'm riding with my queen. Enough said." Fenwith crossed her arms and glared at Chelyss, who sighed.

Solace was still reeling from the news that Fenwith had been a lady rider when Evryst said, "If you're set on leaving in the morning, perhaps we can ask Peka and Alyn to join you?"

Solace nodded. "Aye, it would be great to have them along. Thank you."

"Alright then. Solace will ride out to intercept Rhees and see what she can do to expedite his return. Meanwhile, we'll plan to meet Neuss with as much force as we can muster," Evryst looked at Chelyss and Ghrier, who murmured their agreement. The three men returned to their maps and battle plans, Chelyss casting a worried glance at his wife.

Solace rose early the next morning, saddlebags packed and ready to leave before first light. The spring weather was cool, and she slipped her traveling cloak over her navy-and-gray striped tunic, navy vest, and gray leggings. Fenwith saddled Caya, who seemed to sense the importance of her mission and snorted a few times while waiting for Solace to double-check that her slings were handy—one looped around her saddle horn, the other tied around her waist—and finish saddling Jenx. As they left the stable yard they heard the sound of a single horse approaching. Although Solace hoped it was Rhees, she knew better, since he'd be riding back to Shulamorn with Kryss and the other northerners.

"What brings you out so early, neighbor?" called Fenwith, recognizing Marek's horse.

In his right hand Marek carried a flagpole that sat inside a holster bolted onto his stirrup. An azure flag flapped at the top of the pole. The flag's round seal displayed a lion's head sitting above a pair of crossed swords, surrounded by a circlet of olive leaves. Marek held his horse's reins lightly in his left hand. "Figured it was time the king's colors flew again in Shulamorn."

Solace and her companions—Fenwith, Peka, Alyn, and Marek—followed the route Rhees had mapped out before he left. They entered the western side of the Orpash Plain, now dotted with the campsites of the rebel army: the gray tents of the Tor monks, the green tents of the former king's knights, and an assortment of patched and quilted tents and lean-tos belonging to the laborers and miners and farmers and their families. Solace heard babies crying in some of the tents and wondered how they'd ever be able to protect the children in that camp when Neuss arrived. Several men and women carried jugs of water from Chelyss and Fenwith's private well to the camp, while others stoked dormant fires back to life.

An elderly man spotted Marek holding the old kingdom's flag aloft and blasted out a single note on his battered horn. Everyone stopped their early morning tasks, put down their water jugs and cooking utensils, and stood at attention. Solace glanced nervously at Fenwith, who nodded and said, "They're honoring you, lass. You're our water diviner and now, our warrior queen."

"I'm a hill girl from Yelosha."

"A hill girl who's sparked a rebellion." Fenwith added, "And captured the hearts of us all."

Solace swallowed down a lump in her throat and led them slowly, single file, through the extensive campsite. As they passed by, every man and woman raised their right fist, pounded their chest once, and then flung their hand outward, flicking all five fingers into the air. Their hands fluttering in the morning breeze reminded Solace of a flock of mourning doves taking flight. Her heart twisted at the sight. Transferring her reins to her left hand, Solace pounded her chest with her right fist and then flicked her fingers outward in response. A trilling cheer rose from the crowd, a roar of defiance and hope.

The cheering followed them as they rode through the camp, echoing across the plain. Once they cleared the last of the tents, they rode as hard as their horses would allow, stopping at midday near an abandoned farm, where the horses grazed on wild grasses and they ate lunch—cheese, jerky, and fresh hunks of bread—in the shade of the only tree. Alyn handed Solace a spyglass and showed her how to use it. They took turns peering into the hills that ran along the northern edge of the Orpash Plain, checking and double-checking Rhees's route.

Alyn frowned. "I don't see so much as a puff of dust."

"Could Rhees have changed routes? Perhaps he's been

discovered and is hiding out somewhere in the hills." Solace hesitated and added, "Or perhaps he's injured and unable to ride."

Alyn sighed. "Perhaps, but even so, *some* men and women would ride down from the north to join in this fight. They've been among the most rebellious, and the most oppressed as a result."

"Then we've no choice but to ride into the hills after Rhees."

Alyn swung the spyglass back and forth along the entire northern perimeter, and paused to focus on the hills to the northeast. "When did Chelyss expect Neuss's army to arrive in Shulamorn?"

"Neuss was two days behind Chelyss, or thereabouts."

"Take a look." Frowning, Alyn handed the spyglass back to Solace. She stared at the size of the army heading toward them, a fist of fear slamming into her stomach.

Refocusing, she looked closer and saw a number of makeshift flags—blue bits of cloth tied atop sticks and spears —fluttering as their riders held them aloft. A tall rider wearing a black duster and a wide-brimmed hat rode in front. Grinning, Solace handed the spyglass back to Alyn. "Rhees chose another route. Let's go meet him!"

They scrambled onto their horses and rode northeast, Jenx and the other horses sensing their riders' excitement and straining at their leads. Knowing they still had to ride back to Shulamorn and stay ahead of Neuss's army, Solace kept a steady pace but not one that would exhaust their mounts. It took every ounce of her self-control to hold Jenx in check, since all she wanted was to fling herself into Rhees's arms.

The rebel contingent from the north slowed down and finally halted as the five riders approached. Scowling, Rhees and Kryss rode ahead to greet them. His scowl deepened when he recognized King Meade's colors fluttering above their heads. Glancing from the flag to the lead rider, Rhees's brown-black eyes softened, their wariness gone.

Riding up with a tender smile that took Solace's breath away, he said, "It's good to see you riding again, my love, although I didn't expect to see you this far north!"

"It's good to see you again, my love, and I wouldn't have ridden this far north if you hadn't been late," she replied with a soft chuckle.

Laughing, Rhees started to reply when a single rider came galloping from the direction of Urhl and pulled up his horse in front of Rhees. He gasped, "Neuss and his men are little more than a day's ride behind and are gaining on us."

Rhees shouted to his northern rebels, "Press on to Shulamorn!" Turning back in his saddle, he said to Solace, "Together." Nodding, she joined Rhees at the head of their rebel contingent. They didn't push either their horses or their rebels too hard on the way. Tomorrow would be time enough to push back against Neuss with all their strength and resolve.

Shortly after sunset, the sky painted in dusky streaks of dark pink and peach and blue, they neared the patchwork of tents and campfires sprinkled across the Orpash Plain. Word spread rapidly that Rhees, the rightful heir to the throne, was approaching with a rebel army from the north. Men, women, and children gathered at the edge of the campsite to see and cheer their true king.

Solace slowed down. "Go on ahead, Rhees. Your people have sacrificed everything to fight by your side tomorrow. They need to see their king tonight."

Rhees slowed down to keep pace with her and Jenx. "But why can't we greet them together?"

Fenwith, riding next to Solace, overheard him. "Lace used her gift, and nearly sacrificed her life, to bring us this moment. Our people are ready to rise up and fight. And now the rest is up to you." Pausing, she looked at the man she'd helped to raise and said firmly, "Ride into camp as their king and commander."

Rhees glanced back at Solace. "What about you? You look exhausted."

"I haven't ridden this much since before my injury." Evryst had warned her she'd tire more easily, and she felt like she could sleep for a week. Every muscle in her body screamed from the exertion.

"I'll look after Lace. She needs her rest, is all," said Fenwith.

Peka rode up on the other side of Rhees. "They'll stay with me tonight. I have a large tent."

The northern rebels that had ridden with Rhees had already reached the edge of the camp and joined the men and women lining up to cheer their king. The entire ragtag rebel army, which stretched out across the plain all the way back to the Stoneguard boulders, seemed to be holding its collective breath, watching and waiting for Rhees to arrive.

Rhees exhaled a puff of air, squared his shoulders, and rode part way toward the waiting crowd. Then he stopped in his tracks and turned Zirott around to face Solace, who was watching his progress.

The crowd quieted; even the babies stopped crying. Rhees pounded his chest with his right fist, brought his fist up to his lips for a kiss, and then flicked his hand outward toward Solace —a modified version of the Toreszan salute she'd learned that morning. Solace realized he was waiting for her reply. She repeated the gesture and the crowd roared its approval. Rhees nodded and turned Zirott back toward the campsite.

"What just happened?" Solace asked Fenwith as they followed Peka to her tent, which was tucked far enough away from the crowd gathering around Rhees to afford some privacy.

"It's an old tradition, used chiefly by a soldier to publicly acknowledge his lover before riding into battle. That's how

Meade would say good-bye to Ellanora every time he left Shulamorn and returned to the palace."

After they dismounted, Bray and Behn offered to brush down and feed their horses. Solace barely had time to thank them before Peka and Fenwith whisked her into the tent, helped her remove her cloak and boots, and insisted she nap while they fixed something to eat. Solace was too weary to argue and fell asleep instantly. She dreamt of soldiers with bows and spears and swords, fighting men and women armed with nothing but sticks and stones. Waking with a start, she pulled on her boots and cloak and went outside.

Fenwith smiled at her and held out a bowl of stew. Solace took the bowl and sat down near the fire. She was hungrier than she realized and ate silently, listening to Behn and Bray argue about the merits of fighting on horseback versus on foot. Peka finally interrupted them. "What matters tomorrow is we defeat Neuss and you come out of the battle alive!"

"But, ma, why can't we ride with Evryst? Or with Rhees?"

"Because your swords are needed on the ground, fighting alongside the farmers and miners and herdsmen, who fight with little more than sticks and stones."

"What 'sticks and stones' do you mean?" asked Solace, surprised at the choice of words, given her restless dream.

Peka shrugged. "The farmers, herdsmen, and others have staffs and slings and a few daggers, which is why a number of us" —she glared at her sons— "volunteered to fill out their ranks with experienced sword fighters and archers."

"How many slingers do we have?" An idea began to form in Solace's head, a crazy, risky idea Rhees would hate, but it just might help make the difference in the fight with Neuss's army.

Behn scratched his head. "Maybe twenty or so. Why?"

"Twenty in all?" Waving her arm to encompass the campsite, Solace said, "Hill children in Yelosha are given slings as our first toys. Our parents place a piece of cake on a rock. If we want to eat that cake, then we have to learn how to sling a stone at it. Are you telling me that hill children in Toresz haven't been taught to use the sling?"

"Our children learned to sling the same way," said Peka. "From the time they could toddle. But we need Behn and Bray to wield their swords. We don't have enough sword fighters to take on Neuss's army."

"I know we need sword fighters, but we also need slingers."

Fenwith asked, "What can they do that our sword fighters can't?"

"They can disrupt the enemy, bring down numbers of them from a distance, and make it easier for our smaller number of sword fighters and archers to take on the rest." Solace realized she sounded more like her father than a seventeen-year-old hill girl, but she'd been reared on Yeloshan military tactics as much as on her mother's beloved storybooks.

Peka looked at her sons and back at Solace. She asked, "How many slingers do you need?"

"If we could round up fifty or so, we could become a real nuisance to Neuss and his men."

Fenwith asked, "And who will be leading these slingers?"

"I will. I know the tactics as well as anyone—when to advance our slingers and when to withdraw behind our infantry, that is, our foot soldiers. Although I'd like to see our slingers at practice first, so I know our average range."

Bray looked at Solace with his mouth open. "How did you learn all this stuff?"

"My dad. He was a commander in the Yeloshan army. I grew up hearing about his battle campaigns, including how he deployed slingers." Solace wondered where her father was at that precise moment. Was he in bed for the night or sitting up with his pipe, looking out the window for a glimpse of his lost daughter? A thought occurred to her. "Doesn't the Toreszan army use slingers?"

Behn shook his head. "Not anymore. When King Meade asked Neuss to take over the army—this was back when the two brothers were still on good terms—one of the first things Neuss did was to disband the King's Slingers, a special unit that went out to battle with the regular army. Neuss looked down on the slingers as little better than farmers or shepherds."

Solace nodded. "That's a good piece of luck."

"How so?" asked Peka, tilting her head to the side.

Solace rubbed her hands together to warm them up. "This gives us a small element of surprise—if we can find enough qualified slingers." She glanced at Behn and Bray. "Please spread the word. I'll meet anyone who is able to sling tomorrow morning, shortly after sunrise, in the old practice field behind Chelyss and Fenwith's cottage. And can someone get word to Rhees, Evryst, and Chelyss? And Kryss and Alyn too? They'll need to know of our plans. And I also have an idea for the cavalry that just might work."

Bray ran off to recruit slingers and Behn and Peka split up to find the others. Fenwith moved around the fire pit to sit closer to Solace. "Rhees isn't going to like this—you at the front of the line, the first to take on Neuss."

"He won't like it at all, but that's beside the point. If we're going to win, we need to use every tool at our disposal. And that includes slingers."

CHAPTER 24

Rhees didn't like it all. He fumed and fussed and tried to think of a better plan, but in the end, Evryst, Kryss and Peka, and even Chelyss, all agreed that Solace's plan had merit. She and Rhees sketched out the lines of attack in the sandy soil and debated with the others over the placement of the various forces. It was past midnight when they wrapped up, each headed to their own tent.

Rhees waited for Peka and Fenwith to turn in and then stirred up the embers in the fire pit. He pulled Solace onto his lap and she snuggled against his chest. She felt oddly content, despite her worries at facing Neuss the next day, and her anxiety over her father and how he was faring without her. Rhees rested his chin on top of her head. "I need to sleep with my rebels tonight."

"I know."

"But tomorrow night, and every night after—"

She pulled back slightly and put a finger to his lips, silencing him. "Focus on defeating Neuss once and for all."

He nipped her finger, sending a warm rush through her body. She cleared her throat. "I said focus."

Rhees laughed. "Who knew when I snatched a water diviner, I'd actually taken a brilliant military commander? How could a future king get so lucky?"

Solace smiled and peered into his brown-black eyes, which crinkled at the corners when he laughed. She brought her hand up to the side of his face, his dark beard longer and bushier than usual from his forty-six days on the road. "Some kings get all the luck."

"And some kings and queens need their rest!" called out Fenwith from inside her tent.

"She's right, you need your rest," Rhees said, kissing her on the mouth, a long, lingering kiss that made Solace ache for more. "Above all else, be safe," he whispered with a hitch in his voice. "I'll not lose you again."

She rose reluctantly, tugging Rhees up with her. "And you as well. No last-minute heroics. If we stick to our plan, we will defeat Neuss."

Rhees brushed a stray wisp of hair from her face, kissed the tip of her nose, and turned away. Strolling toward his tent, he whistled an old hill lullaby. Solace strained her ears until she couldn't hear the tune any longer.

She woke just before dawn to an empty tent; Fenwith and Peka were already up and dressed. Solace's stomach knotted with fresh fears at what the day would bring. Would they really be able to defeat Neuss and install Rhees as the rightful king? In the cold light of early morning, all their plans seemed as far-fetched as something from her mother's storybooks.

Solace sighed. She knew better than to start second-guessing. She smelled coffee and hurried to smooth down the same rumpled tunic, vest, and leggings she'd worn the previous day. She finger-combed her black hair and then wove it into a single braid. Taking her slings, Solace wrapped one around her waist and the second around her forehead, tying the cord behind her head. She attached her drawstring bag filled with stones to her belt, pulled on her boots, and left her leather cloak behind in the tent. The days were warming, and she wouldn't need her cloak once the fighting started.

Fenwith handed Solace a mug of coffee, a hard roll, and some jerky as soon as she exited the tent. "I'd still feel better if I was by your side, instead of sitting on a horse behind Chelyss," said Fenwith.

"We discussed this last night. We're only putting slingers out front for the initial skirmish. And you're not a slinger. Besides, we'd be wasting your skills as a lady rider."

Fenwith pursed her lips. "A lady rider whose skills are a mite rusty."

"Even rusty, your skills are better than most." Pausing, Solace added almost shyly, "Whatever happens out there today, Fenwith—thank you for everything."

Fenwith's eyes widened in alarm. "Don't you go thanking me as if we're not meeting again! I'll have none of it!" She turned away from Solace with a sniffle, and Solace threw her arms around Fenwith's waist, hugging her from behind as she used to hug her mother.

Solace traversed the campground until she reached Chelyss's old practice field. She rubbed her eyes, wondering whether she might be sleepwalking. Bray had recruited close to a hundred slingers, all of them waiting to demonstrate their skills for her.

Behn, Bray, and Solace split the slingers into three groups and tested them first for their accuracy. Solace insisted that accuracy trumped everything else, and so they eliminated about twenty slingers. Solace thanked them for volunteering and sent them back to the campsite to assist Governor Ghrier, who was overseeing the evacuation of the children and the elderly, relocating them to the provincial headquarters and elsewhere inside the town of Shulamorn itself. True to his word, the governor had jailed Neuss's guards and opened the town's well to the public.

Next, they tested the slingers' ability to hurl stones long distances, and they sent another twenty or so slingers to Peka, who would intersperse them among the infantry's sword fighters, staff fighters, and archers, where the slinger's short-range accuracy would be more effective.

"How many do we have left?" Solace asked Behn when they were finished.

"Sixty-three, including us."

"More than enough to disrupt Neuss's front line when they come after us." Solace recognized a rail-thin woman standing behind Behn and walked toward her. Lowering her voice, she said, "Are you sure about this, Maysel? Wilhm is already fighting in Peka's unit. What would happen to your children if—"

"Aye, I'm sure." Maysel thrust out her jaw. "My children are staying with my sister and her husband, who love them as their own. Besides, what kind of future will my children have if we don't stand up and fight? They'll all fall the way of my Wils." Maysel stared eastward, in the direction of Urhl.

Solace realized Maysel desperately needed to fight back and reached out to grip Maysel's hand. "We're grateful to have you here with us." Maysel nodded wordlessly, a look of defiance in her large brown eyes.

After they drilled for another hour, Solace reassigned the slingers so the three groups were evenly divided, in terms of skill and endurance, and she asked Maysel, Behn, and Bray to each lead a unit. Solace marched the columns of slingers past the Stoneguard boulders that marked the entrance to the Orpash Plain, reminding them to refill their pouches with stones along the way.

She led them past the mostly deserted campsite, past the horses snorting as their riders saddled them, past the infantry —the sword fighters, staff fighters, and archers, as well as the short-range slingers, nervously chatting in small clusters—and gathered her slinger units at the front, where they'd hurl stones as Neuss's army approached from the east and attempt to stay out of range of his archers for as long as possible.

Rhees rode over to inspect the slingers and thank them for volunteering to skirmish at the front. His eyes met Solace's, and she blushed at the heat behind his glance. Nodding, his voice gruff with emotion, he said, "Well done," before moving on to inspect the remainder of his rebel army.

And then there was nothing to do but wait. The slingers sat down in their columns, passed water and bits of jerky between them, and sorted through their stones. Every time Solace thought of the coming battle, her heart thundered with a fresh wave of fear and her mouth dried out. To distract herself, she walked up and down the three columns of slingers, asking each man or woman to tell her their names and where they hailed from.

A lookout perched in the low hills nearby blasted a hollow note on his battered trumpet. Everyone scrambled to their feet, the riders calming their anxious steeds before mounting them. Solace wished for Alyn's spyglass to see the size of the army heading their way. Then she spotted a cloud of dust on the horizon and watched as it grew, spreading across the entire eastern end of the Orpash Plain. *Neuss is throwing everything he has into this fight. He wants to eliminate the only remaining heir to the throne and crush the rebellion before it spreads further, before it reaches beyond his gnarly grasp.*

When Neuss's sword-wielding foot soldiers and archers were twelve hundred feet away, Solace shouted to her three commanders, "Line up!" Bray, Behn, and Maysel spread out their slingers across the dry, dusty plain, so that each man or woman had the space to wind up and hurl without impeding the slinger next to them. Solace wished she had twice as many slingers now that she saw what was heading their way. Rhees's entire rag-tag rebel army, including her three slinger units, could be swallowed up thrice over by the troops charging toward them. They needed to pick off as many of the crafty king's best fighters as early in the battle as possible— something she hoped her untested slingers would be able to accomplish.

At eleven hundred feet, Solace untied the sling from her waist and pulled three stones from her pouch. "Ready yourselves!" Her fear fizzled out, replaced by a steady calm. She heard the sounds of the soldiers' boots striking the hard ground, running with their swords drawn.

At one thousand feet, Solace yelled, "Set!" Placing a stone inside the cradle of her sling, she ran her middle finger through the loop at one end of her cord and gripped the knot at the other end between her thumb and forefinger. She picked her target, an enormous man with full armor bearing down on her. Rotating her sling in an arc above her head, she shouted, "Hurl!" and released the knotted end. She heard the whoosh of sixty-odd slingers hurling stones at metal shields and armor and sent up a silent prayer they'd be able to slow down the enemy's advance.

As the stones pinged on metal, Neuss's soldiers began falling to the ground. Their comrades, confused that a group of unarmored men and women could bring down well-trained fighters, faltered, slowing their charge. This enabled Solace and her slingers to reload and hurl repeatedly, striking more soldiers down. Neuss's front line of well-trained soldiers seemed almost hesitant to push ahead and Solace pressed the advantage. "Keep hurling, lads and lasses! Double-time, whilst you can!"

Neuss's archers ran forward, regaining some of their lost momentum on the battlefield. When the first arrows hit the ground near Solace's feet, she shouted, "Fall back!" and the three slinger units slipped behind their own line of archers, joining the rest of the ground force for the short-range fighting. Her slingers were now fighting alongside the sword- and staff-wielding rebels, and flanked by the archers, who fired off a slew of arrows before retreating to rejoin the rest of their line.

The two infantries collided, and all Solace could do was concentrate on loading her stone in the cradle, rotating the sling, and releasing. *Load, rotate, and release.* She repeated the words in her head fifteen, twenty, thirty times, losing count. Good men and women fell to the ground on either side of her —including Bray, Maysel, so many others—and Solace wanted to run over and check on each one, but she forced herself to focus on the battle—loading the next stone into the cradle, rotating her sling in a wide arc, aiming at the next swordsman in armor hurtling toward her, releasing the stone with split-second precision, and then watching as another of Neuss's soldiers fell to the ground.

Solace moved back a few paces when the rest of the rebel line retreated, and pressed forward a few paces when they managed to advance, a strange sort of dance that lasted far too many hours. She heard shouts and cries and metal clanging against metal, the hiss of an arrow whizzing past, and the sickening sound of another friend tumbling to the ground. At some point she pushed back her hair and her hand came away bloody, but she wiped off her fingers and carried on, slinging stones and shouting encouragement to the others up and down the line.

Solace wondered how Rhees and the cavalry were faring but

she had no time to glance about and try to see through the haze of dust kicked up by all the fighting. What she could see gave her no comfort—for the Orpash Plain was littered with men and women, armored soldiers and plainclothes slingers and rebel fighters, lying where they'd fallen—and she had no idea whether Rhees's rebel army was winning or losing.

CHAPTER 25

Load, rotate, and release. Load, rotate, and release. Solace's arms and legs ached, and fresh twinges tugged at her chest. Even so, there was no time to rest, no time to step away from the constant barrage of flying arrows and charging sword fighters. The two armies fought past sunset and moonrise. Eventually, both camps lit torches and the skirmishing continued through the night. Solace thought the rebels may have lost some of their earlier drive, but then again, they were fighting with no sleep and very little food. She wondered how much longer they could last without rotating fighters and allowing some in the front lines to take breaks.

A man's hand gripped her shoulder and for a moment she thought it might be Rhees, but Evryst shouted to be heard above the tumult of battle. "Follow me please, milady."

She turned her head to glance at Evryst. His robe was torn and his face was grimy with dust and perspiration. Her stomach tightened, turning to a fistful of lead. She swallowed hard, her mouth dry. "It's Rhees, isn't it? He's been injured?"

Before Evryst could reply, a tall soldier lumbered toward

her, sword pointing at her chest. Evryst stepped in front of Solace, his blade raised and knees flexed. The two men lunged and parried, their swords swishing and clanging, Evryst meeting and countering every blow. Solace dropped a stone into her cradle and held her sling at her side. She scanned the immediate fighting circle to ensure no one else charged into the fray. All around her were friends and foes, locked in hand-to-hand combat with swords, staffs, spears, short blades, and daggers. Arrows continued to fly, although more sporadically, since the archers had expended most of their supply in the earlier hours of battle. Meanwhile, her remaining close-range slingers continued flinging stones and picking off Neuss's fighters where they could.

Another armored soldier ran toward them, shouting a string of oaths. Solace blocked out all the sounds around her and concentrated on the act of rotating her sling until it whirred overhead, faster and faster. Careful to avoid Evryst and the others skirmishing nearby, she hurled her stone, striking the oncoming man between his eyes. He crumpled to the ground at the same time Evryst's sword sank into his opponent's unprotected flank.

Evryst withdrew his sword and tugged Solace away from the constant din of clashing blades, drawing her behind the front lines. Healers were attending to the wounded on the field and in tents set up at the rear of the campsite, where Evryst appeared to be headed. It was quieter here, away from the skirmish, where shouts and screams gave way to whimpers and moans from the wounded.

Solace's ears rang and she found it difficult to speak in a normal tone. She whispered the one name that had been carved into her heart, the only name that truly counted, for without him nothing else mattered, for the rebels, for Toresz itself, but especially for her. "Rhees?"

"Rhees is fine. He has a cut above his eye and a flesh wound in his left arm, both of which I've patched up."

Solace closed her eyes, overwhelmed with relief. *Rhees is safe for now!* Her head spun and she opened her eyes quickly, to find Evryst examining her, concern etched in the lines of his face. "But you're not fine. You've pushed yourself too hard and need to rest a bit."

Solace waved her hand. "How can I rest while the battle still rages, when my friends need me."

Evryst guided her into the nearest healer's tent. "Rhees needs you, alive and well. But if you carry on like this, without giving any thought to your own health, you will drive yourself into an early grave—without any assistance from Neuss."

The master healer nodded at a clean bedroll on the ground and asked her to sit down so he could examine her wound. Solace complied, but asked, "What wound?"

Evryst arched an eyebrow. "The gash near your hairline that's still bleeding."

Solace vaguely recalled seeing blood on her hand when she'd pushed her hair out of her face. Evryst withdrew his silver tube, and Solace scowled. "That's not for my forehead."

"I'll get to your gash, but I'm more concerned about your chest pains."

"Why do you assume I have any pain?" Solace wasn't ready to acknowledge the aches in her chest and arms. After all, everybody else was equally exhausted.

Evryst ran a hand over his bald head. Perhaps she was exasperating the normally patient monk. "Because I've observed you rubbing your chest at least three times since I arrived. Are you telling me you have no chest pain whatsoever?"

Solace's shoulders slumped. She wouldn't lie to the man who'd saved her life. "Alright, you win. I've had some twinges in my chest, and my arms are really achy, but I'm sure that's from all the slinging."

"May I examine you and clean your wound?"

When Solace nodded, Evryst said, "But first, have some water."

After she slaked her thirst—she'd drained her water skin hours earlier—she closed her eyes. She preferred not to watch as Evryst worked. "Tell me how the cavalry is faring."

Evryst spoke as he cleansed her wound. "Your suggestion that we split up the cavalry was brilliant. We're hiding out with our horses in the low hills on either side of the plain. And we've been able to hold our own, surprising Neuss's riders by attacking from the sides, rather than straight on as they expected. Your strategy is also keeping Rhees out of the worst of the skirmishing on the plain, which I suspect was part of your plan. Of course, Rhees is itching to ride down out of the hills, especially when he sees how much damage Neuss's army is inflicting on the rest of you. He ordered me to come find you. He's beside himself with worry, particularly after we received reports that half our slingers were down."

Solace gritted her teeth as Evryst stitched the gash in her head. "We've lost good people today, with many more wounded. It breaks my heart to see so many of our friends fallen. I keep reminding myself that everyone standing with me on the plain volunteered to be there, and not a single woman or man ran from the fight." She paused and added more softly. "'Tis true I wanted Rhees well away from the main skirmish, not because of my personal feelings, but because Toresz needs a king—the one true, rightful heir to the throne—the one man who can begin to right the wrongs committed by Neuss. It makes no sense to send Rhees into the worst of the skirmishing until Neuss shows himself. While Rhees may want to join the battle now, he knows the true fight is yet to come—Neuss's arrival will be Rhees's cue to ride down from the hills."

"Aye, and let's hope that crafty old fox shows his face soon."
Evryst used his silver tube to listen to her chest. Neither of
them spoke until Evryst packed his tube away in a pouch he
carried on his back. "You are straining your heart. You need to
drink plenty of water, keep dried fruit and nuts at hand to
snack on throughout the day, and you need to take breaks, as
you are doing now."

Solace started to object but thought better of it. Evryst was
right—she'd pushed herself to near exhaustion. Nodding, she
said, "I'll do as you say."

Evryst patted her shoulder. "Lie here for the next hour and
close your eyes. You lost more blood than you realize. I'll send
someone in with a hot meal and then you can rejoin the other
slingers. But be careful—Rhees will have my poor, hairless head
if anything happens to you."

"How can he possibly hold you accountable? That makes no
sense."

Evryst snorted. "It may not make sense, but then a man in
love rarely does."

Solace called out as he was leaving, "Tell Rhees...tell him to
make sure he keeps a sharp eye on Neuss. He can't be trusted,
especially if he's losing."

She closed her eyes, only to be awakened by someone
jostling her arm. A wizened, elderly woman with a blue
kerchief on her head helped her sit up and handed her a bowl
of thin broth and a fresh water skin. Solace thanked her and
after she'd eaten, left the tent. The sky was lightening in the
east, a gentle spring breeze stirring the air—a perfect day for
tilling and planting, for cleaning out stalls and airing out
mattresses—for nearly any chore imaginable, anything other
than killing one's neighbor for the right to dig a well.

Solace set her jaw and marched toward the skirmish line,
which was thinner than the evening before, with more losses
on both sides. She gathered more stones as she went and

dropped one into the cradle of her sling. She took up her position between a Toreszan farmer carrying a staff and an old soldier with his sword, both of them friends of Peka. The three of them fought side by side throughout the day, spelling each other so they could each take short breaks.

When Solace returned to the same position after her break around midnight, she discovered an arrow had struck the farmer, although the soldier thought he'd survive. About noon on the third day of fighting, Neuss's infantry rushed across the field, screaming war cries at the rebel forces. Solace thought this signaled a change in the battle, a final surge to quell the rebellion before Neuss rode onto the battlefield.

Load, rotate, and release. She hurled her stones and shouted encouragements up and down the rebel line to the weary men and women she'd grown to love over the course of the past few days. When a husky man in chainmail dashed toward Solace, the old soldier pushed her out of the way and took the killing blow. Another rebel sword fighter took out the husky king's man, and Solace's eyes welled up as she sent up a silent prayer for the old soldier and all the others they'd lost on the battlefield.

She heard a series of trumpet blasts a few hours later and another cloud of dust filled the plain as Neuss's cavalry rode into sight. *Finally,* thought Solace, *the man himself.* Grateful she had taken Evryst's advice and rested just before the last surge, Solace was ready to face Neuss, ready for whatever came next.

Neuss's mounted fighters arrived, and although she knew Rhees, Chelyss, and the others had been thinning their ranks, Neuss still commanded a large contingent of horses and knights, all itching for one final battle. They kept coming and Solace wondered, heartsick with worry, whether the rebels' cavalry had been defeated without her realizing it. Rhees and the other rebel riders should be fighting on the Orpash Plain by now too.

Then she saw them, riding on either side of Neuss's army and driving his forces closer to the center of the plain. All the rebels—mounted or on foot—pounded the enemy with arrow, sword, staff, and stone, squeezing them on three sides. *Load, rotate, and release.*

Neuss's cavalry tried to pull back, only to find Rhees's band of mounted warriors had circled behind them and closed off their escape route. Surrounded on all sides, Neuss's army had no choice but to fight to the last man or surrender. Solace believed Neuss was too cowardly to fight to the death—particularly his own.

A few more hours, and Solace saw several white handkerchiefs fluttering in the air, and then several more, until there was a blast from another horn, somewhere inside Neuss's line, and the enemy lowered their weapons. Solace held a stone in her left hand, ready to load it into the cradle, but she dropped her right hand, her sling dangling harmlessly at her side.

A large man in full armor, accompanied by four knights, one of them bearing a white flag, rode to the front of the enemy's line. The rebels stood still, weapons drawn, watchful and on edge. Solace slipped in front of the rebel swordsmen and archers to have an unobstructed view of Neuss's surrender.

Five rebel horses emerged from behind the enemy line, where they'd cut off Neuss's retreat. They rode through the ranks of the rebel army, sending a ripple of movement—horses shifting, men and women stepping out of the way—and as the rebels saw it was their new king riding past them, fists pounded chests, hands flicked outward, and a roar rose from their lips.

When Rhees and his four horsemen, one of whom was Marek bearing the old kingdom's colors, circled around to the front, the crowd grew quiet again. Rhees and his riders squared off about fifty paces in front of the defeated king and his men, and Rhees ordered them to disarm. Neuss dismounted, removed his helmet and handed it to one of his riders. He pulled his sword from its scabbard and laid it on the ground. Neuss's soldiers and riders, following his example, dropped their swords, bows, and spears on the ground.

Rhees dismounted and handed his sword and wide-brimmed hat to Kryss, who'd dismounted as well. Rhees and Neuss walked toward each other slowly, deliberately, neither one in a hurry. When they were twenty paces apart, Neuss stumbled forward and bent down to catch his balance. As he steadied himself, Solace saw with horror he held something in his right hand—a short sword that he'd pulled out of his boot—and now he was charging an unarmed Rhees. Solace felt herself moving as if in a dream, her left hand fingering a stone, her right hand raising her sling. *Load, rotate, and release.*

The stone smashed into Neuss's armor, shattering his collarbone. He screamed as he fell backward, crumpling onto the ground. Rhees ran over and picked up Neuss's fallen blade. Calling Zirott with a whistle, Rhees climbed onto his horse and raised the sword above his head. He bellowed at Neuss's army, "I am King Meade's only living son, and I claim the throne of Toresz!"

The rebels shouted and cheered. Rhees waited for them to quiet down before he continued. "Commanders and senior officers, report to the front of the line now." Neuss's most trusted men moved to the front, where Kryss placed them under arrest and marched them away. The rest of Neuss's army murmured among themselves and shifted their feet nervously.

Rhees pointed the sword at the sky and they quieted down. "As for the rest of you, from this moment forward, you are no longer my enemies, but my subjects. You are free to leave. Take nothing with you but your water skins and your provisions, and go home." A collective gasp escaped from Neuss's army, shocked the new king was showing them mercy.

Behn had slipped behind Solace and tapped her on the shoulder. "You're the best slinger I've ever seen. I know you could've killed Neuss with a single shot. Why didn't you?"

Solace squinted at the former king, moaning as Evryst and his warrior monks led him away. "Because that would have been the easy way out for him. I want to see Neuss stand on trial for his crimes." She thought about the number of people he'd killed, families he'd destroyed—either directly through murder and assassination, or indirectly through greed and neglect—and she knew nothing could ever truly balance the score against a man like Neuss. But a public trial might help the healing process for those who'd suffered, including Rhees.

"You can only hang a man once," said Behn.

Solace didn't want to think about Neuss any longer. He was the past. "What's the word on Bray?"

"He took an arrow to the shoulder, but he'll be fine. My mother's with him now."

"That's good news. I'm going to try to find Maysel and see how she's doing." Solace knew Rhees would be busy for hours yet, questioning Neuss's commanders and then meeting with his rebel leaders. It was enough for her to know Rhees had survived. In fact, he looked remarkably well, sitting atop Zirott wielding Neuss's blade in his right hand.

Solace searched for Maysel among the healers' tents, scattered about haphazardly toward the back of the campsite. Many of the injured recognized her, and Solace stopped to thank them for their bravery or to console those who'd lost loved ones. She eventually found Maysel and stayed with her until Wilhm arrived, worry lines creasing his brow. Maysel would recover, but she'd likely have a permanent limp due to the sword wound in her upper thigh.

Although night had fallen by the time Solace emerged from the last healer's tent, a full moon and numerous campfires provided plenty of light. She ran into Fenwith, who wrapped her in a bear hug. "Rhees has been looking for you. Everyone's talking about how you brought down Neuss with your sling and saved Rhees's life."

"Where is he now?"

"Having supper with the rebel leaders. Evryst wants to conduct a formal coronation next month, which Rhees has agreed to. Rhees has appointed Ghrier as his chancellor, and he's asked Chelyss to return to Urhl as the royal trainer again and train a new generation of knights."

"What about you? I thought you liked living in Shulamorn."

"I'm thinking there might be an opening for a lady's rider at the palace," Fenwith grinned.

"I think that could be arranged," Solace laughed. "But first, I need your help with something." After she explained what she needed, Fenwith was beaming.

"Can you ask Rhees to meet me by Stoneguard in two hours, then?"

"Gladly, lass. In the meantime, please come with me."

Solace followed her back to Peka's tent, where Fenwith had placed an urn of water, a small pot of stew, and a change of clothes—a long, flowing purple and gold tunic with pale gold leggings and a matching, ankle-length overcoat. Solace realized how hungry she was and quickly polished off the stew, then stripped out of her grimy clothes, rolled them into a tight ball, and took a sponge bath. After dressing, she unbraided and combed out her hair, letting it fall in loose waves around her shoulders.

Solace arrived early at Stoneguard. When she heard Rhees's footsteps approaching, she stepped out of the shadow of the boulders to greet him. He ran the last few steps and pulled her into his arms, threading his fingers through her hair as his mouth found hers. Between kisses, he thanked her for saving his life.

He paused to catch his breath. "We did it, Lace. We defeated Neuss! It never would've happened without you." Kissing her again, he added, "And tomorrow, we'll ride to Urhl to begin the hard work of rebuilding this country, together."

Solace stepped out of his grasp and folded her arms. "Aren't you forgetting something?"

Rhees stared at her blankly.

"You promised to take me back to Yelosha and my father. Remember?"

Rhees frowned, his dark eyes clouding over. "But I thought—"

"You thought I'd forget about my father?" Solace asked, her voice quivering. "I've been gone so long, he's probably given up all hope of ever seeing me again."

Rhees ran a hand through his unruly waves and dropped his gaze to the ground. Compressing his lips in a straight line, he said through gritted teeth, "I keep my promises. I'll speak with Evryst about the annulment in the morning." Rhees turned away from her abruptly.

Solace stared at his broad back, shaking her head. *Really, the man is now King of Toresz, but he can be so dense sometimes.* "Who said anything about an annulment? I want to *see* my father, not *stay* with my father."

Rhees spun around and gripped her arms. "You mean you're not leaving me?"

"Of course not."

"But what about your father? He's in Yelosha, and I'm in Toresz. I'll need to rule from here."

Solace sighed. "You're overthinking this."

"How so?" he asked gruffly.

"We're going to bring my father back to Toresz to live with us at the palace, and Barley too. It's time for my father to retire for good and deed the farm to Arik."

"You've thought of everything, haven't you, my love?"

Rhees's voice was barely more than a whisper, but his yearning punctuated every word.

"Hmm." Solace stood on her tiptoes, grasped the lapels of Rhees's duster, and pulled him toward her. After kissing him firmly on the lips, she said, "Husband, I'm to bed. It's been a long day. Are you coming?"

Rhees breathed her name, "Solace," a sigh of need and desire.

She led him by the hand to the same tent they'd slept in during their travels across the hills of Toresz, but instead of two separate bedrolls, there was one larger bedroll spread out on the ground.

Kryss intercepted them as they were entering their tent. "Rhees, I mean Your Majesty, several of the men are—"

Rhees put up his hand. "My wife...my queen and I are retiring for the night. Could you please see that we're not disturbed for any reason?"

Kryss winked. "Aye indeed, Your Majesty."

They cleared the last hill and looked down at the valley where Solace had grown up.

A farmer and his sheepdog were standing beneath a solitary oak, the dog barking and leaping in crazy circles. The old man looked down at the dog and up at the two riders poised at the crest of the hill. He pushed his floppy hat back from his forehead and stared.

Solace raised an arm and waved.

Rhees cleared his throat. "What if he hates me? I know I'd hate anyone who took you away from me."

"He won't hate you. Not if you tell him the truth."

"The truth makes for a pretty complicated story."

Solace arched an eyebrow at her husband. "But it's a story with a happy ending. Don't you agree?"

Rhees's brown-black eyes twinkled in the slanting rays of the afternoon sun. "Of course, my love."

Riding side by side, they started down the hill as the Yeloshan farmer and his sheepdog ran to greet them.

THE END

Thanks so much for reading *The Lightness of Water*. I hope you enjoyed it! Please visit https://tonicabell.com to sign up for my newsletter and stay tuned for giveaways and new releases, including the next book in the Water Witch Series, *The Way of Water* (2023).

For more action-packed fantasy books, please check out my Serving Magic Series, available for sale on Amazon:

- Lady Tanglewood (novella)
- Lady Apprentice
- Lady Mage
- Lady Liege
- Lady Spy
- Lady Reaper (2022)
- *More Serving Magic books are in the works!*

Thank you,

~Toni

Made in the USA
Monee, IL
08 April 2022

94329002R10152